STEAL AWAY

Books by BV Lawson

Scott Drayco Series

Played to Death
Requiem for Innocence
Dies Irae
Elegy in Scarlet
The Suicide Sonata
Deadly Dance (2020)

Beverly Laborde & Adam Dutton Series

Steal Away
Hide Away
Burn Away

Steal Away

An Adam Dutton & Beverly Laborde Mystery

BV Lawson

Crimetime Press

1

Beverly yanked her luggage through the revolving doorway in annoyance. Already worn out from the trip, the ticketing hassles, and trying to appear inconspicuous, that damned door was one more obstacle she didn't need.

But this place, oh this place, was everything she'd expected it to be. It was the quintessential symbol of luxury pamper-porn.

The sprawling Vermont resort spa bustled with autumn looky-loo tourists, or "leaf peepers," as the train conductor had called them. Syrupy music from hidden speakers matched the complimentary bottles of maple syrup handed out to guests. The columns were marble, the brocade fabric chairs had gold threads, and the light pendants looked like Swarovski crystal. The air reeked of Chanel No.5, sandalwood oil, and money.

All told, it was the perfect place for her to hide in plain sight.

Her gaze landed on a Japanese ceramic vase that she stopped to examine, then she grimaced as she noticed the backstamp. Just a contemporary Prouna piece, probably cost a couple grand, but hardly interesting. Not like the treasure she was in town to steal.

Heading toward the reception desk, she paused to study

the people around her. No one seemed to be interested in her. Good. She waited for the group closest to her to move on until she gave her name to the clerk, "It's under Beverly Laborde."

After the too-cheerful clerk verified Beverly's reservation and checked her in, the clerk motioned to a valet to take the bags. Beverly stepped between her luggage and the valet, saying, "That won't be necessary. They're not heavy," and waved him off. She gripped the maroon leather overnight case in one hand—no rolling along a hard floor for that one—and headed to her room.

Stepping inside, she nodded her approval. Four-poster bed, elegant sitting area with two turquoise and gray damask chairs, a Jacuzzi tub near the fireplace, and a stocked bar in the mini-refrigerator that greeted her with an alluring humming. She scanned a card on the table beside the bed that listed the à la carte spa services. The body wrap with neem black clay and skin-cupping was seven hundred dollars.

Much better than last week's cramped box-of-a-room or the hotel next to the railroad tracks the week before that. She looked out the windows toward the White Mountains. Other areas around the world could boast of snowy-sand beaches or historic pyramids or Amazon rainforests. But in Vermont, it was the autumn leaves in their fluorescent glory.

She gently laid the overnight case on the bed, dialed in the security code on the lock, and unzipped the top, holding her breath as she peered inside. Still there and undamaged. She reached into a pocket in the front of the case, pulled out a manila envelope and map, and settled in one of the padded wingback chairs.

The notes she'd jotted down in the margins on the papers from the envelope were scribbled hastily, and she strained now to read them. Instead of fake reading glasses, maybe she was way overdue getting a real pair.

Next, she picked up old man Kornelson's treasure map and turned it around to compare it to her notes. The yellowing map's edges were only slightly smudged, and the lettering was remarkably vibrant and the printing legible.

She'd looked at the thing hundreds of times—what had she missed? She was just tired, that must be it.

Tossing the map, papers, and envelope on the coffee table in front of her chair, she rubbed her temples. When was the last time she'd traveled with someone else? She couldn't remember. It must have been her grandmother, that trip to the antiques fair near Boston, six, no seven years ago. Three months before Grammie died. Beverly ran a hand across her eyes. She was not going to cry. Not now.

The room phone rang and made her jump out of her chair. No one could possibly know she was here, could they? It was a call transferred from the front desk, a call that made her forget all about crying.

"Is this Beverly Laborde?" the baritone voice asked.

"Who is this?"

"I'm Detective Adam Dutton with the Ironwood Junction PD. I'd like to come by and ask you a few questions."

"If this is about that parking ticket in Hanover, I paid it off," she forced a laugh. "Although I think a hundred dollars was a tad steep."

"Not a parking ticket, no. Would four o'clock be convenient?"

"Of course. I'll meet you in the lobby." Beverly hung up, battling with the part of her that wanted to run away. She'd expected something like this might happen but hoped it wouldn't. Oh well, another cop, another performance.

She picked up the notes and map again, but her blurred vision from lack of sleep made it hard to concentrate, so she gave up and headed to the mini-bar to pour herself a glass of wine. Maybe it would help give her some bottled courage before her appointment with Detective Dutton.

Glancing at her watch, she noted with chagrin that four o'clock was only ten minutes away. She hated to rush the Chablis but took a few hurried gulps of the flinty liquid with its pleasant aftertaste of green apples.

Well. Those few law enforcement types she had not been able to avoid were much the same. This being a smaller town and not Boston or New York, Dutton was bound to be a fat, dumpy, slow-witted Cro-Magnon type with a beer belly and low brow ridge. He probably went home every night to his cold-fish-of-a-wife and four rambunctious kids, two boys who were into Little League, and two girls who were cheerleaders.

She slid the wine glass onto the table where it made a disapproving ping. Fine, then, have it your way, Chablis. She grabbed the glass, took a few sips, walked to the door, and then stopped and listened. Was that someone coming down the hall? It was, but when the steps came and went, she relaxed and gulped down the rest of the wine.

After a quick touch-up of face powder and perfume, she headed downstairs, ready to bat her eyelashes coated in sapphire mascara and to smile with lips plumped with Fuchsia Fever. The poor unsuspecting detective wouldn't know what hit him.

She spied the receptionist talking to a man and then turning to point at Beverly. That must be the cop she was expecting? If so, he was hardly a Cro-Magnon and definitely no low brow ridge. He was actually quite . . . appealing. Part of her hoped it was him, part of her hoped it wasn't. She sucked in her stomach and straightened up.

The man in question headed toward her, his lean frame sporting a casual suit and tie. He strolled with a lanky, confident walk, not so much a caveman as a panther in an urban jungle. His thick sandy-colored hair, combed carelessly to one side, matched the light stubble on his face. Handsome in a well-seasoned, combat-carved way. At least, she'd have something nice to look at during her ordeal.

"Miss Laborde?" he asked, and she nodded. "I'm Detective Adam Dutton. Is there some quiet place where we could go to talk?"

"I just checked in, myself. But I noticed a tea room over there." She indicated a room off to the right.

He looked in that direction and studied the room for a moment. "That'll be fine." He held out one hand, indicating the way. "Shall we?"

She maneuvered around him to get in front. Beverly Laborde never followed anyone. Looking around, she spotted a table in a corner away from other diners and headed for it.

"Tea room" was a misnomer since the place also served coffee, smoothies, and alcohol. She craved more Chablis but opted for a staid serving of chamomile. After all, suspects never drank chamomile, did they?

Apparently, detectives on duty didn't drink anything, even if it was non-alcoholic. Dutton refused a drink at first until the waitress recognized him and offered him a cup of coffee on the house. Beverly watched him closely as he stirred in some sugar, his spoon clinking rhythmically in the cup. Then she said, "I didn't know I was meeting with a local celebrity."

He shrugged. "I arrested her husband once."

"I'm surprised she didn't throw the coffee at you. Unless she's trying to stay on your good side."

"She was glad to get rid of him." Dutton took a sip of the coffee.

"You must see all kinds. And get all kinds of cases. I can't imagine it ever getting dull." This is where she'd ordinarily bat her eyelashes. But in this instance, she didn't. His steady gaze was unsettling, and her sixth sense was telling her that he wouldn't fall for the vixen routine.

He replied, "The work is interesting enough. And as for the cases, let's say I don't think I'll be out of a job anytime soon. You'd be surprised at how much trouble is attracted to this area." He studied her over his cup with a half-smile.

"And here I was thinking a nice spa vacation would be pleasantly dull."

"You don't seem like the spa type."

"Oh? And what exactly is the spa type?"

"Middle-aged, married," he glanced at her bare left hand. "And a little heavyish."

"Sexist *and* ageist, Detective Dutton?"

He laughed. "Profile-ist. I'm only talking about the law of averages. It's the outliers you have to watch out for."

"Outliers like the mild-mannered Lizzie Borden?"

"Not that extreme."

Beverly traced the rim of the warm cup with her finger. Dutton was wearing a cedar musk cologne or aftershave. Why did he have to smell so distracting? She cleared her throat. "I assure you I'm no Lizzie Borden, Detective. Just a tired girl in need of a massage and a pedicure."

"Maybe if Lizzie had gotten a massage and pedicure, she wouldn't have taken an axe to her parents."

Beverly bit back a laugh. "Touché." She needed to focus, play along. But the caution alarms were screaming inside her head, and the urge to flee was overwhelming. Should she stay? Should she run? For the first time in quite a while, she didn't know what to do.

Then she remembered her grandmother sitting in the nursing home, not eating, staring out into space with unfocused eyes that were like cloudy window glass. When they ruined her grandmother's antiques business, they ruined her life—she hadn't lived long after. Even the hospice nurse said it was clear she died of a broken heart. Beverly was doing all of this for her, and she wasn't going to back down now.

She took a deep breath, counted to five, and batted her eyelashes at Dutton. Just another performance, another day, another town. But she didn't have the chance for any more stalling tactics because he got right down to the point. "I'll tell you why I'm here today. I'm looking for a scam artist. Perhaps you can help me find her."

2

Beverly Laborde kept staring at him after he dropped his little bombshell question, and Adam Dutton decided to let her sweat for a moment as he looked around the Apple Valley Resort. This was only the third time he'd set foot in the pricey spa where rooms started at two-fifty, and he still wasn't sure he liked it.

Okay, so it wasn't the typical folksy decor in the lobby, but this looked more like a set out of a sci-fi film. Clinical, cold, impersonal. Fortunately, the tea room had soft chairs instead of some hard metal contraption. And it smelled like coffee and muffins, not fake potpourri.

Beverly Laborde wasn't what he'd thought she'd be, either. She was hardly the model of a con artist, with her knee-length gray skirt, starched white blouse, and flat-heeled shoes. Throw in the brunette hair pulled into a bun contrasting against her porcelain skin, and she could have stepped out of a 1930s photo, the demure debutante.

But an air of sophistication about her made Detective Adam Dutton all too aware of his JC Penney suit and tie, complete with a mustard stain from his hot dog lunch. He pushed those thoughts aside. Let the interrogation begin.

"So, you arrived on the Amtrak train this morning and checked in at the Apple Valley Resort, not more than an hour ago. Is that correct, Miss Laborde?"

She smiled and picked up her chamomile tea from the table between them. "Such a lovely view, don't you think?"

He followed her gaze out the wraparound windows to the Presidentials in the distance, across the New Hampshire border. Ah, that kaleidoscopic quilt of autumn leaves. Easy to take for granted, which is why he never did. "Is that why you're here—for the view?"

She inhaled the chamomile aroma, then slowly exhaled with a smile. "I'm as much here for the view as you're here to chat about the architecture of this place."

Her cornflower eyes studied his face so intently, he felt as if he were the one suspected of passing off fake artifacts. The thick emotional skin he'd evolved, thanks to his ex-wife and a string of ex-girlfriends, wasn't much of a shield against Beverly Laborde's soul-piercing gaze.

"I'm here, Miss Laborde, because a disgruntled collector was bilked out of forty-thousand dollars. A woman approached the guy saying she had a genuine Paul Revere silver bowl. Even let it be appraised. Once she sold it to him, he discovered she'd switched it with a replica."

"What did this woman look like, Detective?"

He leaned back. "The victim, Reginald Forsythe the Fourth, described her as tall, slightly heavyset, with red hair and dark glasses."

"How tall?"

"About five-ten."

Beverly set her cup down, took a mirror out of her purse, and held it in front of her. "No red hair. I'm only five-eight. And I do try to adhere to caloric restriction, so I hope I'm not heavyset. Your description doesn't sound like me, does it?"

"Forsythe got the impression it might be a disguise. At the risk of sounding like a TV crime show, I have to ask where you were two evenings ago, around eight?"

Without hesitation, she replied, "Two nights ago, I was at a play by myself. I think I have the ticket stub around here somewhere." She dug into her purse. "Here you go."

He took it from her, wrote down the info, and handed it back. The theater wasn't anywhere near Boston. She couldn't have met with Forsythe at his shop there and made the two-hour trip to Hanover in time for that play. Unless she simply tore the ticket in half and never attended the performance.

Laborde added another spoonful of organic honey to her tea and stirred. "Have you ever played Fox and Geese, Detective Dutton?"

"What?"

"Fox and Geese. A board game popular in Colonial days. One piece represents the fox, and thirteen pieces represent the geese. The geese can't capture the fox but can win by hemming him in. For the fox to win, he has to capture and remove geese one by one, so they can't trap him."

Okay, maybe Adam's first impressions of Beverly Laborde hadn't been on the mark. Maybe she was one brick shy of a full load. "I don't see the connection with our female thief."

"This collector of yours, the one who made the complaint. Do you know much about him?"

"The basics. Middle-aged, very rich. Owner of a successful art and antiques gallery near Boston. Again, I really don't see—"

"Is it likely that someone that successful could be duped? And why didn't your female suspect just take the money and run? Why the switch?"

"To sell it twice. Two con jobs with the same item, and you've turned forty-thousand into eighty."

"The art world isn't all that large, Detective. Don't you think someone would spot this scheme? The FBI has a division for art fraud now. So I've heard."

"It's possible our thief is planning to sell the Revere bowl to one of those collectors off the grid. Someone like a rich Wall Street inside trader who buys artworks just to have them around. The status of it all."

"Sounds like you speak with the voice of experience, Detective."

An image of Adam's father sprang to mind, the once-proud carpenter fading into a dried-up husk of a man after sinking all his savings into a Ponzi scheme. He lost every dime. The rich bastard who ran the operation escaped to South America and was undoubtedly living the high life—wine, women, and more gambling. With prized artwork hanging on his walls, and a Paul Revere bowl or two on a credenza, no doubt.

Adam turned his attention back to business. "The buyer told Boston police officers he saw an Amtrak ticket receipt in the con woman's purse. We've been warned to keep an eye out for women arriving on the train from out of town. Primarily those asking about antiques. And you're the only one so far who fills the bill."

"I hardly think antiquing is a crime, Detective. If that were the case, then my sainted grandmother and thousands of others like her are guilty."

"Harlan Wilford, who owns the local Tossed Treasures shop, said you'd telephoned asking about silver artifacts. That you'd been doing some research. What kind of research would that be?"

"It's quite fascinating. I don't suppose you've heard of Rogers' Rangers in the eighteenth century?"

He shook his head. History was never one of his strong suits.

"They were dead set on preventing Indian raids on

Canadian and New England towns. So, some of the Rangers slaughtered the natives in a French-built Indian village."

He blinked at her. "I don't see the connection to a silver statue."

"The Rangers stole a silver plate, candlesticks, and a solid silver statue of Our Lady of Chartres from a church. As the story goes, an Indian guide leading the Rangers back through Mount Adams abandoned them. Only one Ranger made it out alive, his knapsack filled with human remains."

"The survivor turned to cannibalism?"

Laborde waved her hand in the air. "There were rumors to that effect."

"And I take it the silver pieces were in that knapsack, too?"

"No one ever said. However, the candlesticks were recovered near Lake Memphremagog in 1816. The statue was never found."

"Your research hasn't turned up anything?"

"Not much other than spirits of the Rangers are said to cry in the woods. And a hunter once had a ghostly vision up on Mount Adams—of Indians in a church under a floating silver statue."

"Why all this interest in ghost stories?"

"I'm a student of history. I think it's a fascinating subject, don't you? I mean it was either that or philosophy. If it hadn't been for my art history classes at the Hood, I might be another Susanne Langer or Simone de Beauvoir."

"The Hood? You mean the Hood Museum of Art? Dartmouth?"

"It's the main reason I got my art history degree. Are you a Darty, too?"

"Too rich for my blood. I worked my way through community college."

Miss Laborde's gaze had rarely wavered from his face, and

he'd gotten more at ease with her scrutiny. Now he was aware of a change, a look he interpreted as pity. Or amusement. Or both.

Deciding this interview was going nowhere fast, and not entirely convinced it wasn't a dead-end, he quickly drained his coffee and got up to leave. "I think that's all for now, Miss Laborde."

"You'll be keeping an eye on me, I presume. At least I hope you will."

He stopped in his tracks. "And why is that?"

She tipped her cup in his direction. "Because you have such nice eyes, Detective."

He put those eyes to good use to stare at her, to remind her who was in charge here. He nodded at the waitress on the way out, and a quick look back at Laborde told him she remained sitting there looking through the window.

Was she only here for the spa as she'd said? Somehow, he didn't think so. It was entirely possible she had nothing whatsoever to do with Forsythe and his damned Revere bowl, but her arrival was a thorny coincidence. And having that ticket stub to prove her alibi was too convenient.

Out in the parking lot, he grabbed some Black Jack chewing gum from the glove box and popped one of the aniseed-flavored sticks in his mouth. It was times like this, he missed his Marlboros. He'd have to settle for an after-work beer, or maybe he'd indulge in some of that Cognac he'd been saving.

He cranked up the engine as he took in the landscape. From here, the resort rose up like a miniature city sculpted out of white pine siding, red clay tennis courts, and azure pools. Red, white and blue. Rah. Not the type of place to make him want to stand up and salute.

Okay, so he'd interviewed Beverly Laborde as he'd

promised the chief this morning. Why this was the department's problem all of a sudden, he hadn't a clue. No, that wasn't entirely true, was it?

Forsythe reported the bowl switch at his store in Boston, but his primary residence was in this county—or half of it since it straddled the border with Hartford. Everything was local when you were dealing with the Vermont version of William Randolph Hearst. But squirrelly investigations or not, Adam wasn't about to be outsmarted by a smug high roller. Or a beautiful scam artist.

3

Beverly drove her rental SUV down Maple Avenue—couldn't they have come up with a more original name?—and marveled at the relative lack of traffic. Not a car horn to be heard. The smallish town of Ironwood Junction, population seven thousand except during leaf-peeping season, was a far cry from her recent big-city haunts.

No building was taller than three stories. And all were of the stereotypical stone or red Vermont brick style, standing proudly, but slightly tattered, like old soldiers in a Civil War reenactment. There was even a town square in the middle of the downtown with a cannon perched in the center. The cannon sat on a granite base, and the cannon's rusted bore, weeping an orangish-brown liquid down the side, made it look like a hemorrhaging tombstone.

She headed north where the town soon turned into forest. It should be unsettling for someone not accustomed to the country to be traveling alone in the boonies, shouldn't it? She hardly passed one car per mile, and with only the trees and birds for company, it was amazingly quiet.

In some ways, she felt safer here than in the big city with all the crime. She'd been mugged and nearly sexually assaulted in large towns, and she'd rather take her chances with a black bear. Or perhaps her courage came from the gun she always kept hidden in the purse slung across her shoulder—positioned diagonally across her chest, naturally, to make it harder to steal.

Beverly turned the rental SUV off the main road and down a washboard unpaved lane. It was getting closer to twilight, so she dare not dawdle if she wanted to see anything. Time to stop for a moment to check the map.

She knew the route would take her into the back end of nowhere, but this was slightly to the back of the back end of nowhere. She rolled down the window to take in some fresh air, with its hints of dried leaves and acorns smelling like an herbal tea.

The image of tea made her think of her meeting with Detective Dutton. She smiled at how wrong she'd been about him, especially his appearance. Neither did he seem the dim-witted type. And no wedding ring. Her smile turned to a frown as she pushed away the image of the attractive Adam Dutton. She needed to stay focused on avenging her grandmother's death, and right now, Dutton was just another obstacle in her way.

A small cabin rose into view as she pointed the car along a curve to the right, and she steered the SUV in front and parked. The cabin looked abandoned, but just in case, she forced herself to concentrate on every sound, every slight movement in a circle around her.

According to her interpretation, this was one of the possible spots Kornelson referred to on his treasure map. Which is to say, she hoped it was. They didn't have GPS back at the turn of the twentieth century when the map was drawn up, so she was learning fast how to translate compass points and map coordinates. Magnetic declination, azimuth—she should have taken an orienteering course.

Beverly headed toward the cabin and peered inside the windows. The place looked empty. She held up a hand to the window. Cool to the touch. No signs of heating or a fireplace. She gave a quick look toward the forest for any signs of being watched, and then she tried the door latch. It opened with a groan.

Pushing her way inside, she examined the interior. Rustic didn't describe it. Something akin to what Currier and Ives might have created in the throes of a nightmare. An old potbelly stove graced the middle of the room, but that was about the only furnishing save for one string-and-wood bed frame. Rotting wood in one corner reeked of mold and stale animal urine.

She paced around the room, looking for cracks in the floor or any sign something might be buried there, but it appeared to be a bust. The notes she'd taken from Kornelson's hints had mentioned a monument, hadn't they? This was certainly far, far from that. Surely she hadn't read the map wrong?

Then, she spied a dark clump where a wooden beam intersected the ceiling. She dragged the bed frame over to the wall and stood on it. The bed was wobbly, and her pulse rate climbed a few notches when she teetered and came close to falling off. Sliding a pencil flashlight out of her pocket, she shined it up toward the clump.

Without warning, a cloud of gray and black flew at her, surrounding her with an ear-splitting peal of swishing, flapping, and squeaks. Her pulse soared off the charts when something shot right at her and almost got tangled in her hair. She swatted at it, and it managed to avoid her and fly off with the other creatures through the open door. Bats.

Beverly checked her hands, looking for bites. None, thankfully. Realizing how lucky she was and how much of a huge disappointment and waste of valuable time this had turned out to be, she followed the bats in escaping outside.

She'd only stepped one foot out the door when a dark figure lurched around the corner of the cabin. Beverly wasn't aware she'd pulled the gun out of her purse until she realized she was pointing it at a man wearing earbuds and sporting a raven-haired ponytail.

The man gaped at her. "Whoa there, missy." Then he raised his hands up in the air. "If it's loot you're after, I've got fifty dollars in a back pocket and this," he slowly lowered one hand and eased a small device out of a shirt pocket. An audio player. The motion of maneuvering the device turned up the volume, and Beverly heard music coming from the earbuds.

"Is that Mozart?"

He grinned. "Symphony thirty-nine. Most people say forty-one is the best, but I like the minuet and trio in thirty-nine. What didja think it was, Johnny Cash?"

"I don't meet too many mountain-men types who listen to Mozart."

"Didn't have TV growing up. Only a radio with three stations, including Vermont Public Radio. And just how many mountain-man types have you met, little lady?"

Beverly lowered the gun and then shoved it back in her purse. She hoped her instincts were as sharp as usual. They'd certainly saved her neck on more than one occasion. "You remind me of a song from my childhood. 'In a cabin in a wood, a little old man by the window stood.'"

She studied his ponytail, where she now spied a few strands of gray hair woven through it and hints of crow's feet around his eyes. "Though you're not terribly old."

"Older than you by half, I'd say. Now, are you going to tell me what a lovely young creature like you is doing way out here in the boonies with a gun like that?"

"Would you believe looking for a retirement home to buy?"

He laughed. "Nope. But I'll take the hint. You passing through or do you live around here?"

"Neither. I'm staying in town, in the Junction."

"If it's leaves you're hunting," he waved his hand around, "We got plenty of 'em. Pick your color. They're all there."

"What's your name, if you don't mind my asking?"

"I don't. And it's Zachery Storich, but people call me Stork."

"Is this your cabin?"

"I can't say it is, or I'd be lying. I'm a handyman. This cabin belongs to a gentleman I do some work for. I was checkin' up on it."

"That's not very exciting. I was hoping for something more thrilling, an escaped convict, or a real mountain-man type."

"I do descend from Rogers' Rangers. Or so the family story goes. You familiar with them?"

Beverly tried not to let her excitement show on her face. "Yes, it's ringing that faint bell. Something about a raid and a treasure?"

Stork snorted. "Don't you go around believing everything you hear, certainly not that treasure. The raid part is sadly true. Can't say I'm proud of my ancestors for that. But those were different times. Like my friend Adam, for instance. His great-grandfather was a slaveholder in the South, but his ancestors, disgusted with that lot, moved up here."

"Adam?"

"Adam Dutton. He's a cop, but I don't hold that against him. We go way back to childhood. He's had some hard knocks, but he turned out okay."

Beverly hid her surprise that this man knew Dutton. "That's good to know. This area is full of noble souls. I feel safer already." She smiled up at him.

"You don't strike me as the type to get lost, but is there something you were looking for in particular?"

Beverly thought of the map in her car but wasn't about to tell him that. "Just getting the lay of the land."

"Lots of land around here for that." He turned and pointed. "North, ya got Phantom Lake State Park. South, it's Putney State Park. Then there's east, which takes you to the edge of the Junction and some other state park. West, is, well you get the idea. In-between, we have this little cabin here, built around nineteen ten." He chuckled. "Parks, trees, grass, and cows. That pretty much sums up Vermont."

"Don't forget the maple syrup."

He grimaced. "I hate maple syrup. It's heresy, I know. But to me, it tastes like burnt bark."

"Do other Vermonters, like your friend Adam Dutton, secretly hate it, too?"

"Adam's got a sweet tooth, but if you should run into him, don't tell him I said so. He's been on more of a health kick the past two years, ever since . . ." Stork gritted his teeth. "Let's just say he's wicked fond of maple fudge."

When Beverly noticed the late-afternoon sun angle and felt a cool breeze, she decided she should start heading back. But first, she apologized to Stork again for the gun.

Stork waved his hand in the direction of the road she'd driven down earlier. "One tip, then. On the way back, be careful to take the right-hand side when you get to the 'Y' in the road. The right'll take you back to the main drag, the other'll head off to an area it's best you stay away from. The souls there ain't all that noble."

He started to head into the cabin but turned around to add, "Oh, and you might want to take the safety off that gun next time if you plan on using it."

She stared after him before climbing back into the SUV. Her shooting instructor at the Castleman Range in Hanover would have flunked her if she pulled that during his course. She was slipping. Maybe it was the constant looking over her shoulder, maybe it was the long succession of nights in cold beds in strange rooms getting to her. She shook off her gloom and pointed the car back toward the main road.

When she came to the "Y" that Stork mentioned, she slowed down. She was more confident now that nothing had happened at the cabin. The left fork didn't look all that threatening. Perhaps Stork didn't want her to discover something valuable the locals kept to themselves. Should she give it a try?

Tempting though it was, she needed to do some more research. Her treasure map obviously wasn't complete, and it was long past due that she speak with an expert. Time to talk to Harlan Wilford, owner of the Tossed Treasures shop, in person. But that would have to wait until tomorrow.

She turned on the radio to find some soothing music to steady her pulse, which hadn't returned to normal after the bats and bumping into Stork. As she passed the intersection, she heard what sounded like a gunshot followed by the wail of a wounded animal.

Stepping on the gas, she made it back to the main road twice as fast as when she'd traveled in the opposite direction. Most likely, a hunter. But she kept a close eye on the rearview mirror as she sped away.

4

Adam Dutton sat in his office, eyeing a Jenga-like pile of folders. He resisted the urge to pull one out at random and see if the pile teetered over.

During the drive back to the police department from Apple Valley Resort last evening, Adam had considered the enigma of Beverly Laborde. He was pretty sure she knew about the Revere bowl switcheroo. There was the timing of her visit, and her answers too oblique. Plus, she was so maddeningly sure of herself, it was like watching an actress on stage.

When he woke up bright and early, he'd determined to research whatever he could find on her background. It was slow going, but he did confirm her attendance at Dartmouth.

Other than that, she didn't have much of a paper trail, and he hadn't found any employment records. An inheritance? He hadn't uncovered anything about her family background to tell. Still, the two-fifty per night at the resort wasn't chump change.

That family background thing bothered him. A scant few Labordes were scattered around New England, but no Beverlys. Not a trace. No birth, wedding, or divorce records, no mentions in newspapers or professional directories. He found a few Beverly Laborde death records, but they dated back a couple of decades and beyond. He broadened his search to the entire U.S., but no luck there.

Where had she come from? It would be hard to get a subpoena from a judge for Adam to take at a look at her Dartmouth records without a good reason. And that was pretty much all he had to go on right now.

Beverly had asked what he knew about the swindled collector, so he dug around there. Much more interesting, that. The collector "victim"—Reginald Forsythe, IV, or "Reggie" as he was known to avoid confusing him with his father—was dogged by hushed allegations he dealt in stolen and plundered artifacts.

He was rich, he had an army of lawyers at his beck and call, and he'd sued a few of those gossips for defamation. And won. Maybe it was all sour grapes, then. The antiques world was filled with cutthroat buyers and dealers? Who knew?

Adam found something else interesting. Reginald Forsythe, III, was accused of similar corruption, and like his son—no charges, no jail time. Both Forsythes belonged to the Northeastern Antiquities League, a group that included two other collectors who'd filed reports of being swindled with replicas. Both those collectors also had black clouds of ethical suspicion hanging over them.

What the hell was going on in that organization? And what was Beverly Laborde's connection? Trying to picture her as a criminal mastermind wasn't working too well for him. Perhaps she really was a simple history and antiques buff?

He didn't have time to ponder those questions as his fellow detective Eliot Jinks wandered in and plopped down on the chair in front of his desk. She pointed to the remains of his half-eaten kielbasa breakfast sandwich. "You gonna eat that?"

Not waiting for his reply, she grabbed it and scarfed it down. "My doc has me on a low-sodium diet. He says to me, 'you know African Americans have an increased risk for high blood pressure, so lay off the salty foods.' But have you tried unsalted potato chips? I'd rather have that heart attack."

"Guess I won't have to throw away that Norwegian lutefisk I ordered for you for Christmas," he said with a grin. Adam once asked Jinks how a skinny little black girl from the Bronx who'd moved to Vermont could know anything about lutefisk. She'd said her college roommate gave it to her as a gag, but the joke was on her after Jinks got addicted to the stuff.

Jinks got up to get herself a cup of water from the water dispenser in the corner of Adam's office. "You get anything out of that woman staying at the Dilly Dally resort?"

"Dilly Dally?"

"Seems like a better name to me. It's on a hill, not a valley, there aren't any apple trees for miles, and those people have time and money to burn."

"Yeah, it reeks of pretense when you walk in the door. But to answer your question, I didn't get anything helpful. Laborde doesn't fit the description of our scam artist, but she struck me as resourceful. The type of woman who could charm the dilly off a guy if he wasn't careful."

"Oh?" Jinks raised her eyebrows. "Sounds like she got under your skin, my friend."

Adam fiddled with a pen on his desk. "I just think she may know more than she's telling."

"Better come up with a concrete clue, because I came here to warn you. I saw the mayor walking into the building a few minutes ago. And he didn't look happy."

Her words were underscored by the chief's administrative assistant, Cherry, who poked her head in with a summons from The Man himself. Jinks gave Adam a sympathetic look, then got up to straighten his tie for him. "Cheer up. Zelda wasn't with the mayor."

Adam grunted. "Thank god for small favors." Not that

he'd expect Zelda to come with her new husband this go 'round like she'd made a point of doing after the man was elected two years ago. Adam knew it was for his benefit, one final exclamation mark on that chapter of his life.

When Adam entered the chief's office, Mayor Lehmann was standing next to the chief, and they were laughing, but the two men got quiet as soon as they spied Adam. Chief Phineas "Phinn" Quinn pointed at one of the overstuffed faux-leather chairs, and Adam took a seat. The mayor continued standing near the chief—a united front, no doubt. Towering over the peon detective to make sure he knew his place.

The chief asked, "Did you interview that woman who's staying at the resort?"

Adam cleared his throat. "She says she doesn't know anything about the bowl switcheroo, and she doesn't match Reggie Forsythe's description. But I'm checking her out, just in case."

"You do that. Even if she's not our thief, we need to be on the lookout for any suspicious woman in our jurisdiction who could be our female Robin Hood."

"Robin Hood?"

"It's what Reggie Forsythe called her. Forsythe's agitating to see this woman is caught and forced to make restitution. I don't need to remind you Forsythe is a wealthy and powerful man. He could make trouble for our department if he so chooses."

The mayor piped up. "Yes, but we're also fortunate to have Forsythe in this part of our fair state. He's an ally we want to keep on our side."

Adam bit his tongue to keep from saying, "No, Forsythe is the type of man you want on *your* sorry-ass side."

It was no secret Mayor Titus Lehmann had grandiose aspirations. The Mayorship was only the first step. Next, it was the governor's mansion. And one thing a candidate needed to make it to the top job in the state was some heavy-hitting backers. Feeding Reggie Forsythe's ego was all part of that plan.

In his research, Adam read that Forsythe had backed several candidates for various offices. Buy them off, and they'll perform for you on command. It was a formula as old as cavemen, bartering food or trinkets to become the clan elder.

Adam looked both men in the eye in turn. "I'll pursue every lead I can."

"You do that." Chief Quinn studied his face. "If you want me to assign someone else other than Jinks to help out—"

"If I need help, Jinks is fine. She's working that missing-person case right now. But I know I can count on her if need be."

The chief seemed somewhat satisfied and turned to Lehmann. "Are we still on for that golf game Sunday morning?"

"Sure thing, Cal. I'll see you around nine-ish."

Lehmann didn't give Adam one look as he strode out of the office. Adam gave the slimy eel plenty of time to slither away before he said, "I don't understand one thing, chief. Okay, more than one, but why didn't this Forsythe guy simply go to the FBI since this may be a multi-jurisdictional thing?"

"He said he didn't want to involve them if he didn't have to."

"Did he now? Why not?"

"He didn't elaborate. But it's probably a reputation thing. Forsythe is all about reputation."

"Yeah, I got that. Just like the mayor." Adam got up to return to his office, but Quinn stopped him.

The chief said, "I meant what I said about Jinks. How are the therapy sessions going?"

Adam's smile faded. "Fine. I'm down to once a month

now."

"You know the department will continue to pay for those as long as you—"

"I've been thinking about stopping them altogether."

"Whatever you think is best." The chief rubbed his chin and added, "You know, as rich as Forsythe is, you'd think he wouldn't be this upset about one silver bowl. Even if it was crafted by Paul Revere himself."

"Forsythe sounds like a man who doesn't like to be crossed. Someone got the better of him. He won't stand for that."

"Then, I hope we catch this thief before he does."

"So do I, Chief. So do I."

Adam stomped down the hallway to his office and dropped into his chair. Jinks poked her head in to see if he was back. "How'd it go?"

"What you'd expect. Quinn's got a monkey on his back. And the monkey—"

"Is an ass, if you're referring to the mayor."

"The brain of a monkey and the tail of an ass."

Jinks made the sign for "correct." She'd learned sign language when her father had gone partially deaf from meningitis. Adam had picked up a little bit so they could communicate silently on stakeouts, but he was nowhere near as fluent as Jinks.

He signed back, "Idiot," and she signed back something he doubted she'd want her kid to repeat. Trust Jinks to make him feel a bit better.

§ § §

Adam made a quick trip to the Amtrak station to see if there'd been any more reports of women traveling alone who might have been seen carrying silver or maybe talked about it. The manager said no, but he did recall Laborde carting one large piece of luggage and a smaller overnight-style bag. He said he'd remembered because he'd thought the unusual blue floral fabric on the bags was perfect for such a lovely lady. Score one for Laborde's charms over the male sex.

An overnight bag was commonly used by women for toiletries and makeup. But it was sort of bowl-sized, too, wasn't it? Fat chance of Adam getting a search warrant based on a tourist who happened to be in town and was interested in history and antiques. Forsythe's clout aside, most judges would laugh Adam out of the courthouse for that.

Adam also stopped by the local library to see if they had any books on silver pieces, mostly those from the Paul Revere era. They had one he checked out and began to read in his car. Hopefully, he'd learn enough to know a real piece when he saw it.

The history of it all was more interesting to him than the actual pieces. He had no idea Paul Revere worked copper and brass and printed currency in addition to his silversmithing—that even included false teeth.

Truth be told, most of the antique silver pieces in the book's photos looked alike to Adam. It was a mystery to him why some collectibles were valued so much more than others. Rarity was a factor, sure, and ownership history. But other than that, a bowl was a bowl was a bowl.

He needed some advice from someone far more expert at this antiquing thing that he was. There was only one person he trusted about these matters, the "Antiques God," as Adam called him.

Talk of bowls and antiques aside, he'd told Jinks he believed Beverly Laborde was hiding something. But if it wasn't this Revere thing, what was it? Adam sighed. He'd almost prefer to have a good old-fashioned murder case right now. He chastised himself for that thought, knowing there'd be plenty more of those in his future. A little bowl-bother might not be so horrible, after all—if only it didn't have Reggie Forsythe's paw prints all over it.

5

He was Santa Claus, pure and simple. At least, he looked the part, and when Beverly introduced herself to Harlan Wilford, he was as jolly as his doppelganger. "So glad to see you are as lovely as your voice on the phone, Miss Laborde. You were asking about silver antiques, I believe. Are you a collector?"

"Of a sort, yes." She stopped to admire a seventeenth-century Dutch ebony table clock resting on a pedestal in the front of Harlan's Tossed Treasures store. "I've been looking into silver lately. Early American, for the most part. Dummer, Winslow, Revere."

"Antique Paul Revere piece ay? I don't know if you heard, but a Revere bowl went missing recently. A collector named Reggie Forsythe believed he was buying the real deal, even had it appraised. But when he got the piece, it was a fake."

Beverly's shoulder's tensed at the mention of the name. Maybe Harlan didn't notice. "Forsythe, yes, I recall the name. He's a multi-millionaire, isn't he? I'd guess he can buy a carload of Revere bowls. Or anything else, for that matter." Including people, or so she'd heard. Bowls, people, lives. They were all the same to a man like Reggie Forsythe. Just interchangeable commodities to be bought and sold.

Harlan frowned as if reading her mind. "I know I shouldn't speak ill of folks, 'specially those that might be customers one day, but I'm no fan of Forsythe. There's philanthropist rich people, and there's useless-as-a-screen-door-on-a-submarine rich people. Forsythe is the latter kind. But I digress. What can I interest you in? A silver clock or a lamp?"

"Forsythe hasn't been in here yet, looking for old treasures?" She pointed to the Tossed Treasures logo in the window. "It is on your sign."

"I do have some items the likes of him might be interested in. Honestly, I'd prefer selling them to someone more deserving. Someone who'd appreciate them, not look at them like scalp marks on a belt."

"Scalp marks? Are you a historian of Native American lore, Mr. Wilford?"

"Harlan. No one calls me mister. Sounds too much like a plant sprayer thingie."

She laughed. "Harlan, it is. I've been researching Indian folk tales in the region. The Rogers' Rangers story is particularly fascinating."

"That the one about a solid silver statue? Some Lady Godiva thing, as I recall."

"Lady of Chartres. You haven't seen anything like that turn up?"

"That's a big no on that one, Miss Laborde."

"Beverly."

He smiled. "You staying in town long, Beverly? We ain't got big-city culture around here, but there's the Ironwood Junction Museum. Some vintage clothing and toy shops. And the Sugar Train restaurant makes mouthwatering maple pecan-glazed trout. This time of year, they have these killer pumpkin biscuits."

"I only got in today, but I may take you up on your suggestions. There are a lot of interesting people hereabouts. I ran into one earlier, a Detective Adam Dutton."

Harlan beamed. "Ah, Adam. I knew his father, you see. I've watched Adam grow from a sullen, serious little boy into a sullen, serious young man. Of course, he's not that sullen anymore. And not as young." Harlan chewed on his cheek. "He hasn't had it easy. He's good at what he does, mind you, but it's dangerous. There was that incident two years ago . . . "

"Incident? What do you mean?"

"I really shouldn't talk about it. I don't think they released many details in the papers. Protecting Adam's privacy, don't you know. And the police department's reputation." Harlan licked his lips. "It was a drug bust gone bad. Adam was kidnapped and tortured, and . . . let's just say it wasn't pleasant."

Beverly thought back to her talk with Adam. He'd seemed so professional, so self-assured, and she hadn't noticed any scars. Tortured? In what way? She'd hoped to weasel out of Harlan everything he knew about Adam Dutton but hadn't expected anything whatsoever like this.

She considered herself a good judge of character and had an inkling Dutton wouldn't want her pity. Still, she wanted to learn everything she could about him. It was always prudent to get intel on your opponents. And he was clearly an opponent if he came between her and her revenge mission. She rubbed her eyes briefly to banish the image of his mocha-brown eyes staring at her.

"In your ad in the paper, Harlan, it said you also deal in antique documents. Maps, letters, diaries?"

"My former partner got me interested in those. He spent many a day with his nose buried in some archives, forgetting to come up for air nor food."

"Would you be able to authenticate a document, then? Tell whether it was a hoax or not?"

"Depends upon the document. Easier if it's English, for instance. Old English is fine, too."

"Oh, it's in English for sure." She reached into a case she wore on a strap and retrieved a plastic sleeve with a yellowed paper inside. "This is what I'd like you to look at. I'd be happy to pay you."

Harlan flipped the reading glasses parked on top of his head into position and peered at the paper. "Looks a little fragile. And I'll need some better light with these aged eyes, you know. Why don't we go to my office? If a customer comes in, they'll know where to find me, or my assistant can handle it." Harlan headed toward the back of the store.

And for once, Beverly followed. They wound up in a room like the Old Curiosity Shop, and she even thought she saw some manuscripts peeking out of a grandfather clock in a corner. A sweet smell of lacquer mingled with musty fabric and hints of lemon polish. Beverly wished she could bottle up antique store aromas into a perfume.

She also caught a whiff of popcorn. Popcorn? Then she spied a vintage popcorn machine labeled "Eat Butter Kist Popcorn," and it was full of freshly popped kernels.

Harlan pulled out a giant magnifying glass mounted on a stand, then carefully removed Beverly's yellowed document from its sleeve and slid it under the glass. "This an original?" he asked.

"Circa 1900." Finding this particular piece was a massive stroke of luck. After getting all the info she was able to glean out of the Kornelson estate, she'd gone to a used bookstore in the same town. There, buried in the stacks of old papers in a file box all but ignored under some stairs, she'd stumbled across this little gem of a map. She wouldn't have given it a second glance if she hadn't spied Kornelson's name written in the margin.

Beverly felt a little guilty keeping it, but Kornelson didn't have any heirs. And the man's papers were largely forgotten, crumbling piece by piece in a library few people visited. Beverly was quite protective of that map, one of the last traces of a man no one missed.

Harlan went over to a shelf and pulled off a book, flipping through it until he found what he was looking for. He put the book side by side with Beverly's document and pointed. "Wear lines along the folds. Looks like a cerograph, popular after 1880 or so. Printed on a banknote, a good sign. That's what you'd expect for pocket maps of that era."

"That sounds promising."

"It is. Also, there's no date on this map. Another good sign. Forgers tend to put dates 'cause they think that makes it look authentic. But that's not something mapmakers around the turn of the century would do."

He peered over his glasses at her. "Got any supporting documents?"

She pulled another piece of paper out of the case. "This is a photocopy. Not an original. But it supposedly relates to that map."

He studied it for a moment. "Can't make heads nor tails out of that text. A poem?"

Beverly reached over and underlined part of the text with her finger. Harlan squinted at it. "Quite interesting. It does mention some of the features on this map. Where did you find this little mystery?"

Beverly filled him in on her discovery, and he smiled. "Estate archives are treasure troves. I'll give you that. Well, Miss Beverly, short of radiocarbon dating, I'd say your map here is likely not a fake. Does that help any?"

She gave him a hug. Maybe this wasn't an exercise in futility, and with any luck, it meant she might be on the right track. Now, if she could just stay one step ahead of Detective

Dutton and find her treasure before Reggie Forsythe did, she'd be home free. Easy peasy, right?

6

Adam didn't waste a minute after his meeting with the mayor and Chief Quinn. He called enough antique stores from Boston up to Montreal to feel like he was becoming an expert on antiques, himself. As long as they were silver. The 1730 Marston Schaats Tankard, punch bowls by early Boston silversmith John Burt, Governor Stoughton Cups created by New England silversmith Jeremiah Dummer. The first mint masters of the Massachusetts Bay Colony, Robert Sanderson, Sr. and his partner John Hull. And of course, Paul Revere.

But no one had seen the tall, red-haired woman or anyone matching Laborde's description, nor had the Revere bowl turned up for sale. Why in the world did the thief go to such an elaborate switch if not to sell it?

Yeah, he knew he'd told Beverly Laborde that the thief might sell it to a private collector and no one would be the wiser, but he'd hoped he was wrong about that. Otherwise, it would be impossible to trace. Game over.

After Adam's research on the Forsythes, father and son, and some of the other members of the Northeastern Antiquities League, Adam was beginning to wonder if there were any honest antique dealers. But as he headed to Tossed Treasures in the center of town, he was convinced old Harlan Wilford was one of them.

He'd known Harlan for years. When he was a boy, Adam called him Uncle Harlan whenever he joined Adam and his father on their fishing outings. Adam felt a pang of guilt when he realized he hadn't stopped by for a while. He already owed Harlan a lunch or two he'd bailed on due to work.

Adam waved at Harlan's assistant, Prospero Rigas, and headed back to Harlan's office, where the man didn't look surprised to see him. "And there you are, Adam, right on time. She said you'd be along shortly."

"She?" Adam hid his irritation. He had an idea who the "she" was and felt like a goose in Beverly Laborde's Fox and Geese game. He was always one step behind her while she stage-managed his investigation to her benefit.

"That young lady who was just here, Beverly. Said you'd taken an interest in her." Wilford winked. "With a figure like that, I can see why."

"That's not the kind of interest she was referring to." Or was it? What had she meant by "nice eyes?" It was all likely an elaborate ploy on her part. And he wasn't going to fall for it.

"Then you must be interested in the vision of Mount Adams she was asking about, Adam. And that silver figure they never found."

"What did you tell her?"

"That I don't know much about it, myself. But she mostly wanted me to help authenticate some documents."

"What documents?" She hadn't mentioned any documents to Adam. Yep, he was definitely a goose. Or should he say, a gander?

"A map and papers originally rescued from the estate of a man who died childless around 1900. They mentioned a silver Lady of Chartres statue stolen by Rogers' Rangers, those papers did. It wasn't among the deceased's effects."

"Why would the documents refer to it, then?"

"It was a puzzle, you see, those documents. Mentioned a 'safe place' or a secret storehouse, I believe it was. All very cloak and dagger. Not my line of work. More yours, I'd say."

"I don't suppose the location of this hidden storehouse was in there?"

"Not spelled out, A-B-C, no. It was part of a poem I couldn't make nary heads nor tails out of. Several references to this area, though. Hartford, the Junction, and the Natick Indians."

"Did you keep copies of those documents Miss Laborde showed you?"

"'Fraid not, Adam. I think she's staying somewhere here in town. If she returns, should I have her give you a call?"

"Thanks, Harlan, but I know where she's staying." At Harlan's smirk, Adam, quickly added, "Do you happen to recall the name of that man, the one whose estate the papers came from?"

"Reckon I do. Reminded me of an old friend of mine, the name did. It was Kornelson."

Adam pulled out a pad and wrote the name down. When he looked up again, Harlan was staring at him. "You look a little peaked, Adam. How long has it been since you had a vacation?"

"Vacation?"

"You know, where you go off to the beach, put some zinc on your nose, lie around turning into a lobster, drink piña coladas."

Adam ignored the question. He was getting tired of people thinking he was fragile and had to be treated with kid gloves. "What did you think of Miss Laborde, Harlan? Did she seem suspicious? Anything set off alarm bells?"

"Quite the opposite, I must say. She's highly knowledgeable about antiques. Nicely well-mannered, too. Although . . . "

"Yes?"

"She struck me as being skittish. Not outlaw-skittish, but

more like a filly ready to bolt at the slightest touch. Like one of my nieces. Went through a spell where she was very much the loner. Her parents had a devil of a time getting her to make friends."

"Thanks for your help, Harlan. If Miss Laborde stops by again, you'll let me know."

Wilford understood it was more of a command than a question, and he shrugged. "Best of luck with whatever it is you're after, Adam. Don't forget legends often have a grain of truth to them. As for that young lady," he grinned. "If I were your age, I'd have no problem taking an interest. Just sayin.'"

§ § §

Adam left Harlan's store and grabbed a copy of the *Junction Jive* from a news rack in front of the store. It was close to supper, but he wasn't hungry, so he grabbed coffee and a sandwich-to-go from Miralee's Market. Their coffee and turkey on rye were usually among the best around, but the coffee tasted stale, and the bread was like chewy cardboard with a slathering of brown mustard.

Nothing had gone right for him today. Maybe the black cat of his neighbor, Mrs. Carden, was to blame. Inkspot took every chance to get in Adam's way, crossing his path several times this morning in the yard. Actually, the bad luck was more on Inkspot's side, half-blind and running around on only three legs. Adam and the cat declared a truce after Adam fed him some leftover sardines a year ago. Kitty detente.

Sitting in his car and munching on the dry sandwich, washed down with the bitter coffee, Adam flipped through the *Junction Jive*. One entry in the regional event calendar stood out and waved at him. Reginald Forsythe, III, the alleged theft victim's father, was speaking at a district NAL meeting tonight down in Brattleboro. Adam checked the time. With any luck, he'd make it there before it began. He gave a quick call to Jinks to let her know where he was headed and started down I-91.

He found his way to the venue, a theater and gallery on the main street in town. Outside the modernistic barn-shaped structure, a marquee of upcoming events announced a performance of *The Fantastiks*, followed by a comedian—that was appropriate for the type of people he was checking out— and then a photography exhibit.

Following the sign for the NAL meeting, he walked down a set of stairs into the gallery where he stopped to admire a photo of a nubile woman in her birthday suit playing a harp. Very artistic. He could just hear Jinks snorting her derision, so he turned to study the rest of the lobby with its collage of pipes and glass-covered gauges, which he soon learned was part of the sprinkler system.

The small, amber-lit hall looked to hold about a hundred, and since most of the seats were taken, he grabbed the nearest empty chair in a corner in the back. The man sitting next to him, about fiftyish and wearing a red vest and a gold paisley cravat, turned to him. "I don't believe I've seen you at one of these meetings before."

"I'm, ah, new," Adam smiled. "First timer."

"You chose a bad one." The man waved his hand around the room. "We'd better get our usual country club meeting space back for our next meeting. Forsythe must be steaming that it wasn't available. Some roof leak or whatever. There goes my chance to get in a game of golf tomorrow morning."

Adam mumbled a "Hmm."

"I should have stayed at home watching Antiques Roadshow. These meetings are deadly dull."

Adam took a stab in the dark. "Think he'll mention that

Revere bowl heist?"

The other man's eyebrows almost launched into the stratosphere, and his voice lowered to barely above a whisper. "Better not let him hear you. You don't want to be on his blacklist. Though the way he and his son are like oil and vinegar, you'd think he'd be elated at the chance to gloat."

"Anything like that happen to you?"

"I would never fall for such an amateurish ploy. Forsythe is an imbecile."

Adam didn't have a chance to ask which Forsythe the man meant because a figure marched out on stage to the podium. In his upper seventies, unbowed, a silver wolf decked out in a hide of hubris and disdain—shady business practices would be a natural fit for this man.

To Adam's surprise and that of his neighbor, who Adam saw flinch out of the corner of his eye, Forsythe-the-elder went on a tirade about antiques fraud. Nothing direct about the Revere bowl, just various oblique references. But the message was clear. The NAL, and by extension, Forsythe, were to declare war on "these moles, these infiltrators, these saboteurs."

Adam knew a thing or two about war. Or battles, anyway. He wasn't the slightest bit concerned what Forsythe would say if he found out Adam himself was playing a mole role right then. When the meeting dragged on and turned to tedious business items, Adam entertained himself by counting the types of ties in the room. Bow ties were neck-and-neck with cravats. He was proud of his apostate JC Penny tie.

After the meeting adjourned for "refreshments" in the lobby, Adam grabbed a glass of wine and casually strolled around the room, listening in on conversations. He took the occasional teensy sip for appearances, but he did have to drive an hour back.

He was surprised at how much of the chatter had to do

with Reggie Forsythe's "female Robin Hood." Some of it was outrage, some of it was more on the side of misogyny. Adam looked around and noted the lack of female attendees. Maybe there was a darker reason than a mere lack of women antique store owners.

Adam sidled up to Reggie's father, who pivoted toward him with a look of confusion. "Do I know you?"

"Mr. Adam." It wasn't his best alias, but he was in a hurry. "Enjoyed your presentation. Rogue antiques scam artists. What's the world coming to?"

Forsythe growled. "Makes you long for eugenics." Before Adam could decide how to answer that Hitler-esque remark, Forsythe continued, "Even that wouldn't help. Although my foundation makes a dent through education."

"Your foundation?"

"A little thing I do on the side. An orphanage, a few scholarships."

"I wasn't aware. Sounds fascinating." Shocking was more like it. Forsythe talked about it without a shred of irony. Was there a heart beating in there somewhere? Or was it a mere tax write-off?

Adam took another sip of wine. "Such a shame about your son's Revere bowl. Surely they've caught the scammer by now."

"The police are a bunch of bumbling incompetents." Adam nodded sagely, and Forsythe the Third added, "But so's my son, apparently. Being taken in like that."

Adam winked. "More so since I imagine he's on a first-name basis with deception, wouldn't you say?"

Forsythe's eyes narrowed. "What did you say your name was again?"

Adam was about to offer up his pseudo-fake name when an intense man with frizzy white hair like an exploded snow globe grabbed Forsythe's arm and mumbled in his ear. Adam caught a few words, "Salvage, black market, and discreet," before the snow-globe man and Forsythe hurried off.

As Adam turned around, he caught a figure weaving through the crowd, headed for the door. A female figure. Once more, Adam was reminded of how few women he'd seen at this meeting, making this one particular woman stand out in the crowd.

She had her back toward him, letting him see she had coal-black hair tied in a French braid. He didn't think he'd seen her before, and yet, there was something familiar about her.

He decided to catch her before she left, but an elderly man bumped his arm, causing Adam to spill wine down his shirt. After brushing off the man's apologies as best he could, Adam sprinted after the woman, but when he reached the street level, she'd vanished.

7

Wednesday, September 15

Her first night at the Apple Valley Resort had helped to justify Beverly's decision to come to Ironwood Junction. The bed was as comfortable as a cloud, and the Jacuzzi tub worked miracles on the tension knots in her shoulders.

She studied the resort's spa menu. Avocado polish, caviar facial, color-and-light wrap with aura imaging—that was a new one—but she put it back on the table with regret. No time. Too much to do.

The trip yesterday to Harlan's was the second reason justifying her decision to come to the Junction. He was the first helpful person she'd run into in years, and she'd felt more at home in his shop than in this pleasure palace. Plus, he'd helped her see she was on the right track with her map. The odd thing was, everywhere she turned in town, she bumped into someone who knew Adam Dutton. Fate or bad omen?

She didn't have the luxury of trusting Dutton. She'd been careful to cover her tracks, and his questions hadn't led to her arrest thus far, but she knew she'd be watched. Best behavior and all that. She could have waited a month or two to come, but she had a strong feeling the window of opportunity to find her treasure would soon slam shut with a bang.

Grabbing a lemon poppy seed muffin from the tea room, with the passing thought her figure was to become muffin-shaped if she kept this up, Beverly made her way to her rental car. She put the map and the document she'd shown Harlan in its plastic bag under a fake floor mat she'd rigged up beneath the passenger seat. Just in case anyone broke into the car.

She used the car's GPS to find her way to an address she'd seen in the newspaper and parked in front of a one-story building with alternating bricks of red and yellow. A taxidermied eel grinned at her from the store-front window. She traced a tinkling sound to a wind chime above the door with dangling black bats. Two mannequins guarded the entrance, one dressed as a Viking, the other as a Goth. She already liked this place.

Ducking through the orange-painted glass door, she spied what she was looking for and headed toward the racks. The clerk, looking like a fish out of water in her blue gingham smock, approached Beverly. "Can I help you find something specific?"

Beverly smiled. "Looking for Halloween costume fodder."

The clerk pointed to a corner, "Victorian is over there, and . . . " She indicated another area, "S&M is other there. In-between, we've got, well, everything in-between. And there's a special wig and makeup section in the back. If you don't see what you need, we have it buried somewhere. Feel free to ask."

Beverly thanked her and headed toward the wigs first. Her hand hovered over one with long, wavy red hair, then fingered another with realistic-looking brown curls. Grabbing that, she checked out a rack of skirts, choosing a long navy blue number she held up to her waist. It dragged the floor and would hide heels. Perfect.

Next, she chose a pair of black shoes left over from the '60s with five-inch stilettos. The store also had a small special effects case of face prosthetics she snapped up. Fortunately, she had plenty of makeup, false eyelashes, and contact lenses in her kit, but she cast a wistful eye on some violet lenses. Too memorable. She paid cash and bundled her purchases into the trunk of her rental.

She sat in the car, recalling a similar store she and her grandmother visited when Beverly was nine. Another child there with his mother and father asked where Beverly's parents were, and she'd snapped at him, "None of your beeswax."

Her grandmother was embarrassed, but not at her outburst. She'd been proud of that, Beverly could tell. No, Grammie was embarrassed by the hard truth in that little boy's words. But Beverly wasn't.

She couldn't remember her parents, and Grammie was the only happy memory left from her childhood. The same Grammie who was crumbling to dust in a graveyard, gone far too soon. Beverly pounded the steering wheel over and over and over. The universe seemed to be mocking everything good she'd ever known.

Peeling out of the parking lot, she wandered aimlessly down a back road before pulling over to get the waterworks under control so she could see to drive. It wouldn't do to drive absentmindedly into some tree or pond. She shuddered at the thought of driving into a body of water. One of her worst nightmares—that or ending up in an orange jumpsuit making license plates with surly inmates.

She retrieved a picture out of the wallet in her purse and traced the outlines of the smiling woman's face and her more-pepper-than-salt hair fashioned into a bun. Gently replacing the photo, Beverly pointed the SUV toward downtown Ironwood Junction.

The cloudy day muted the fall colors, but it matched her mood, so she didn't mind. She made another stop at a small general store, the type you didn't see much anymore except in New England. The muffin hadn't sated her hunger, so she purchased an ice-cold bottle of Moxie and some roasted pumpkin seeds. She said to herself, "Not quite those killer pumpkin muffins you mentioned, Harlan, but it'll have to do."

She was immediately drawn to Harlan. She didn't know if it was the Santa effect or the fact he reminded her of Grammie, but whatever the reason, she knew she'd be back to his store soon. She ran the risk of running into Detective Dutton, but it wasn't a crime to sightsee or buy antiques the old-fashioned way, was it?

Detective Dutton. Adam Dutton. A nice masculine, no-nonsense name. He was fun to flirt with, she had to admit. Usually, it was more of a chore, a distraction. He wasn't like anybody she'd met before, not necessarily a bad thing.

But men were so easy to play. All it took was a sexy, come-hither smile meant "only" for them, and that universal key to the male psyche unlocked barriers to the frontal cortex, giving you instant access to the limbic system. Once in, you had free rein to take whatever you wanted. Sex, money, favors, trust. Everything except love.

A familiar head of hair caught her attention, and she pulled down the car's sun visor and sat up tall to avoid being seen. Speak of the devil. Her curiosity getting the better of her, she risked a peek around the visor at Dutton, who was standing in front of a wine shop. Was he buying some Chablis? Waiting for someone? Looking for her?

A woman with short auburn hair, carrying Prada and wearing an Yves St. Laurent dress Beverly had seen at Saks, hurried out of the wine shop and grabbed Dutton's arm. He whirled around toward the woman, and she smiled up at him.

Beverly knew that smile. Not casual, not motherly, not we're-just-friends. That woman knew Adam, as only one who's intimate with someone can.

Beverly made a U-turn toward the resort. She needed a nap or some tea. Make that Cognac tea. Or skip the tea and stick with the Cognac. Adam Dutton obviously had his hands—and god knows what else—full, and she needed to consult her notes.

What she didn't need was another full-blown headache. Headaches, heartaches, funny how they all ended up the same way. You got over them, eventually. If they didn't kill you first.

8

Adam stared at Zelda Lehmann. If he'd known she was in the deli, he would have walked on the other side of the street to get to the bank. Waking up with a stiff neck should have been a tip on how his day was going to go. The stiff-neck omen. He'd have to remember that for next time. Maybe take the day off.

Zelda's hair was redder than the last time but had hints of the black and gray roots. He'd liked it when her hair first showed wisps of gray, but she didn't believe anyone would take her seriously if she looked too "old." Did he look old to her now? Then again, her husband, the mayor, had shaved the last traces of hair off his nearly bald head, hadn't he?

Zelda grabbed his arm, but when she saw him staring at her hand and at the diamond boulder on her ring finger, she released his arm to reach inside a bag from the deli. Pulling out a bottle of Russian River Valley Pinot Noir she said, "Your favorite."

Funny, he hadn't had a glass of that since the divorce. Guess he knew why now. "As I recall, you weren't all that fond of Pinot Noir. Unless you're buying that for the mayor?"

She stuffed the bottle back into the bag and set it on the ground. "He's more of a champagne man. The wine is for me. I've developed a taste for it."

"Goody for you."

"Adam . . ." She gazed up at him with those soft, brown doe eyes of hers, in the way she did when they first started dating. He'd half-believed her when she once said she'd cast a spell on him because those eyes bewitched him whenever she looked at him that way.

"Adam, I've missed you. That sounds trite, I suppose. It's just . . . I know we had something special back then. And I wanted to tell you that."

What was he supposed to say? Thanks oh-so-much for reminding me that we had something great until you decided being first lady with your cop husband wasn't enough? That richer was better than poorer? And "until death we part" was only a suggestion?

Adam glanced at the bottle of Pinot Noir in the bag. He used to like the wine's taste—dry, smoky, dark, complex. A lot like his marriage.

He squinted at holes in the cloud layer that allowed peeks of blue sky and sunlight to show through. "I've got to get going. Your husband laid down the law yesterday in the chief's office. A case he's got a personal interest in. For some odd reason, he's taken a dislike to me. Wonder why?"

Zelda pushed her bangs out of her eyes. "Your famous sarcasm is alive and well, I see. Titus has a mountain of pressure on him right now. It's nothing personal."

Dutton laughed. "And your talent for denial is still razor-sharp. Like hell, it's personal."

"Is that the Forsythe case, the one with the high-stakes thief? I heard Titus talking. It sounded like there was a woman involved. Or an organized ring, and the woman is the distraction."

"Could be. I don't like to discuss cases I'm working."

"How well I remember." She tilted her head, and the morning sun on her hair matched the light glittering on the red maple leaves. "What is this femme fatale like, Adam? She must be gorgeous to be such an effective distraction."

"The description is vague. But I'd guess she's attractive."

"You'd better look out then, lest she get her claws into you," she replied, touching his arm lightly this time. "Adam, I do admire you, you know that." When he started to reply, she put a finger on his lips and added, "No, not just admire. A part of me will always love you."

Picking up her bag, she hurried to her car and was out of sight in less than a minute. Adam stood staring after her for a good two minutes longer, not knowing whether to curse her or run after her. He continued his interrupted walk to the bank, when a familiar nasal voice said, "Are you trying to win back your wife, Dutton? If you are, there's no chance in hell it will work."

Adam whirled around to face the mayor, whose pretense of calm was shattered by the red blotches on his cheeks and nose. He was a bald strawberry. "Why would I want to do that, Lehmann? You won, I lost. End of story."

"Oh, I doubt it's love you have in mind. Perhaps you hope to make me look bad in front of the voters. Keep me from winning the governorship. Get back at me for marrying Zelda and for putting pressure on your beloved police force."

"If that's what you believe, feel free to file a formal complaint with the chief. I couldn't care less."

"We'll see about that. And don't believe for a minute I'm going to go easy on you about the Forsythe case. I know what you think. You think he is lying about the whole affair and had a hand in it. And other antiquities thefts, to boot. But you're wrong. You need to chase after that mystery red-headed woman. That's your thief."

"I never said anything about Reggie Forsythe lying. And this mystery woman is probably in Canada or Mexico right now."

"Or under our very noses. I expect results, Dutton. Chief

Quinn is pushing the council for money to fund new cruisers and other gear." The man sneered as he added, "Maybe some new radios?"

Adam counted to ten to avoid smashing Lehmann in his bright red nose to give him some bright red blood to go with it. That was a cheap shot, and Lehmann knew it. If Jinks were here, she'd have kicked the guy in his nuts for that. Turn his whiny tenor into a bleating soprano.

Adam felt a trickle of sweat down the back of his neck and took some deep breaths like his therapist instructed. One, two, three, four . . . The same doc who said, "It can take a while for PTSD to resolve, Adam. Give it time." Time, Adam had in abundance. Patience, not so much.

Adam looked Lehmann in the eye. "I will never betray my badge, my integrity, my character, or the public trust. I will always have the courage to hold myself and others accountable for our actions."

Lehmann blinked slowly, and Adam added, "That is part of the oath I took for my job. Perhaps you should revisit the oath you took when you were sworn in, sir."

With that, Adam finally made it to the bank, grateful for the escape it afforded from an old-but-new problem. And trying not to worry about a possible worse one. Why, oh, why did Zelda take that moment to accost him in the street? He had a bad feeling it was going to come back to haunt him and not in a Halloween sort of way.

What was that Chinese curse, "May you live in interesting times?" He could use several degrees less "interesting" in his life right now. Maybe Harlan was right, and Adam just needed a vacation. But never in the middle of a case, especially this one. That stopped him for a moment—why this case? It was an ordinary one, a stupid stolen bowl. With a beautiful suspect in the center of it all.

Adam thrust his hands into his pocket and fingered the miniature police badge on the keychain his father had given him when he was sworn in. It was there to remind him that whenever he felt down or distracted about a case, he had a calling to see it through.

He was a cop first, and everything else came in second place. That's what Zelda hadn't understood—he was married to his job, and she was more like a mistress. The divorce rate was pretty high among cops, go figure.

Adam checked his watch. He was running late for work, thanks to his encounters with the troublesome Lehmann duo. As if he needed another reason for the chief not to trust him. Laborde, Forsythe—he'd get to the bottom of it sooner or later if they'd just let him do his job.

§ § §

Let it never be said Adam Dutton wasn't thorough in his job. *If* he knew exactly what the job was, that is. A theft case that may, or may not, have anything to do with his jurisdiction. And his main suspect was a woman who may, or may not, have anything to do with said theft. There were far more critical cases, but power and politics did have their privileges.

Fine, then. He'd do what was expected to get the mayor off the chief's ass, and the chief off of Adam's. Which meant it was oh-so-fun database time. Searching computer records was part of the job, but it wasn't his favorite part. Bits and bytes didn't have the same tangible thrill of pounding the pavement and talking with people.

He guzzled some lukewarm coffee he'd picked up from the break room on the way to his office and grimaced. Bitter brew to go with his bitter mood. After Beverly beat him to the punch yesterday at Harlan's shop, Adam had returned to the Apple Valley Resort to see if he could get any additional info on Beverly and was rewarded when he saw her getting out of a car. He jotted down the tag. Not that it mattered that much since it turned out to be a rental SUV when he ran the plates.

He didn't have probable cause for hauling her in for further questioning without any evidence. It would also make it hard or impossible to get subpoenas from the courts for accessing various personal records. He didn't have any hits on a Beverly Laborde in either the National Driver Registry or the federal NCIC database, but he did have a hit on one and only one Beverly Laborde in NLETS records that indicated a Massachusetts driver's license.

After checking the address from the license on the internet, it looked to be a house subdivided into units. When he called the owner, she told him that a woman matching Beverly's name and description did rent a space, hardly more than a "big closet with a small bathroom." But the woman rarely saw Beverly, who'd paid up her rent in cash for the entire year.

Pretty smart on Beverly's part—you couldn't get a driver's license with only a P.O. box. It was likewise good for passports, but Beverly hadn't been charged with a crime, so he was out of luck getting those records.

It brought up an interesting insight into Beverly Laborde, who feigned innocence but essentially used a dummy address to obtain her license. If she had a more "normal" address, she'd surely have used that. She appeared to want to be as invisible as possible, so what game was she playing? He had a feeling it was far more complicated than her Fox and Geese and that she was quite good at it.

It made the claims by Reggie Forsythe and Mayor Lehmann more credible. But there was a long stretch of investigative road between a woman who wanted to keep a low profile and a serial crook. People with legitimate reasons might benefit from being hard to track—a victim of domestic violence, for instance.

He thought of the waitress at the resort. Her husband had put her in the hospital several times with broken bones, a punctured lung, and burns before he landed in prison for forty years. Adam wouldn't have blamed her for wanting to disappear and start a new life somewhere else. Beverly Laborde was also haunted by something—he knew that look in her eyes, one he'd seen too often in his career.

Why couldn't a filthy rich SOB like Reggie Forsythe just write off one damn bowl and be satisfied with his other expensive toys? Because it wasn't about money, that's why. Adam had come across too many men like him. Cold hard cash wasn't really what drove them on, it was cold hard revenge even for slights others would deem meaningless. And thanks to Mayor Lehmann, Adam was now a tool for that revenge. Hip hip hooray.

9

In the research she'd conducted on the Forsythes, Beverly had come across one name, a man identified only as "Mr. X." The shadowy figure sounded even more intriguing when she read between the lines and figured out he'd parted ways with the Forsythe clan after a falling out.

Another former disgruntled Forsythe associate had confirmed to her that Mr. X was someone she needed to talk to if she wanted salacious details about the Forsythes. The contact didn't have a number or address, and it had taken some sweet-talking on a false pretense to the telephone office for her to get Mr. X's phone number.

Now, she only hoped the thirty-minute ride to meet the enigmatic Mr. X would be worth it. She drove most of the way without seeing another car, one of the things she loved about Vermont. It was just her, some yogurt bars, Led Zeppelin tunes, and the open road.

She followed the instructions she'd jotted down over the phone. Mr. X said the GPS would be next to useless, and he was right. She counted eight different turns, four without road signs, until she reached the end of the road. As she pulled into a long, winding driveway, the scene before her was wholly unexpected.

What could best be described as a mini-castle rose out of

the rolling green landscape, complete with a small drawbridge across a moat filled with water, more decoration than barrier. She walked up to the front door, looking around for a button or knocker, when a disembodied voice said, "Beverly Laborde?"

She replied, "That would be me," and waited. Nothing happened. She scanned the pasture to the right, noting a pair of large, shaggy creatures. Bison? No, too small. A special breed of cow? Then she heard a click, and the castle door swung open.

Two things she noticed right away—the first was that the entry resembled the yawning opening of a cave, complete with a slick, rock-like surface when she touched it. The second was the curious man standing in the middle of the opening. Not troll-like, not dressed in armor, nor wearing a crown. He looked to be around fifty, wore black slacks, a plain black shirt, and a black scarf around his neck. The black made his pale skin and platinum-colored hair stand out like a neon sign. "Do come in," he waved toward the hallway behind them.

The interior hardly matched the castle theme, either, with beige walls and furniture that could have hopped out of a Boca Do Lobo catalog. They passed by an iridescent green, blue, and red vase with a pedestal base in the shape of a female figure.

She stopped to take a closer look. "That's Hungarian Zsolnay, with eocin glaze, isn't it? Early twentieth century? These are hard to find. Where did you get this?"

"I travel all over the world looking for interesting things. Believe it or not, I found this in a Budapest flea market. But I see you know your antiques." As if to punctuate his statement, he perched on the edge of a green leather British Chesterfield armchair. "Have a seat."

"Thank you. But I have to ask, what does Mr. X stand for?"

"Xenakis. But everyone calls me Mr. X."

The man hadn't smiled once since she arrived, and his gaze

was unsettling. She didn't know much about Mr. X, and yet here she was, with this odd stranger in his bizarre house in the middle of a lonely countryside. What would Adam Dutton think of that?

She asked, "What were those two shaggy creatures outside?"

"Yaks. I call them Yin and Yang. Yaks have lean meat. One-sixth the fat of grain-fed beef and forty percent more protein."

"You eat them?"

"They're popular in the Himalayas. I bought them thinking I'd farm them to sell their meat to Tibetan restaurants, like the one in New York. But I couldn't bear to slaughter them. I drink their milk."

"Their milk? Isn't Yang supposed to be the symbol for male?"

"They're both female. But don't tell them that. Yin is a bit on the butch side." He hopped up from his perch. "Want to try some yak hot chocolate?"

Hoping she wasn't making a huge mistake either from the taste or potential poisoning—accidental or otherwise—she agreed. She heard him banging around in the kitchen, and then he reappeared within a couple of minutes. "Specialty of the house. I hope you don't mind if I included a few shots of chocolate liqueur."

She accepted the drink with a smile and took a tentative sip. "Yum. This is good."

Still no smile, but Mr. X tented his hands together. "Glad you like it." He kept staring at her intently. "You said you wanted to discuss Reginald Forsythe. Would that be Forsythe the Third or Fourth?"

"Both, although I have a particular interest in the Fourth."

"Not that it matters since they're cut from the same

cheesecloth. Soiled cheesecloth at that."

"First, is it true you worked for the elder Forsythe?"

He parted his lips, and for the first time, she saw that he had a row of silver bottom teeth. "For ten years. Ten lucrative, heady, but ultimately unsatisfying years."

"The lucrative and heady I get. Traveling the world buying and selling pricey antiques and artifacts would be stimulating. But why unsatisfying?"

"When I write my tell-all memoir, I'll send you a copy. But long story short, I got tired of being at the beck and call of a man with less of conscience than my yaks. He didn't mind how he got his precious trinkets, be it beg, borrow, steal, or kill."

"Kill? Did it come to that?"

He rubbed his hand along his thigh. "I drew the line there. But I wasn't his only operative. And his son is as bad, if not worse."

"You've kept tabs on them since you left? The contact I was telling you about on the phone said if I needed to know anything about them, you were the one to ask."

"I don't know if you noticed the security features around here, did you? Probably not. Motion detectors, volumetric alarms, night-vision cameras. The control panel for it all looks like it belongs on a starship."

"That's the reason for the castle?"

"No, I just like castles." He peered over at her cup. "Need a refill?"

"I'm still working on this one. But thanks. Does all the security have something to do with the Forsythes?"

"They were none too pleased with my decision to leave the Third's employ. I assured them of my intention to retire quietly."

"I heard a rumor. I hoped you could tell me if it's true."

He waved his hand in the air for her to continue.

"There's a legend about Rogers' Rangers and—"

"The Lady of Chartres silver statue?"

Beverly took a sip of chocolate to cover her surprise but choked on the drink and had a coughing spell. When she could speak again, she asked, "You've heard of it?"

"I know about most of the fabled treasure legends hereabouts and around the world. It's come in handy in the past."

"Is Reggie Forsythe aware of it?"

"Not only aware, actively seeking it. Has been for years. The man is OCD when it comes to silver."

Beverly set her mug down on the table next to her chair. She'd lost interest in having any more. She'd only heard hints before that Forsythe was interested in the statue, the main reason *she* was interested in the piece, but here it was verified in black and white. It underscored the importance and urgency of her treasure hunt and felt like a kick in the gut.

Mr. X tilted his head at her. "This is not happy news?"

"Reggie Forsythe has his talons into everything I care about."

"He hasn't located it, you know. If it exists."

"Do you think the legend is true?"

"I hope it is. And I'd rather that statue fall into your hands than his."

She smiled at that. Maybe she had one person in her corner. "From what you're telling me, sounds like the Forsythes have plenty of enemies and few friends."

"Their type don't believe in friends, only conquests or allies. The elder Forsythe did have one fellow he seemed fond of. Lowell Steen. Long retired, now."

Mr. X rubbed his chin. "It did my heart good to hear that Reggie was bested recently. By a woman, no less. Wearing red hair and dark glasses. I'd love to meet her in person."

"You would?"

"Indeed." And Mr. X's lips formed into something that might be close to a smile. "I'd tell her I'd like to give her a medal. But to be careful. And that if she ever needed anything, day or night to give me a call."

Beverly thanked him for the information and the hot chocolate as he walked her back to the front of the "castle." Before climbing into her car, she headed over to take a closer look at the yaks. One of them strolled over to the fence right in front of her, and Beverly gingerly reached out to pet the shaggy head.

"Thanks for the milk," she said with a smile.

She didn't know whether to be encouraged or discouraged by her little chat with Mr. X. She'd known the Forsythe duo to be formidable, but she hadn't realized how dangerous they really were. Crime, yes, but also maybe murder? Was Mr. X even telling the truth? Perhaps he was still in their employ, and she'd just made the biggest mistake of her life by trusting this man—who'd likely go running back to the Forsythes and tell them all about her.

But no, she had to trust those gut instincts of hers. They were all she had. And as with Harlan, she had a good feeling about Mr. X. He'd seen right through her, she knew that. And he certainly had good taste in antiques.

The main takeaway from her meeting was that Reggie Forsythe was pursuing the Lady Chartres statue for real and had been seeking it for a long while. She'd counted on having some time for her search and that she was the only one seriously interested in the missing artifact.

As Grammie used to say, "The people who get on in this world are the people who get up and look for the circumstances they want, and, if they can't find them, make them." It wasn't until years later she found out those words came originally from

George Bernard Shaw.

But she didn't care, they were good words, survival-words. If there was one thing she'd gotten pretty good at it, it was surviving despite long odds. And she wasn't about to let a pampered, soulless scoundrel stand in her way of success—and revenge.

10

Jinks called out as Dutton walked by her office. "Why the long face? Someone cleaned out your bank account?"

He stepped inside, balancing a briefcase in one hand and a cardboard container with two cups of coffee in another—after he'd gone out to get something better than the bitter sludge he'd had from the breakroom earlier. He dropped the briefcase to the floor. "I was going to put that on my desk first, but . . . "

He handed her one of the coffees. "How do you keep so fit drinking coffee with six sugars and three creamers?"

"I've been going to the gym every day at five. Felicia gets the kids ready for school while I get ready for work. Then she gets ready for work. Mornings at our house could use some air traffic control." She took a sip of the coffee. "You didn't answer my question."

He flopped down on a chair. "I ran into Zelda. And then I ran into the mayor. He accused me of trying to win her back to make him look bad. And then to show what a nice guy he is, he threatened department funding over this Forsythe business." Adam wasn't about to mention Lehmann's crack about the radios.

"Oh, is that all? I was afraid he'd gone nice on us because that's when we should start to worry. At least we know where he stands."

"He likes to stand on other people. Comes from being the only child in a long line of lawyer-politicians. Bet he's never had to clean his own bathroom."

"Or clean up baby puke." Jinks smiled. "And the uber-privileged wonder why we don't bow down and worship at their pedicured feet."

"Think he gets a pedicure?"

"Oh, yeah. A girl Felicia works with saw him at her salon."

Dutton blew on his plain black coffee before taking a sip. Zelda always said he had scratchy feet. No more scratchy feet for her. Just shopping trips to Fifth Avenue in New York and Newbury Street in Boston, and foie gras at lunch every day if she wanted.

Jinks tilted her head. "So, what did Zelda have to say?"

"Not much. Bought some wine. Says she misses me. Asked about the case."

"Misses you? Was the mayor half-right? Would you get back together with her after she dumped you for a social-climbing turd?"

If she'd asked him that a few months ago, he might have said yes, pathetic as that sounded. You didn't live with someone for ten years without forming a bond. But now he wasn't so sure. Maybe he was finally ready to move on.

"I'm holding out for you, Jinks."

She laughed. "You've got good taste. Who wouldn't want a half-Asian, half-black lesbian cop?"

He and Jinks had come up through the ranks and made detective at the same time. They were the only two detectives in the small force, but she'd earned his trust a hundred times over. It hadn't been easy for her, either, due to what she called prejudice times four, or "quad-udice," for being in not one, but four minority categories. He'd heard the rumors, especially after his kidnapping.

"How's the case with the missing husband going? Any breaks?"

"After talking to his wife, I'd bet he's in the Caymans getting himself a new identity to get away from her. But their two kids are adorable. Be hard to leave them behind. We haven't ruled out murder, yet, since he had a couple grand on him when he disappeared." She picked at the rim of her cup. "And the Forsythe case?"

"Beverly Laborde is my best lead. She's hiding something, I just don't know what."

"Anything interesting in her background?"

"Nothing to tie her to Forsythe yet. But she's calm and cool, that one. Intelligent, too."

"I don't know. Don't think it's all that bright to stiff Reggie Forsythe, if she did stiff Forsythe, from what you've been telling me. Sounds like he's John Gotti, Junior."

"Possibly. All that chatter about him might have some truth, or it might turn out to be jealousy. Unless I come across something telling me otherwise, he's the official victim in all this."

Adam drained the last of his coffee and hopped up to throw the cup in the trash. "I got a lead from Harlan Wilford. Wish me luck."

"You bet. And hurry up, will ya? The chief is making noises about pulling me off my case to work on Forsythe, too. I don't want to disappoint those two kids, you know?"

Dutton hurried back to the office to work the phone and computer. A couple hours later, he was standing by the fax, tapping his foot. He'd identified the Kornelson guy Harlan told him Beverly was researching, the owner of the document she'd wanted him to authenticate. Then, he dug up the name of the library where Thaddeus Kornelson's papers had ended up and extracted a promise from the archivist for copies.

By now it was late in the day, and he debated whether to pore through the materials this evening or wait until tomorrow. Making up his mind, he headed for home, first stopping for some C&S Pizza, heavy on the peppers and onions. With his feet propped on his coffee table, a pizza slice in one hand and one of the faxes in the other, he started to read.

It was detailed stuff, but he got all the way through and re-read it several times. Like Harlan Wilford said, the part about the silver statue was written in verse he strained to decipher. Adam glanced over at his guitar on its stand. Maybe some music would help him think?

Grabbing the remote control to the TV, he instead flipped through the channels hoping to clear his head. But the endless stream of shopping channels, so-called news, and bad cop shows with their *GQ* pretty-boy detectives made him even more irritated. He stopped at an unassigned channel that was all snow.

Through the hypnotic blur of white dots and hissing static, slivers of an idea began to coalesce in his brain, and he fumbled for his laptop on the floor. The verses mentioned a vault which at first he'd thought meant safe deposit box. And also a *sacellum*, the Latin word for "monument," which he'd assumed was referring to the statue itself. But now he believed the words meant something else entirely, so he researched the internet for references to the history of Quechee Gorge.

He checked his watch. Nine-thirty. Too late to scope it out now since the gorge park was closed. He'd have to wait twelve hours. He found one cop show that wasn't half-bad, but his eyelids kept closing, and before he knew it, the remote fell from the couch to the floor with a "thunk."

Adam rescued the remote, even as he cursed it for waking him up, and flipped to another channel. He landed on a sports channel broadcasting a cricket match. His mind wandered as he stared at the action without really watching. "Cricket" the word came from cricket the game. As in fair play, honorable. As in what Mayor Lehmann most certainly was not. The Forsythes, too, if they turned out to be as bad as he suspected. And Beverly Laborde?

He'd interrogated black-widow types before. He'd arrested female criminals for everything from embezzlement to murder. But none of those women could match Laborde's poise, her composure. Perhaps she really was some master criminal, heartless, uncaring, orbiting through her own shady universe. An icy comet—make that a human icy comet—leaving trails of debris behind wherever she goes.

Adam looked at the clock again. Only ten. Some geezer he was turning into, going to bed so early and then falling asleep in front of the TV. Okay, not so much bed as couch. He hadn't slept in his bed much since the divorce. Probably should sell the house. Or get a new bed. At least, Beverly Laborde was sleeping soundly tonight in her two-fifty-a-night king featherbed.

11

The moon was in first quarter, which was enough to provide a little bit of light, but not enough to give her position away if she was careful. Beverly studied the Kornelson document using her red-light headlamp. The northwesterly winds flapped the edges of the paper, making it harder to read. The gusts also threatened to blow her black hat off her head, and she cinched it tighter to keep it in place and to cover up most of the headlamp.

One good thing—it was above freezing. Barely. The light from the moon dimmed for a moment as a few stray clouds passed overhead, turning the trees into ghostly shapes flailing their limbs in the breeze. It may be bustling with tourists during the day, but it was a lonely place at night.

Beverly's conversation with Mr. X earlier today had left her light-headed once her blood stopped boiling and settled down. So Reggie Forsythe was definitely after the Lady of Chartres statue. Not surprising, since silver pieces were his obsession.

But she'd be damned if she'd let him get his hands on it first. For him, it would be just one other piece among many. Sitting on a shelf, covered in dust-mite dander and largely forgotten, except to be hauled out once every few years and cooed over.

Dear Harlan had largely authenticated her map, which

meant she wasn't wasting her efforts with someone's antiques-version of a snipe hunt. She still didn't know Kornelson's full connection with this area. Nor could she decipher all the verses in the maddening puzzle Kornelson left behind in his papers.

But she was convinced he'd found the Lady and buried it somewhere. Why he'd done it, she didn't know, but she suspected it had to do with the fact his only potential heir was a detested ne'er-do-well nephew. But wouldn't it be easier to sell the Lady so the nephew wouldn't inherit it? Right now, she didn't care about the why only the where.

What she was doing was risky. Sneaking into the Quechee Gorge Park and the trails at night after it closed to day-trippers might be not the brightest idea she'd ever had. How would she explain the metal detector and shovel to a park ranger?

If caught, she'd say she lost her way from the campground—which used to be mill's recreation area. And with any luck, it would be a male ranger, and her dim damsel-in-distress act would fool him. It usually did with depressing regularity.

Kornelson's documents had mentioned a monument, and not too many of those existed in the areas surrounding Ironwood Junction. But Quechee was a natural monument, of a sort. It was a long shot, but Beverly's life was one string of long shots. After consulting the map and matching it with the history of Dewey's Mill before it was torn down, she narrowed her target area.

Pulling a pair of earbuds out of her pocket, she fitted them in and plugged the end into the audio port on the metal detector. Between the spooky light, the earbuds sticking out from her head, and the black hat, she felt like a Frankenstein-monster prospector, but she set to work using a grid pattern.

First up, check the site of the former mill. The muted roar of the nearby Mill Pond Falls added to the eerie feeling of being too near the one-hundred-sixty-foot drop down into the gorge.

She knew her prowling might take her closer to the pond and falls, and that almost prompted her to turn back. Being this near to bodies of water made her nervous. When one of the Apple Valley Resort's staff tried to get her to check out the heated pool, she'd snapped at him. It wasn't his fault, and it wasn't her finest moment. But you could easily drown in a pool—one bad leg cramp was all it took. Didn't he know that? She shuddered, then steadied her nerves and pressed on.

Checking to make sure the metal detector's discrimination was turned off to increase the depth detection, she began sweeping around the mill site. Thanks to practice runs, she'd gotten good at ruling out nails, bullets, coins, and metals she didn't care about—iron, foil, nickel. Plus, the target ID feature would help find only those objects that were about the same size as the foot-tall statue.

She'd purchased what was supposed to be a light-weight model, but after lugging the detector around for forty-five minutes, her arms started getting tired. Not to mention the heavy folding shovel in her backpack weighing her down, along with all the headgear. And so far, nothing to show for it. Except for being cold, tired, sleepy, and wishing she was back in her room's Jacuzzi.

There were potentially hundreds of acres in the park to cover, but she'd decided to concentrate on areas Kornelson would have targeted. Namely, places he might be able to find later since GPS didn't exist around 1900. The old mill still existed back then, but all that was left were a few stone remains of the mill and dam at the head of the gorge.

Concentrating on each blip through the earbuds, she didn't hear the sound of an approaching car motor until it was close by. It stopped her up short, and she switched off her headlamp and ducked as fast as she could behind a rock outcropping.

Adam Dutton should see her now, flopping around clumsily just like Frankenstein's monster. Too bad Dutton wasn't there—he looked like a man who could use a good laugh.

She lay low to the ground, hugging the detector and hoping her backpack didn't peek out over the top of the rock. The motor came closer and then slowed as it approached her position. A vehicle here, at night, likely meant a park ranger in his jeep. Hopefully, it wasn't a couple of young punks looking for trouble.

Not wanting to use her damsel-in-distress routine if she didn't have to, she waited as the jeep pulled up parallel to her position, holding her breath until her lungs were on fire. With the jeep's motor idling, she heard how quiet the park was at night in autumn. The wind barely rattled the leaves, and no crickets, no nocturnal fox or coyote sounds, not one screech owl disturbed the silence.

Finally, she couldn't wait to exhale any longer, even if it meant possibly giving her position away. But then the motor revved up, and the ranger and his jeep continued along the trail. Beverly let out her breath in a drawn-out exasperated sigh. This was going to be a long, cold night.

12

Thursday, September 16

The morning dawned gray and drizzly, the type most people hated. But Adam liked the views of the White and Connecticut Rivers with the fog rising between the banks. Made him think of early mornings as a boy when his father took him fishing.

He headed west along US 4 and knew he was near his target when he came to a stop behind a line of cars approaching the bridge in front. He could practically hear the locals rolling their eyes about the tourists gawking at the sight from the bridge. Fortunately, the rain had stopped.

He wasn't a hundred percent sure why he was here instead of calling more antique stores, but his hunch told him Beverly Laborde was at the heart of this Forsythe mess. And if she was interested in that Lady of Chartres statue, then *he* was interested in that statue.

He wasn't sure what it looked like or where to hunt for such a thing, but Kornelson's cryptic verses referred to a place sacred to the Natick Indians. Add to that mentions of a deep chasm, and Quechee Gorge filled that bill. If crazy old Mr. Kornelson had decided to bury or hide that silver statue for whatever reason, Quechee was a possible place, but where? The environs looked vastly different back in Kornelson's day.

The gift shop wasn't a likely hiding spot, but he hadn't had breakfast. He grabbed some coffee and a Snickers bar and had no sooner stuffed the change in his pockets when he literally bumped into Beverly Laborde.

"Fancy meeting you here, Detective Dutton."

Adam was so busy admiring the way her tight jeans set off her legs that he barely avoided spilling coffee on her surprisingly sensible hiking boots. "Taking in the local sights, Miss Laborde? Or are you more interested in sacred Natick Indian stories?"

She linked one arm through his and led him over to a picnic table and chairs. It wasn't until they sat down that he noticed her empty hands. "Did you want some coffee?"

"Had some at the resort. Is that your breakfast?" She pointed to his candy bar.

"Portable bachelor chow." He grinned.

She folded her arms across her chest in reply. "You should do that more often."

"What, eat bachelor chow?"

"Smile. It sets off your eyes nicely."

"You seem obsessed with my eyes."

"Windows into the soul."

"What are they telling you about my soul? Small-town police detective, whose idea of culture is a spinning rod and twister-tail lure?"

"A strong, honest man who's seen his share of pain and suffering. A man who tilts at windmills even when he knows there are giants he can't slay."

"Are you sure you didn't get a philosophy degree from Dartmouth?"

"I learned all I need to know about human nature from my grandmother."

"The antiquer?"

"Antique store owner. She loved it with a passion. Until someone in the Northeastern Antiquities League shut down her business seven years ago due to obscure legalities buried in the state business code. She had to sell everything for a pittance and died not long after."

Adam squinted at her. "Sounds like a good reason to hold a grudge against the likes of shady NAL member Reggie Forsythe. Or his father, for that matter."

She looked away, toward a group of tourists. "First you spout Natick Indian lore and now the Forsythe family saga—you've been a busy little detective bee, haven't you, Adam Dutton? Seeing as how you're in busy-mode, and I'm willing to bet a large sum we have the same objective in mind, why don't we go exploring together? Never know what kind of buried treasure we might stumble over."

"I don't know about that. What did you have in mind?"

She pulled a folded paper out of her pocket. "This area was once the site of the A.G. Dewey wool mill. It was active around Kornelson's death in 1901 and didn't become a state park until 1962. Remains of both mill and dam are at the head of the gorge."

She showed him a copy of an old photo of the mill on the piece of paper. "Did you know Dewey wool was used to make baseball uniforms for the Red Sox?"

"You weren't kidding when you said you love history." He smiled again. Despite his best efforts, he was having a hard time not smiling around Beverly Laborde. And that wouldn't do. He forced a more professional expression on his face and considered his options. Should he join her or not? The chief wanted him to keep an eye on this woman, and this was certainly one way to do it.

They headed along a trail to the crystal-blue Dewey's Mill

Pond, ringed by tall grasses and red pines, where it tumbled over a small dike forming falls that cascaded into the river below. With the trees at maximum "Crayola," with vibrant reds, oranges, and yellows, the area was colored like a typical Vermont tourism postcard.

Despite her sensible hiking boots, she tripped over a log at one point, and he grabbed her arm to steady her. Okay, so he wouldn't have done that for a male suspect, but it wouldn't help anything to have his only suspect in the hospital, would it?

Laborde had a rather nice smile, too, as she expressed her gratitude. "Looks like we're at the old Dewey's Mill site. Too bad they didn't restore it and keep it as a museum."

It hadn't taken long to get there, but one look around the place made Dutton feel it was a wasted trip. He'd been here years ago and forgot how empty the place was. Not much in the way of ruins at all. And most of what was here was built long after Kornelson's era.

"If this is your treasure hiding place, Miss Laborde, then it vanished when they tore down the mill. Or it's buried in the middle of six hundred acres and lost for posterity."

She appeared neither surprised nor concerned by his gloomy assessment. He faced her square-on. "You knew there wasn't anything to find. You've already been here, haven't you?"

"Last night after sunset."

He ignored the fact—for the moment—that she'd broken a few regulations by entering the park after hours. "Then why the wild goose chase today?"

"I wanted to get to know you better." She smiled at him over her shoulder as she turned to head back the way they'd come. Adam didn't know whether to arrest her for wasting his time or ask her out on a date.

Reminding himself he was potentially following an expert

con artist, he shrugged off his un-detective-like thoughts and concentrated on her as a suspect. When they reached the parking lot, he leaned up against the driver's side door to her car, blocking her entry. "I've got a businessman who, as far as the law knows, is a legitimate antiques dealer with a complaint about being scammed. The only suspect we have so far is you. And I'm not willing to play the role of small-town hick detective who's just part of your goddamn Fox and Geese game."

She stood very still and gazed toward the perilous drop from the bridge to the bottom of the gorge. "I'd never take you for a fool, Adam." She reached over and gently brushed off a leaf that was clinging to his shirt. "Besides, I find you more foxy than goose."

With a wink, she walked around to the passenger side of her car, opened it, and slid over to the driver's seat. He moved away from the car, and she rolled down the window as if to add something. But then she waved, started up the engine, and drove off.

Beverly was here last night in the dark after hours looking for the statue? What did she use, a flashlight and a metal detector? Or did she have some "magic" statue-divining rod? That woman was seriously obsessed. What would a long-ago piece of plunder from a Rangers raid have to do with a Paul Revere bowl? Other than the fact they were both silver.

Adam climbed into his Subaru and slammed the door. How did she know he'd be here today unless she followed him? Was it merely a case of "keep your friends close and enemies closer?" Or was she purposely trying to get under his skin and sabotage his investigation? Either way, he was disgusted with himself right now. And he had a good idea the chief would concur—right before busting Adam back down to beat cop.

When his stomach rumbled, he decided bachelor chow

wasn't going to cut it this morning. He'd have to scrounge up some emergency rations. It had been too long since he'd hit up the Crossroads Cafe and its fist-sized bacon cheddar muffins and homemade chorizo hash. Maybe they'd have a low-salt donut for Jinks. He peeled the car out of the parking lot, scanning for vehicles that might be following him. He wasn't about to let Laborde get the jump on him again.

13

Beverly knew she shouldn't have tailed Adam Dutton. Even more so after she'd only had a couple hours of sleep after her unfruitful scavenger hunt last night. But when he'd headed toward Quechee, she couldn't help herself.

Her smile at the endearing confusion on his face faded as she pulled up in front of her next target. The shop wasn't at all like she remembered.

Dark trickles of slime and grime seeped down the white cast-stone facade like black blood on a Madonna statue. The sign that spelled out "Antiques" was loose from its mooring and clung desperately in a losing attempt to hang on. The store windows were broken in some places with BB holes in the center of tiny glass craters that branched out into spider-web patterns.

The door was open, thanks to a splintered lock. She poked her head in to take a peek. The miniature dollhouse town, the collection of seasoned cast-iron cookware, the old wax cylinder phonographs—all the things from years ago were long gone.

A scratching noise got her attention. She followed it toward the door in the back that led to the basement. As she approached, the door opened with such force, it slammed into the wall and pieces of plaster fell to the floor. Two young men strutted into the room, stopping when they caught sight of her.

The first, the taller of the two, wore a black beanie and had a beer in one hand and a crowbar in the other. He winked at the other youth and said, "Look what we have here. A city girl with a nice big purse."

The shorter youth dropped a green pillowcase sack he was carrying. "Looks like pricey swag. A chick who can buy that must have a shitload of money."

His friend laughed. "Yeah, a nice big purse with a nice big wallet full of nice big bills."

Beverly pulled her purse off her shoulder as if getting ready to hand it over. But with a quick snap, she flipped it open and pulled out her gun. She slowly, and dramatically, clicked off the safety. "You forgot the nice big gun."

The shorter boy looked to the other, who was chewing on his lip. He said, "Look, lady, we was playing around. No bigs, 'kay?"

Beverly kept the gun pointed at them and moved off to one side. "No bigs if you get out of here and don't come back."

The boys gave each other a quick look and a nod. Then they both took off running through the doorway. Beverly followed them, watching and waiting until they were out of sight before she put the gun back in her purse.

She walked over to the pillowcase bag on the floor and peered inside. A few copper wires, some coils, and other metal parts she couldn't identify. Destined to be sold for scrap, but she doubted such a haul would bring much cash. But junkies needed all they could get, and judging by the boys' bloodshot eyes and hand tremors, she guessed it was either potential drug or alcohol money lying in that bag.

Grabbing the bag, she headed outside and walked around the building, where she spied a staircase leading to the top floor. With one last look around to determine the young toughs were nowhere in sight, she climbed the stairs to the top. This door was locked. So, she knocked.

To her surprise, the door swung open to reveal a petite elderly woman dressed in a blue paisley dress with a purple felt cloche hat. She squinted at her visitor and said, "Beverly?"

Beverly smiled at her. "Mrs. Framm."

"Agnes, dear. You're old enough now to skip all those old-fashioned manner rules. Come on in. Let me get a look at you."

Agnes looked her over and smiled. "Always knew you'd turn out to be a stunning woman someday. You've got your grandmother's skin and eyes."

"That's the nicest compliment I've had in years."

"Have a seat, rest your feet. I'm afraid I don't have much in the way of refreshments. You should have called first. I would have made one of my famous mincemeat pies."

"It was a whim of sorts. Grammie's been on my mind lately. Since I was in the area, thought I'd drop by and see how her best friend is doing these days."

Agnes motioned her over to some overstuffed, faded club chairs, which were like slipping into a pillow. That made her think of the boys' pillowcase, which she showed to Agnes, telling her how she came by it.

Agnes settled back in her chair. "I've called the local police dozens of times. But those vagrant types keep coming back. Can't afford private security. There's not much to be done about it."

"When did you close the store?"

"Going on five years now. Feels like yesterday."

"Was it the Northeastern Antiquities League? Did they force you out?" Beverly realized her hands were balled into fists. She willed them to relax.

"You're thinking of what happened to your grandmother. But no, it was more eBay. People don't want to buy local. Just a few clicks on a computer, and whatever you want is delivered to your front door."

"And the Forsythes didn't pressure you?"

"I got a visit from someone who said he was from the state licensing board, but I knew better. He asked odd questions a board representative should already know if he were genuine. The shifty type. Had this eye twitch. He was nicely dressed, much nicer than a government employee."

"What did you tell him?"

"That since my shop had a bakery and deli, it didn't fall under that new law. That I'd asked around, and I was grandfathered in."

"If that's true, Grammie could have done something similar."

"I don't think so, dear. The way it was worded, it wouldn't have applied to such changes after the law took place. They saw to that."

Beverly closed her eyes for a moment. Images of her grandmother lifting her up for a better look at Agnes's Christmas dollhouse display sprang to mind. Grammie had always loved Christmas.

The older woman's voice gently got her attention. "Your grandmother was a wonderful woman, and she loved you to pieces. I know how you miss her, but she wouldn't want you to be bitter. In fact," Agnes paused for a moment as if choosing her words carefully. "Guinevere confided to me when she was ill there, toward the end. Said she was worried about you."

"Worried about me? But why?"

"Feared you were losing your way, becoming colder, harder. She wanted me to tell you not to let those bastards win."

No problem there, Beverly had no intention of letting those bastards win. Just not in the way Grammie intended. She swallowed her grief and anger to study her host. Agnes was about Grammie's age, seventy-ish. Her orange hair must come from a bottle or salon, but along with white strands dappled through, it gave her the appearance of a ginger cat. "After you closed your store, why didn't you sell it and move?"

"Not the best timing for real estate." She held up two fingers, pinched together. "Got this close to a deal with a young couple to turn it into a used bookstore and live up here in the apartment, but it fell through. Bookstores aren't in plentiful supply, either."

"What about those punks? I hate to think of you here by yourself with their lot around."

"You sound like my son. He wants me to move to Florida to be closer to him. I hate beaches. And I would miss the seasons. Vermonters are sturdy folks, and Florida is for wimps. But it would be nice to see more of him and his family."

"You could open up an antique store down there."

"The whole state is full of antiques. And I'm not talking about the stores. It's the new Mecca for white-haired acolytes. If you'll pardon the mixed-religion metaphors."

Beverly felt more relaxed in Agnes's presence than she had with anyone in . . . she couldn't remember how long. Unless it was Harlan. Part of her longed to stay here, to swap tales about her grandmother and reminisce. But the bastards who'd sent her grandmother to an early grave were still out there and still a threat to others. They had the potential to do an order of magnitude more damage than those two young thieves could ever dream of.

She reluctantly gave Agnes a hug and a promise to return soon. But Beverly couldn't keep putzing around armed with only a few old, cryptic documents and half-baked clues, tantalizing as they were. No, she needed to shake things up. And that meant sneaking into the lair of the monster himself.

14

Adam had no sooner stepped out of his car in the PD's parking lot when he was hit by a pint-sized missile. He glanced down at the culprit, a boy of about three or so, who'd bounced off Adam's leg and onto the ground. Rather than cry, the boy looked up at Adam with wide, shiny eyes.

"Andrew Baylor!" A woman's voice called out, with the woman herself soon coming into view. On one side of the woman was a girl around seven, and on the other was Jinks.

Adam said to Jinks, "Who's your friend here?"

The female trio caught up to him, and the mother of the boy swooped him up into the crook of her arm. Jinks nodded at her. "This is Priscilla Baylor and her daughter Patricia. And you've met little Andy. This is the family involved in the case I'm working on."

The missing-man case. If not for the distraction of the boy-missile, he'd have guessed. The mother, Priscilla, wasn't wearing any makeup, save for some haphazard mascara that had recently run and been wiped away, leaving tiny smears like black eyes. Her shoulders were hunched as if too heavy to hold up, and the hand she clasped around the girl's was white-knuckled. But it was the little girl's eyes that disturbed him the most. Too old for her young age, heavy-lidded with a torpor resembling blinds over leaded glass.

Adam said to the mother, "You've got the best working on your case with Detective Jinks, here. If anyone can find your husband, it's Jinks."

Priscilla managed a brief smile in Jinks' direction. "We're grateful for her help. It all feels like being trapped in a nightmare. A non-stop nightmare. And with the holidays coming up ... " The black mascara tears threatened a new cascade.

Jinks patted her on the shoulder and gave Andy's hair a ruffle. "We're gonna follow up this new lead, and if that doesn't pan out, there will be more. We'll find him. You can count on it."

Jinks walked the Baylors over to their car and helped get the kids situated, then waved as the family drove off. Adam asked, "New lead?"

"A source," she drew air quotes with her fingers, "Says the father might be doing drugs. That he was pals with Derek Cotter."

"Cotter, ay? That means a trip up to the Pittsbury neighborhood."

"The 'pitts' is right."

"Need some backup?" Adam hoped his voice sounded nonchalant, even as his pulse was racing. Pittsbury had its share of small drug houses dotting the woods, abscesses on the picturesque landscape. It had been a while since he was involved with a drug case. Not since *that* case. Whether the chief kept him away from them or they were forked over to be handled by the DEA, he wasn't sure. He hadn't asked.

Adam and Jinks ducked back into the PD offices to pick up some gear. Sergeant Moody was passing by and overheard their plans, laughing, "Got your radio, Jinks?"

Jinks retorted, "Got your brain, Moody?"

But when the cop was out of earshot, an awkward silence

hung over Adam and Jinks. Adam said, "He didn't mean it. Just cop jokes."

"Yeah. Jokes. Funny, haha." Jinks held up her radio at Adam and shook it side to side. "Let's go."

They made the fifteen-mile drive to Pittsbury without saying much, listening to the occasional crackle of the disembodied dispatcher's voice. When they pulled up in front of their destination, Adam smiled to himself. In scenic Vermont, even the crack houses were quaint. This particular house was a vacation cabin owned by a Burlington businessman who leased it out to tourists during the summer and anybody else during the winter. More often than not, the "anybody else" was the likes of Derek Cotter, perpetual drug addict.

They approached the cabin, its brown cedar shake siding and white shutters with cutout hearts making it look like a gingerbread house. Too bad its inhabitants had a taste for drugs instead of sweets. Jinks knocked on the door. They waited. Thirty seconds, one minute. She knocked louder, but again, no answer.

Adam reached over to try the doorknob, and it opened with one twist. They drew their guns, stepping inside, side by side.

Adam had seen the worst that drugs, poverty, and squalor could do to people and places, but instead of piles of ecstasy pills, packets of meth, and a vacuum cleaner full of MDMA powder, this house looked eerily normal by comparison. Wood floors, wood paneling, a wooden fireplace surround. One pink futon, a coffee table made from a slab of granite, and a suit of armor standing in one corner.

Jinks shook her head at Adam and headed toward the back rooms. Adam kept an eye on her progress while trying to surveil the way they'd come. No signs of Cotter, no signs of the missing Baylor. Adam felt a chill running up his spine, but he was sweating. He wiped his brow with his sleeve and pushed past Jinks toward a bathroom at the end of the hall.

There, seated on the floor between the tub and toilet was a semi-conscious man, his shaved head covered with a rash, and he had red eyes to match. He wore a t-shirt with holes and, from the smell of it, recently soiled underwear. Since he was the only occupant of the house, Adam holstered his gun and bent down to lift the man's chin up to look into his eyes.

"Derek Cotter, you must be a devil with the ladies."

Cotter gaped up at Adam. "Bite me." The man's voice was so unsteady, it sounded like he'd said "Blot me," which would be handy, given the underwear.

"If I had one of our police puppies with the nice big teeth and jaws, I could oblige with the biting part."

Cotter's eyes swung wildly around the room, finally focusing behind Adam. "Where? You wouldn't sic a dog on me."

Adam half-wished he'd brought along the K-9 unit, but replied, "Answer a few questions, and we might let them eat their regular puppy chow instead."

"Don't know nuthin.'"

"I'll be the judge of that. Tell us about Bobby Baylor."

"Who?"

"Robert M. Baylor. Mutual friend of yours said you and Baylor liked to socialize together. As in crack open some crack."

Cotter started rocking his upper body. It was oddly hypnotic. "Don't know no Baylor. Don't know no Bobbies or Bobs or Roberts. Must have the wrong guy."

Adam glanced at Jinks, who stepped closer to Cotter to ask, "You staying here all alone, Mr. Cotter?"

"Got a girl who comes by from time to time." He glared when Adam smirked. "Hey, I can get me some tail whenever I want."

Jinks said soothingly, "So just this girlfriend? No roommates to help pay the rent?"

"My Dad pays the rent."

"Your father knows you're here, Mr. Cotter?"

The young man slid down further against the tub. "Don't tell him, okay?" His pleading eyes swung from Jinks to Adam. "He thinks I'm using the money to go to school. Take some classes at VCC."

Adam asked, "Why aren't you?"

Cotter's reply was cut off by a prolonged coughing spell. Adam looked around for a glass, spied a used one on the sink and took a chance by filling it with water to hand to the man. Cotter gulped it down without taking a break. Had he had anything to eat or drink today? Or was his money all going to the rent and drugs?

Adam hauled Cotter up and slapped some handcuffs on him to be safe. "You'll get some medical attention at the jail. And a hot meal."

He and Jinks were often on the mental wavelength, so he wasn't surprised when Jinks pulled a card out of her pocket and tucked the card into Cotter's t-shirt pocket. "This is the number for a drug rehab in Barre, for when your lawyer gets you out on bail. No questions asked. Rent's about the same as here."

After Adam had bundled Cotter into the squad car and closed the door, he asked Jinks, "Think he's telling the truth about not knowing your missing man, Baylor?"

"You do, don't you?"

Adam nodded. "Yeah. Damn it all. Another lead, another bust."

He knew she'd meant it, even believed it, when she told the Baylors she would find the missing husband, and they could count on it. But he also knew if they did find the man, they'd be as likely to discover him in a body bag in a morgue as much as they'd find him alive. The chance of finding any missing person after the first seventy-two hours was around seven percent if you got lucky.

Adam realized he hadn't thought about his own case the entire time he was helping Jinks with hers. Too bad Reggie Forsythe and Mayor Lehmann couldn't go missing. Adam chided himself. But only a little bit.

§ § §

After dropping off their drug-addict prisoner and making sure Jinks had what she needed to add to her report, Adam decided to have a little chat with an old "friend" of his. When he pulled in front of Dragon's Teeth Bar, it looked about the same as when he'd last been here. It would look the same forever—dingy brick facade, sagging reddish-pink awnings, and a tired neon sign that buzzed and flickered.

The inside made the exterior look ritzy, but it was dark so you couldn't see it in all its glory. Adam crunched his way over the spent peanut shells and snagged one of the bar stools that wasn't held together by wood glue. He'd picked a good time. It was before the influx of workers from the lumber mill and stone quarry.

Proprietor Bryce Garrow ran a rag over the countertop, blazing a trail through a wasteland made of up layers of grime and grease. He squinted up at Adam. "You aiming to stay awhile? No offense, but cops tend to spook the regulars."

"You have regulars?"

"Haha. You should be a standup comedian." Bryce tossed the rag into a sink filled with gray water. "Since you never come here unless you're on a case, I won't offer you a drink."

A blessing in disguise. Bryce's "regulars" should be so lucky. "You've been out now for what, nine years?"

"Ten. Don't you dare take one of those hard-earned years away just like that. And I been clean ever since."

"I know, I know. But you still have friends in low places. Meaning you might have overheard—quite by accident, of course—a few rumors about some interesting people."

"What kind of interesting people?"

"A father-son duo. Name of Forsythe."

Bryce picked up some glasses from a cart and crammed them into shelves behind the bar. He didn't answer right away, so Adam prompted him, "Ever heard of them?"

"I'd like to stay out of prison, Dutton."

"I take it you have heard of them. Look, it's only you and me in here right now. And I'm not wired. Tell me what you've got."

Bryce pinched his nose. "You probably know it all. Or you wouldn't be here."

"Try me."

"I don't got much on the elder one. But the younger one, he's a piece of work."

"Reggie."

"Yeah. Friend of mine worked as his gardener. Forsythe made him sign one of those non-disclosure thingies."

"An NDA to be a gardener? Whatever for?"

"Beats me. My friend said he saw weird shit going on, though. People stopping by at odd hours. And they often came in with cases of stuff but didn't leave with 'em."

"Reggie's an antiques dealer. Hardly sounds suspicious."

"Yeah, but these guys often didn't come alone. Had bodyguard types."

"So, they're expensive antiques."

Bryce shook his head. "My friend, Dale, he recognized one of those bodyguards. Was in prison 'bout the same time as me. And several of 'em were packing. I mean, do people go around hijacking antiques or something? 'Cause that seems over the top, you know?"

"The one who spent time in prison—what did go in for?"

"Second-degree murder. Said it was self-defense, so he was out in eleven."

"Did your friend see anything else unusual?"

Bryce picked up a glass and rubbed it with his sleeve then put it back on the counter. "Limos."

"Limos?"

"The kind with tinted glass. Several of 'em pulled up, but nobody ever came out of those limos in front of the house. Always inside the garage after the door was down."

"Maybe the potential buyers preferred to remain anonymous." Adam's excuses were starting to sound thin even to him.

"Yeah, well, when Dale worked there, I asked around a few places. Curiosity and the cat, you know. I'm not dead yet, but someone I asked about the Forsythes told me if I wanted to keep on not being dead, to stop asking questions."

Adam pulled a couple of twenties out of his wallet and stuffed them into the glass on the counter. "Thanks, Bryce. Next time, I'll stop by the bank first."

"Yeah, you're Mr. Moneybags Detective. And don't come back asking for more about the Forsythes. This place may not be much, but I've grown attached to it. And who'd tank these guys up day after day if I'm six feet under?"

Adam waved at him as he left and then cranked up his engine and pointed his car back out onto Henry's Hollow Road. He slowed down as he passed some earth mounds off to his right, about a quarter-mile in the distance. Native American burial mounds, or so the experts said. Were they for Natick Indians, the same natives old man Kornelson's map and verses talked about?

When Adam's cellphone rang, he pulled over on the side of the road parallel to the mounds. He kept staring at them as he took the call from his FBI friend, Roger "Mac" McInturff. Just because Forsythe didn't want to ask the FBI's help didn't mean Adam couldn't make an "unofficial" request.

Mac said, "You were asking about the art fraud division. I checked with them about Paul Revere antiques and other silver bowls that were reported stolen in the past couple of years."

"Find anything?"

"One Revere bowl was stolen from an elderly woman, Coral Dockett. Hasn't turned up since."

"There's a record of ownership for these things?"

"Not a national database, no. Auction house records, sure, but the black market stuff is often untraceable. From pawn shops to unethical collectors, to a few appraisers who undervalue items so they can get their hands on them and sell them for their real value. Make thousands in profit."

"This stolen Revere silver bowl. Can you describe it?"

"Old-looking, silver, about ten inches diameter. Has a small, jagged scratch on one side and REVERE etched in all caps in a rectangle on the bottom."

"No suspects, Mac?"

"None. The poor, dear lady was beside herself. Never thought to put it in even a locked cabinet. No home security. A cat could have sauntered in and grabbed it. Might as well have had 'rob me' written in bright letters on the front of the house."

"And that's the only Revere bowl reported stolen?"

"In the past five years or so, yeah. You got a lead?"

"I don't know. Maybe. If it works out, I'll let you know."

"You do that. Our fraud guys love to cross one off the list."

Adam thanked him and hung up. Two stolen Revere bowls or one Revere bowl stolen twice? He rubbed his temples. He much preferred Jinks's case. Better to look for missing people than missing bowls. Still, he owed it to the chief. And maybe Beverly Laborde, too. If she were innocent.

That whole stunt at Quechee had caught him by surprise—and he didn't like being caught by surprise, especially by suspects. Anyway, the whole fraud matter would most likely be wrapped up in a few days. What else could possibly go wrong with one lousy, stinking stolen bowl?

15

Beverly put down the binoculars for a moment to rest her aching arms. How long had she been sitting here? It felt like hours, but when she checked her watch, it had only been thirty-five minutes. She rubbed some caked dirt off the bottom of her slacks where she'd half-tripped on the carpet of slimy pine needles.

Parking her car a quarter mile away in a different neighborhood had felt like a good idea, but not only were her arms aching, the ground was ice cold. And so far, she hadn't seen anything to help her decide how to proceed.

This home wasn't a castle to match Mr. X's, but it fit the definition of a mansion. Tree-lined drive, animal topiaries, and Greek-god statues in the garden in front, columned portico, and a house crafted of brick and stone in the Norman or Tudor style. Not many visible signs of a security system, but she couldn't imagine Reggie Forsythe not having one. She listened. No dogs, or so she hoped.

She rubbed her hand on her slacks. Her feet and legs may be cold, but her hands were sweating. What was she thinking, believing she might have a chance to gain access to Forsythe's domain? Especially since he was home, too, as she'd discovered when he drove his Jag into the garage a half-hour ago. When she'd called his office on a pretext earlier, his secretary said Forsythe would be on a conference call locked in his office for the next several hours. So much for that.

Beverly picked up the binoculars again, training them on the front of the house. Eerily quiet and not even a ghosted silhouette in any of the windows. Thanks to her research, she'd learned Forsythe had servants, but they weren't live-ins and should have left by now. She'd tracked down one former servant, a maid, but the poor woman had refused to talk about her former boss. After what Mr. X told Beverly about the man and the way he treated his staff, she wasn't all that surprised.

Just as Beverly was about to call it a day and head back through the forest of bayberry shrubs and red maple trees that barely provided cover, she heard the distinctive sound of a motor. She recognized it as the same garage door motor cranking up she'd heard when Forsythe's Jaguar entered only fifteen minutes ago.

Hesitating only a second, she dropped her binoculars, scrambled to her feet, and ran through the side yard, dodging a few statues. With her heart racing, she hurled herself behind a tall topiary shaped like an evergreen layer cake.

She was only two feet from the front of the garage, and she got a good look at Forsythe as he sped out of the garage with his Jag in reverse. At a dangerously high speed.

She also saw his dark, clouded expression as he recklessly navigated the circular driveway, coming close to hitting a lamp pole. Why did he leave his meeting early and drive all the way home just to zip in and out of his house in a virtual blur?

This time, she didn't hesitate as she rolled under the garage door like a limbo expert, landing on her stomach as the door closed behind her with a definitive thud. Well, she'd come here in hopes of getting in, hadn't she? Not quite this way, but it would do.

After covering her hand with her sleeve to avoid leaving prints, she approached the door and turned the knob cautiously. A peek through the crack in the door looked promising, so she slipped inside to find a blue-tiled entry with chestnut paneled wood. One way led downstairs, the other up to the kitchen. She chose the kitchen.

Then she stopped. Two hallways branched out from the kitchen, giving her more decisions to make. It was like being in a treasure-hunter movie—one way led to gold, the other to certain death. Which to choose?

A series of paintings on the wall of one hallway suggested a route to a more formal area, so she headed that way, looking down to see if she was leaving any flecks of dried mud from her clothes. They might serve like bread crumbs leading her back to the way she came, but she didn't want to leave any traces she'd been here.

At the end of the hallway, she found a study which looked like an excellent place to start. She used her sleeve-wrapped hand to open various file drawers and flip through the contents. Housekeeping records, a few invoices, bills. Not that she'd expected him to be moronic enough to keep incriminating papers in plain sight, but she had to try.

If he'd found the Lady statue, no doubt it was safe inside some vault. But as she took a look around the room, she changed her mind. Pieces from the silver-obsessed Reggie Forsythe's collection littered the room on various bookshelves, tables, a curio cabinet. Could the statue be among them?

Kornelson's notes weren't all that helpful in describing what to look for. Beverly had researched the Lady of Chartres as depicted in historical paintings and statues and hoped she had a rough idea of what the silver statue should resemble, but this could be different.

She wasn't sure who the artist was—maybe he'd used a girlfriend as a model. Beverly hurried through the study, foyer, and a library with floor-to-ceiling shelves but no joy.

Leaving the study, she headed down another branch of the

hallway, grateful for her rubber shoes on the hardwood floors. One of her shoes caught on a small rough joint between floorboards and made a little squeak. She stopped and listened. No sounds.

She entered the oval dining room, with its elegant, long mahogany table and blue silk-covered chairs, at first admiring the craftsmanship of the table. But then, all thoughts of incriminating documents and silver statues flew from her mind, and she had to fight the urge to flee.

For on the left side of the room, an elderly man lay on his back on the floor, his eyes wide open. Blood trickled from the gaping hole in the top of his head, and a blood-covered silver candelabra lay beside him.

Oh, dear god. Beverly put her hand over her mouth and closed her eyes for a brief moment, as she fought the acidic bile rising in the back of her throat. Then she opened her eyes wide and gingerly kneeled down beside the man, checking for a pulse in his wrist despite what the gory scene was telling her loud and clear.

The man was dead. She wanted to close those staring eyes, wanted to put something over him, a blanket, a sheet, anything to give him one last modicum of respect.

Standing up again, she forced herself to study his face. Even with the bloody wound, she could see his features. He was a handsome man in his 70s with a full head of white hair and eyes clouded with cataracts.

She knew who he was, this man. Reginald Forsythe, III. And apparently, murdered by his own son.

Beverly couldn't stay there any longer. She'd be a suspect, and that would throw attention off the real killer, the man she hated more than life itself. Still fighting the bile rising up in her throat, she took one last look at the body on the floor.

Before turning to make her way out of this damned, doomed house, she whispered softly to the dead man, "Oh, grandfather." And then she stumbled out the way she'd come.

16

Adam knew the summons to the chief's office couldn't be good news when he caught the chief popping some snuff. After a scare with mouth cancer a few years ago, the chief had sworn off all tobacco but imbibed whenever the stress ramped up to Defcon 3 territory. The smell of cloves that wafted in Adam's direction didn't go too well with the chocolate and raspberry cream cheese Danish that Adam had for breakfast.

Chief Quinn motioned toward a chair, but he stayed standing. Adam sat, trying to read between the frown lines on Quinn's face. The chief snapped the snuff tin shut and thrust it into the back of a drawer on his desk. "Got a call from the PD in Hartford. Reggie Forsythe found his father's body on the floor of the younger man's dining room. Someone had bashed the old man's head in with a candlestick."

Adam leaned forward. "Any suspects?"

"Forsythe says he checked his CCTV tape and saw the blurred image of a woman in his yard right before his father was killed. He's blaming it on the same woman who stole his Revere bowl."

"Same description, red hair and all?"

"Not exactly. Brown curly hair, different dark glasses, a little shorter and either heavyset or wearing a bulky coat. The face looked different, too, but wore a hat that covered her eyes."

"And yet he says it's the same person."

"He claims it's the same woman, two different disguises."

"Does he say why this woman would want his father dead?"

"He was vague on the motive but thinks it may have to do with the Revere bowl or some other antique doodad she was after."

"Was anything missing from his house?"

"He said he hadn't found anything. But he was too distraught to make a thorough review."

"Did he call you, or did you call him?"

"He called us."

"Other than rubbing this whole mess in our faces, what can we do? We're working the theft case since it's technically in our jurisdiction if this female thief is here in town. But Hartford isn't our problem."

"Part of his property lies in our county."

"But his official address is in Hartford."

Chief Quinn leaned on his desk. A fitting posture, since Adam had an idea the mayor was leaning on Quinn. The expression on that chief's face looked like he'd swallowed some of that snuff as he said, "I want you to assist the PD in Hartford. Research, legwork, whatever they need. You know Detective Given, right?"

Yeah, Adam was familiar with Given. Nice guy, if you liked sharks and were willing to wear a chum suit. Adam stifled a groan. He knew what the chief was thinking. A relatively minor theft was one thing, but murder connected with such a high-profile person as Forsythe was a whole different can of "worm-snuff." And that didn't include the jurisdictional pissing contest. It was better to stay silent and do the job.

Adam asked, "What about Reggie Forsythe, the son? Does he have an alibi?"

"His secretary swears he was in his office in Hartford on a long conference call."

"With whom? Got any names?"

"An attorney of his who vouches for him."

"No surprise, there. And amazingly convenient."

Jinks slipped into the office and flopped down on the other chair next to Adam. She avoided looking at him, but he didn't take offense. The chief didn't like it when he suspected his underlings were colluding behind his back, keeping him out of the loop.

Quinn said, "Jinks, as I was telling Dutton here, Reginald Forsythe, the elder, was murdered, and Dutton's going to assist the Hartford PD as needed. I'm pulling you off the missing-person case so you can work with Dutton on this."

If Adam dropped a bead of water on Jinks' skin right then, he wouldn't be surprised if it vaporized from the way she was radiating outrage. "Sir, I understand Mr. Forsythe is an important man, but I feel I'm close to a break in my case. And maybe this one wayward husband *isn't* an important man, but he has a grieving wife and two innocent children who need closure. Sir."

Quinn looked fixedly at her for a moment, and then his eyes dipped toward a photo on his desk. It was a photo of Quinn's grandchildren taken at the department Christmas party last year. The chief rubbed his forehead as if trying to smooth out the throbbing vein visible at his temple. "I'll let you continue the missing-person case, if, and only if, you help out Dutton with research or phone calls. It'll mean extra work for you, and we don't have the money for much overtime in the budget right now."

Adam looked at Jinks, who offered a small smile. "Thank

you, sir." She added in the faux-polite voice Adam knew all too well, "Is that all for now, sir?"

The chief nodded, and Jinks quickly left the office. Adam got up to follow her, but Quinn held him back. "Dutton, there's another thing I wanted to discuss with you. Make that two things."

Adam waved his hand for the chief to continue but didn't sit back down and kept one foot poised toward the door.

Quinn said, "The first is that Laborde woman. I want you to shadow her. Find out all you can. I want to know her childhood pet's name, what she was like at Dartmouth, what she eats for breakfast."

Adam didn't reply that he knew for sure Beverly's favorite breakfast wasn't bachelor chow bars. He'd had time to get more perspective on his Quechee Gorge meeting with Beverly, but he still didn't want Quinn to know about it. He felt a little silly just thinking about it, let along putting in a report.

"And the other thing?" he asked.

"Mayor Lehmann claims you've been harassing his wife."

Adam sagged down against the top of the chairback and caught himself right before it fell over backward. "Does he now? On what evidence?"

"Said he caught the two of you the other day down on Main. And that you were holding on to her arm, and that you looked upset. He claims Zelda was upset after talking with you, too."

The Zelda that Adam knew was always carefully controlled. No heart-on-your-sleeve woman, she. But this Zelda had seemed . . . not upset, but confused and troubled. Perhaps she wasn't only trying to patch over the hole she'd carved in his heart. Maybe she really was having second thoughts? What the hell was he supposed to say about that?

Adam felt like he needed a good stiff drink. "As I recall

that meeting, she approached *me* and grabbed my arm when she came out of the deli. Not the other way around."

The chief studied his face. "It's been, what, two years now since the divorce?"

"Just about."

The chief picked up a pencil and stabbed the eraser end on the desk. "I don't like to tell my people how to live their personal lives unless it reflects negatively on the department. Knowing Lehmann, I can believe it's sour grapes. But I want you to try to stay as far away from Zelda as possible for now. Give it a few weeks, and this'll all blow over."

"Yeah. Sure, Chief." Blow like a tornado blows a particle-board house high into the sky, dropping it a half-mile away.

Adam escaped from the chief's office and headed for the safety of his own office. When he passed by Jinks, she made a time-out motion with her hands. They detoured to the coffee machine to load up on caffeine before their upcoming confab—it was going to be a long afternoon.

Jinks grabbed a bottle from her pocket and poured a few drops into Adam's coffee before he could stop her. "What's that?" he asked.

"Energy shots. Extra caffeine, B vitamins, guarana, taurine, and tyrosine. Looked like you need it. I'd have said Quinn kicked your dog if you had a dog."

"Do exes count?"

Jinks tutted. "Zelda giving you grief? You know I can take her, right? Me, her, a pair of boxing gloves and a ring. I'd have her on a TKO in one round."

Adam took a sip of the "energy" coffee and blinked his eyes as they watered. His heart started dancing the Lindy Hop. "I don't know, Jinks. Zelda has a mean right hook."

Jinks looked at him askance.

"She accidentally knocked me over once when we were

cleaning out the garage."

"Accidentally?"

"I believed so then. In retrospect, it was a sign of things to come."

Not that they'd come to blows during the final year of their marriage. More like cold, dying embers than a fiery battle. His long hours were a problem, but she kept saying it wasn't him, it was her, she needed something different. Someone different. Someone who didn't listen to rockabilly CDs or wear an old pair of plaid fleece sweatpants to bed. Someone who knew the difference between Vucana wool and cashmere. Or so he'd thought.

He didn't have the energy or brain cells to waste obsessing about Zelda. It was possible the Revere bowl theft and the elder Forsythe's murder weren't connected. But if they were, it meant their little problem was escalating into something bigger and far more complicated. Forsythe's folly had just morphed into a political fiasco.

§ § §

Adam called the Apple Valley Resort to see if Beverly Laborde was in, but the front desk said they'd seen her leave earlier that morning, and she hadn't returned. On the plus side, she hadn't checked out. On the negative side, he had no idea where to find her.

They say patience is a virtue, but Adam didn't want to hang around the resort and wait for her return. He needed to be proactive, not wasting more precious minutes in nature hikes.

Jinks volunteered to work the databases, her nod to helping Adam with his case to please the chief. Adam called Harlan, but he said Beverly hadn't turned up at Harlan's antiques store, either. Nor had she been seen at the Amtrak station or turned in her rental car.

She might be out with her damned treasure map again or maybe something even worse. He tried not to imagine what the "worse" might be. She gave off an air of being clever and fearless, something that impressed him more than he cared to admit, but he didn't want her ending up like Reginald Forsythe, III.

Before he could do anything, however, he had to call the repair shop to see if his car was ready. When he dropped it off on his way to work, they'd said it would only take a couple of hours. Sure enough, after getting a lift from the shop, he was happy to see the old girl ready.

Petey Peeler, the shop manager, told him the good news, "This thing is built like a tank, Adam. You should hold on to it," right before he gave him the bad news, the bill. For the fifteen hundred dollars Adam would have to fork over, he'd be able to buy a tank. A used one, anyway.

Armed with a newly fixed car, a newly purchased cheesesteak, and a newly emailed address, thanks to Jinks, he was ready to tackle this whole Laborde affair head-on. He only wished he knew what Beverly was up to right now.

17

Another day, another muffin. Beverly sat in her car, staring straight ahead, trying to stay awake. Such a long, mostly sleepless night except for the few nightmares she'd had—with grinning skulls dripping with blood chasing her through Quechee where she'd fallen into the pond. She awoke with her heart pounding and never went back to sleep after that.

The remains of her scant half a bran muffin sat like a lump of clay in her stomach, and the black coffee hadn't helped. But she needed the caffeine. Barely aware of what she was doing, she'd wandered out to her rental car. After driving around for hours trying to decide what to do, she'd somehow found her way to this place without consciously thinking about it. She dragged herself out of the car and entered the door to Tossed Treasures.

Seeing that Harlan was helping a customer, Beverly wandered over to a table of ceramics and absently picked up a Pointon vase, studying the hand-painted cartouches—a Cupid's bow, a pastoral river scene, delicate blue flowers. *So* not representative of her life right now. She felt a hand on her shoulder and turned to see Harlan looking at her with concern.

"That's a nice piece you have there, but you've been staring at it for five minutes without moving." His eyes narrowed. "You look like you're about to fall over. Come with me."

He led her to a room in the back, herding her to a yellow tufted loveseat. He headed over to an urn of coffee on a hot plate, pouring out a cup, then adding a couple shots of something from a brown bottle. "Here you go. That'll warm you up."

She accepted the offering gratefully, aware for the first time she was shivering.

Harlan perched on the edge of his desk. "Want to tell me about it?"

She looked up, with a small shake of her head.

"Does this have to with Adam? He called earlier to see if you'd been by. If he's giving you grief, he'll have to deal with me. I may be his godfather, but that doesn't mean I can't give him a piece of my mind."

Beverly took another sip of the soothing drink. "You said you were good friends with Adam's father?"

"Adam's mother died when he was a wee boy. Aggressive breast cancer. Shame about his father, too. A good man." Harlan sighed. "I've wrestled with guilt over that."

"Guilt? Why?"

"I was the one who told Adam's father about that investment scheme. Didn't realize it was one of those consarned pyramid things. Never would have told him had I known. The poor man lost everything."

Beverly frowned. "But it's not your fault. Look at all the people Bernie Madoff conned. High society people, rich enough to know better."

"Cut from the devil's own piece goods, those types are, the Madoffs, the Zuneys."

"I can add another one to that list. Reggie Forsythe."

Harlan folded his arms across his chest. "Forsythe and his father may be the devil and his son. Never seen two men as morally bankrupt. Their coat of ethics is filled with moth-eaten holes. Not much coat left after that."

"Did you have direct dealings with them?"

"Used to belong to the Northeastern Antiquities League, so I bumped into them now and then. When they took the League in a dangerous direction and attracted others of their type, I gave up and left."

"By dangerous direction, you mean their shady deals, the thefts, the price gouging?"

Harlan scanned her face. "Sounds like you know them well."

"My grandmother owned an antiques shop. A lot like this one." Beverly smiled briefly at the memory. "Forsythe used a loophole in the state code enabling him to shut her down. After the bankruptcy and selling everything off, she was never the same."

"Who was your grandmother? Surely I know her."

"She died a few years ago following a stroke. But her name was Guinevere Glas."

Harlan spread his palms out on the desk as a broad smile dawned across his face. "Guinevere was your grandmother? Well, I'll be. I should have known since you're every bit as beautiful as she was. I had a crush, you know."

"You . . . you did?"

"Indeed I did. Fine woman. Met her about fifteen years ago, I think it was. Yes, that's about right. Even considered asking her out."

"Why didn't you?"

"She didn't seem interested, quite honestly. Told me she'd had a bad relationship once and didn't want to risk it. I never saw her after that."

Beverly bit her tongue, and it wasn't from the coffee. She knew exactly what Grammie meant by that remark. And the reason for it Beverly had just seen lying dead on the floor of his son's dining room with his head bashed in. "My grandmother married her husband when they were young, only eighteen. He wasn't a villain then, but it didn't take long for her to witness his true colors. She was heartbroken."

"Sorry to hear that. She deserved better. But she got some children and grandchildren out of it."

Beverly got up to pour some more coffee, pleased to see her hand wasn't shaking. "Her daughter, my mother, stayed with her. Her ex-husband insisted he take their son with him. Turned him against us, too. She never saw her son again after that."

"Oh, dear. To be separated from your child in such a cruel fashion. The man must be a monster."

They sat without talking for a few moments. The only sounds in the room were the quiet humming from the vintage popcorn machine's motor and the ticking from a roulette wheel clock on the wall. It was a surreal duet, so ordinary and so far removed from murder.

Beverly spoke up, "You weren't too far off when you said Adam Dutton was part of my problem. I might be a target of one of his investigations."

"Are you now?" Harlan cocked one eyebrow, making him look like a cross between Santa and Yoda. "Nothing too serious, I hope."

Beverly curled the hem of her jacket with her non-coffee hand. "He's just doing his job. And he's good at what he does, isn't he?"

"The best. Not the flashy type. Doesn't like attention. Unfortunately, he had more than he could handle of that two years ago."

"The drug bust gone bad you told me about? With the torture?"

"Ayah. The same. Adam was pushed into therapy afterward by the department. A condition of him staying on."

"It was that much of a nightmare?"

Harlan hesitated, then replied, "You could look it up in the local library archives, so I might as well tell you. The man who kidnapped him was a fan of ancient Greek philosophy. He thought it would be great sport to torture Adam with the four elements. You know, the ones Greeks believed made up everything—earth, water, air, fire. The air and water part involved waterboarding. The fire part was a branding iron. And the earth part . . . he buried Adam alive in a coffin in the ground."

Beverly gripped the mug in both hands. As horrible as the fresh image from the senior Forsythe's bloodied body was in her mind, the mental images conjured up by Harlan's description of Adam's torture were worse. "Who found him?"

"His fellow detective, Eliot Jinks. But there lies some controversy, too."

"Why? She should be given a medal."

"She forgot to double-check her radio before they went out on the drug bust that night. She and Adam got separated, she saw him being taken, but it was too fast for her to react. She tried to radio for backup."

"But the radio didn't work."

"Exactly. The other cops on the force started writing her name as Jinx after that. To this day, I'm not sure some of them trust her. Except Adam. He's loyal that way."

Beverly made a note to add Eliot Jinks to her cellphone list. She'd added quite a few names recently, Adam, Harlan, Mr. X, even Reggie Forsythe.

Harlan refilled his cup, adding four shots from the brown bottle, which Beverly now saw was labeled Irish whiskey. He asked, "You coming here this morning—and that investigation you referred to. Wouldn't be tied to that drug thing?"

"No, nothing like that."

"You and he should have a nice sit-down and work all this

out." Harlan slurped more of the coffee. "He's a good catch, you know. Despite what his gold-digging, social-climbing ex-wife might tell you."

"He's divorced?"

"Zelda's her name. Zelda Lehmann. She married our wealthy mayor. Wanted Adam to run for office, but that's not his style. She decided to marry an office instead."

"Does she have short red hair?"

"That she does."

Perhaps that's who Adam was talking to the other day. She ignored the feeling of relief that swept over her at the knowledge. After all, maybe they were trying to get back together? She needed to be like Grammie and foreswear relationships with men. Too much trouble. Too many wasted years.

Relationships—something her late grandfather wasn't particularly good at either. Beverly didn't know anything about Reginald Forsythe's second wife, but it was hard to believe any woman would want to live with a snake. But then, how did you explain women attracted to serial killers in prison?

She asked Harlan, "Reggie Forsythe, the younger, was divorced recently. Do you know why they broke up?"

"Near as I recall, it was due to those 'irreconcilable differences.' It's been a few years now, you see. I think it was the same woman who came with him to one of the NAL meetings. Heard a friend say it was Forsythe's missus, anyway. Never saw her after that."

"Do you remember her name?"

"Reckon I might. One of those famous names. You know, that dictator's wife. Irina, Ivana. No, it was Imelda. Yes, I'm sure that's it."

"What was she like?"

Harlan scratched his chin. "I don't like to speak ill of folks.

Let's just say they were made for each other."

The sound of a bell tinkling at the front door alerted them to a new customer. Harlan made his excuses, and Beverly thanked him for the coffee and the sympathy. She told him it was because he had such a cherubic face, but what she didn't say was that his was the only friendly face she had to turn to right now.

Why, oh why, couldn't her grandmother have married him instead of Reginald Forsythe the Third? But then, Beverly would never have been born. Would she really wish her existence away just like that? She laughed at the irony of that. Here she was getting sucked into an existential crisis when she'd just found her own grandfather murdered. No, what's done was done.

But that didn't mean Beverly was done. Not at all, not by a long shot. She wasn't going to just sit around and wait for the walls of justice to close in and suffocate her. She wasn't a con artist for nothing.

18

Thanks to Jinks and their combined research—starting with antiques stores shut down seven years ago due to "code violations"—Adam had a pretty good idea where Miss Beverly Laborde's grandmother used to have her store. If he was right, her name wasn't Laborde, but Gras.

Ordinarily, the drive to Lakeford would be relaxing. A chance to get away from office stress, especially when the leaves were exploding with color like a fireworks chain reaction from one tree to the next.

Adam usually liked the smells of fall, too, the tobacco-like odor of brown leaves, the straggler apples on the ground fermenting their version of cider. Today, it all smelled like death.

Now the chief wanted him to stay away from Zelda and stick close to Beverly? Like the chief was some sort of dating advisor, if it weren't for the gravity of the situation. Zelda and Beverly, both potential mankillers in their own way.

Thanks to Beverly, Adam was doing more research on the Natick Indians, who viewed women as equals. Caregivers, yes, but adept at making weapons and assisting in warfare when required. Sometimes Adam felt the relationships between the sexes were a series of war games.

Adam pulled up in front of the address from the file he'd made, but a hardware store now stood on the site where haunted look to them, Kora's were bright and clear. Too bright and clear. And green. Probably contact lenses. Kora was pleasant-looking, but compared to Beverly, it was no contest.

He asked her, "I hate to bother you, Mrs. Gilmore, but Mr. Strickland over there said you were friends with Beverly Glas?"

"We were blood sisters." She laughed at his reaction, adding, "You know how kids are. We pricked the tips of our fingers with a pin and pressed mine to hers. Feels like a lifetime ago."

"When was the last time you saw her?"

"At my sister's wedding."

"And that was . . . ?"

"Five years plus change. I've been thinking of her lately, so it's funny you should ask about her now. I mean, out of the blue, I get a letter from her with a ticket to the Chevron Playhouse production of *The Fantasticks*. She said she couldn't go, and she knew I loved theater, so she hoped I could take her place."

"And you haven't heard from her since?"

"No, but thanks for the reminder. I really need to give her a call. Do you have her number? She didn't list any. Or an address."

"I might be able to get that for you," Adam hemmed. He didn't want Beverly to know he'd tracked Kora down. "Is there somewhere I could reach you?"

Kora pulled her wallet out and handed over a business card for an accounting firm. She tapped it with her finger. "I'm there most days. Weekends, sometimes."

Kora hesitated a moment. "Beverly's not in any trouble, is she?"

Adam lied, "No, it's just related to a case I'm working on. Thanks very much for speaking with me. And I appreciate your help."

He watched her drive away, then leaned on his car window, thinking. It wasn't damning evidence, but it made Beverly look more like she'd been setting up an alibi. He was finding it harder to wrap his head around the fact that Beverly Laborde was the granddaughter of Reginald Forsythe, III. The late, murdered Reginald Forsythe, III. Which made Reggie Forsythe her estranged uncle.

If Reggie never had any further contact with her or her grandmother, he wouldn't have recognized his now-grown-up niece if she came to his house—posing as a Revere silver collector with a piece to sell. Doubly so if she was in disguise as the man himself had suspected.

Maybe Adam was right when he told Beverly that Reggie's forcing her grandmother out of business was a strong motive for Beverly being the con woman. Her way of getting back at him. But if true, how deep did her hatred lie? And how far would she go to get back at both Forsythes? Murder, perhaps?

His next thought plunged him in the middle of a dilemma. Did she know how dangerous this man was? If Adam went back to the chief with this intel, Beverly would be hauled in as a person of interest and thrown into jail as the primary suspect if Reggie Forsythe had his way. And if he found out she was his niece ... He and his father had shown their true colors when they ruined Beverly's grandmother's antiques business.

Adam decided to drive by Forsythe's office to take a quick look. It was in a one-story building that took up a city block with a parking lot in back. The man had said he was on a conference call while the murder was taking place, but it wouldn't be hard to slip in and out of a window. Especially if the man lied and if his attorney and possibly his secretary were in on the charade.

Plenty of "ifs" there. Yet, plenty of "real" proof for a mystery-woman intruder on the security footage. And he had a pretty good feeling who a judge and jury would likely believe.

What he needed was a man-to-man with Beverly's uncle. Adam climbed into the car and headed toward another address in his folder. Hopefully, the guy would call off his attack dogs long enough for Adam to have a little "friendly" chat.

19

After a call to Mr. X, Beverly found out that the body of Reginald Forsythe had been taken to the Southeastern Vermont Regional Hospital instead of the usual UV Medical Center, due to a sprinkler mishap in their forensics lab. Perfect. Closer and easier.

For this role, she'd chosen a short, layered wig of light-ash-brown-and-silver to go with her very sensible navy dress and equally sensible black flats. She ducked inside the hospital bathroom for a quick mirror check. The fake "Dr. Liz Smith" ID tag she'd cooked up thanks to materials from an office supply store looked pretty good. And the stethoscope and white lab coat she'd bought from a return trip to the costume store were a nice touch.

As she headed back down the main hallway, she had an anxious moment when a hospital visitor stopped her and asked, "Doctor, my brother was brought here after a car crash. They said he broke his clavicle. Can you tell me anything?"

Beverly put on her best professional face. "You'll have to speak with the Information Desk in the lobby."

When the woman scrunched up her face in misery, Beverly quickly added, "They'll tell you where he is and when you can visit. And don't worry too much about a broken collarbone. They usually take one to two months to heal and may require some physical therapy. But he should be fine."

but who knows how long it would take? She didn't recall Grammie saying he was diabetic. A drug user, like heroin?

Beverly couldn't risk taking any longer, so she put everything back as she'd found it and slipped out the door. Just as she was pulling off her gloves to drop in a trash can, she heard scrubs-guy's voice coming down the hall soon followed by that of the M.E., Lynda. Talk about good timing.

Right before she left the hospital, she stopped by the Information Desk and asked the young staffer, "A man was brought in a while ago with a broken clavicle. A cousin of mine, as it turns out. I understand he's been moved from ER to a room. Do you have that number?" Beverly didn't know he was out of the ER, but the man *should* have been moved by now.

The staffer checked his database. "Room 215."

"Great, thanks. I'll check on him later." Maybe not visit, but perhaps he'd be getting some "anonymous" flowers.

She didn't want the staffer to dwell too long on why a doctor would need to ask the Information Desk about such things and scurried outside to her waiting rental car, which she'd parked at the farthest corner of the lot—and out of the range of any security cameras.

Could her grandfather have been a heroin user? He hadn't shown any of the signs when she was at the NAL meeting that day when she'd barely missed bumping into Detective Adam Dutton. Maybe Reggie the Fourth was covering all bases, shooting up his father after bashing his head in so he could blame a drug dealer for the murder.

But if Beverly ended up being tied to the murder scene, she'd given Reggie a much more convenient and a much better patsy for his crime, hadn't she?

§ § §

Beverly tossed the lab coat, fake ID, and stethoscope in the trunk of the car but kept the wig and added a pair of tinted eyeglasses. Mr. X said her grandfather had one possible friend, a Lowell Steen, and after looking him up, she'd found what she hoped was the right address.

She wasn't entirely sure why she felt compelled to see him. Could be partly curiosity to find the one man who got along with Forsythe senior, and maybe it was partly hope that he'd help her case against Reggie.

But when she pulled in front of the address from her GPS, she had half a mind to drive on by. It wasn't so much the peeling purple paint on the house's facade as the windows with bars over them and blackout shades behind that. Was her information wrong? Then she noticed a rusted, tilting mailbox that read "teen," with the initial S in danger of falling off. Maybe the "S" was trying to escape this place? Beverly couldn't blame it for that.

She couldn't tell if anyone was home or whether they would answer the door if so, but it opened before she had a chance to press the doorbell. She asked, "Are you Mr. Steen?"

The man looked older than her grandfather, but she'd met plenty of people whose white hair and wrinkles came from hard knocks and not long lives. He pulled out a pair of coke-bottle-thick glasses from the pocket of his blue-stained shirt and looked her up and down. "I don't know what you're selling, but I don't need it."

"My name is Barbara Beale. I'm with Human Services and Investigations. I'd like to talk to you about your late friend, Reginald Forsythe."

"Don't think I've heard of your agency—"

"We assist the police department in these cases. To help with the families and friends of the recently deceased."

"I don't know anything about any of that. But I haven't

had a visitor other than the mailman in months, and you're a far sight prettier than he is. You might as well come in and sit for a spell."

If the house's exterior and the man's appearance hinted at "eccentric," the interior sealed the deal. All the chairs were upholstered in various mismatched and faded colors of paisley fabric—gold, red, turquoise, purple—to match the faded orange paisley curtains. And what was the reason for those curtains if he was using blackout shades?

Every single surface held piles of boxes, magazines and papers, and knickknacks like googly-eyed dolls and vintage hand-painted duck decoys. Many were threatening to topple over any minute. If Lowell Steen wasn't yet the textbook definition of a hoarder, he was well on his way.

Beverly gingerly sat down on the edge of one seat. When she got a whiff from a container of menthol rub next to a bowl of rotten apples on a table nearby, she wished she'd chosen another one. She'd have to hurry this along if she wanted to keep from chain-sneezing. "Mr. Steen, have you known Reginald Forsythe a long time?"

"Long enough. We had the misfortune of being placed in the same Gestapo primary school."

"Gestapo?"

"Private school. Felt like a prison. Ruler-wielding nuns like Teutonic terrors in tunics."

"His parents had money, then?" She realized she didn't know the first thing about her grandfather's family. Never bothered to find out.

"In spades. He never saw them much. Private school in fall and spring, military camp in summer. He was an inconvenience."

"Then it's good he had a friend like you. A lifelong friend, at that."

"You could say we've been through a lot together. We both enjoyed hockey and a good hard cider. But there were the weddings, divorces, births, deaths . . . and enemies."

"Enemies?"

He squinted at her. "Who did you say you were with?"

"We're checking into Forsythe's frame of mind. To determine if he might have taken his own life." She had to think fast on that one. Not her best effort, for sure.

"Suicide? The newspapers said murder."

"The police have to check all angles. Insurance companies, you know." She hoped her expression was convincing as she waited to see if he'd bought it.

"Bah, insurance people." Steen took a swig from a glass that held something green. "Rats and snakes, all of them."

Before she could reply, Steen continued, "Snakes, you wanna see snakes? Come with me."

He crooked his finger at her, and she followed him into a back room near the kitchen, somewhat against her better judgment. He pointed at three glass aquarium tanks that held several species of snakes. Then he called her attention to one of the most giant snakes she'd ever seen.

Steen said, "Python. Watch." He went to a cage in the back corner and pulled out something. He tossed a live mouse into the enclosure, which the python promptly gobbled up.

"Reginald and I used to have a little fun naming these mice with people from our enemies list. And then we fed them to the snake."

After Steen had told her about her grandfather's childhood, she'd almost felt sorry for him. But now, he was back to being the indecipherable monster who'd bred a junior monster that ended up swallowing his father just like that python with the mouse.

Not a fan of snakes, animal or human, she didn't want to

stay in that room any longer. She whirled around and headed back toward the living room and sat down again, making sure it was farther away from the menthol-and-moldy-apple table.

Steen followed, took another swig of the green concoction, and sat opposite her. Beverly longed to leave this house, but she had to play the part a while longer to avoid suspicion.

She asked, "You would say his state of mind before his death was one of anger since obviously, he had a great deal of anger toward those enemies of his? But not suicidal?"

"I'd sooner expect Reginald to turn into a cross-dresser than go all suicidal. I spoke to him on the phone only last week. He was fine."

"Did he mention anything about his son, Reggie?"

Steen put down the glass, grabbed a cigarette from a pack, and lit it, taking a long drag. "We never talked about Reggie."

"I heard he was quite successful."

"Too successful."

"I'm afraid I don't understand."

Steen blew a few smoke rings. "Reggie's always thought he's top turd on the wheelbarrow. He was the one snake his father couldn't tame."

There was nothing funny about the situation, but Steen's "wheelbarrow" comment might be amusing on any other occasion. And it was spot-on. "Sounds like they argued a great deal, then."

"He didn't tell me. But I saw it. I'd say you should be asking about Reggie's frame of mind more than his father's."

Score one for a possible witness to Reggie's character and a motive in a murder trial. The smell of the room and the psychedelic paisley were getting to her, so she thanked Steen for his "assistance" and fled back to her car.

She'd learned a little more about her grandfather even if it wasn't altogether flattering. And she'd found someone who could help pin the murder on Reggie, not that Adam Dutton would be interested, coming from her. The same Detective Dutton who was now undoubtedly aware of her grandfather's murder and hopefully connecting the dots back to Reggie.

Feeling like a failure as both a detective and a treasure hunter, she headed back to the resort to lick her wounds. She was tired, that was all. Hungry, too, as she hadn't eaten since her half a bran muffin and coffee for breakfast. She'd have a nice dinner, a nice bath, and resume her pursuit of justice tomorrow. Even avenging angels needed a little break now and then.

20

Reggie Forsythe's house was what you'd expect of the man. Big, bloated, and bombastic. Topiaries? Seriously? The least he could do is make them into something interesting. Or more appropriate. A weasel, maybe, or a moray eel.

Dutton had called Detective Given ahead of time to square it with him, and Given gave his blessing. He literally used those words. So it was Saint Given now. Adam knew Given was aiming for the top, but he'd thought more along the lines of Chief of the Hartford PD someday than a religious icon.

Adam flashed his badge at a police officer rolling up yellow crime scene tape across one end of the driveway. The officer let him pass through. After entering the house, Adam didn't see any detectives, but the CSIs were hard at work.

"Well, well, Detective Dutton. What a pleasant surprise." Forsythe's voice dripped with the verbal equivalent of lye. "It's nice to see Chief Quinn sent along his best."

"Mind if I have a look around, sir?"

"But of course, Detective. Whatever it takes to catch that horrid woman."

One of the CSI techs approached Forsythe, so Adam took the opportunity to walk through the house. Lots of old, musty-smelling books that had probably never been cracked open, lots of king-sized furniture and lots and lots of silver. Silver chandeliers, silver-and-glass end tables, silver mirrors, silver tchotchkes. The tin man looking for a heart?

He found the dining room, the red stains on the floor making it easy to pinpoint where the victim died. Adam spied a heavy candelabra sealed in a plastic bag. More red stains on that, the likely murder weapon.

He picked up the plastic bag. That thing was heavy. When the chief mentioned a candlestick, Adam pictured a smaller one-candle unit. This one had holes for five candles, was about eighteen inches tall and around three pounds. He pictured a woman like Beverly hoisting the thing high enough to bring it down with the force required to crack a skull wide open. She looked fit but not the bodybuilder type.

The tech bending over a wallboard straightened up to look at the plastic bag in Adam's hands. He pointed at it. "My aunt has one of those. Solid silver. She uses it for candles, though, not bonking people on the head. On second thought, I better tell my uncle to watch his back."

Crime scene humor. Adam flashed an obligatory smile, but his heart wasn't in it. He examined the bag again. "Check for prints on this candlestick thing yet?"

"We'll wait 'til the lab. Looks clean on first blush."

"That would mean gloves or our killer wrapped something around this first. That makes it premeditation, not a crime of passion." He placed the bag back on the table. "Do you think a petite woman could have used this as a murder weapon?"

The tech guy frowned. "Women are often stronger than they look. But if I'd seen it before you told me it was a woman who allegedly did this, I wouldn't have guessed."

Adam heard a slight cough and looked up to find Forsythe in the doorway. "If you have a moment, Detective, I want to talk to you."

Deciding to launch a charm offensive, Adam smiled broadly. "Why yes, that would be nice. Wherever you say, sir."

They ended up in the study with all the moldy books, and

Adam pushed the tip of his tongue between his upper teeth to stifle a sneeze. "I was so sorry to hear about your father, Mr. Forsythe."

"Yes, a terrible tragedy. His loss will be felt by many."

"Many" didn't include his son, judging by the slack look on the "grieving" heir's face and the cavalier tone in his words. Adam added, "I know you suspect the mystery woman of being behind your father's death, and we're checking into that. But do you know of anyone else who might have wanted your father dead?"

"Certainly not. The angriest I've seen anyone toward Father was a fellow golfer at the Apple Valley Resort golf course when Father asked to play through."

"You and your father are in the antiques business. Surely there are competitors, rivalries, someone who might not be his number one fan?"

Forsythe pulled a pipe out of pocket, followed by a pouch of tobacco. He slowly and deliberately added the tobacco to the pipe and then struck a match to it. An aroma like singed blackberries wafted through the room. "Naturally, there are rivalries in any business. But businessmen don't go around bashing each other over the head. It's much less messy to simply undermine your opponent."

"Whatever that entails?"

"Business is a harsh reality, Detective Dutton. It's not for the faint of heart."

"Most businessmen don't go to work every day wondering if they're going to get shot in the line of duty."

Forsythe looked at Adam over his pipe. "Perhaps."

Adam leaned back in his wingback chair, his very uncomfortable wingback chair. What was the point of having painful furniture? He surveyed the room. "You have a nice home here, Mr. Forsythe. I understand you've lived here for twenty years."

Forsythe waved his pipe in the air in reply.

"Pleasant area to live. But you weren't born here, were you, sir?"

"I was born in neighboring Riverton. But I haven't kept in touch with my estranged mother's side of the family. I had a sister once. I believe she and her husband died in a car crash. I never knew them."

"Tin man" was the right description for Forsythe, all right. He was as shaken by the mention of his sister's death as one would be shaking snow off their shoes. "What was your mother's maiden name, Mr. Forsythe?"

"It was Gras. Why?

"Just curious. I have family around here, too, and wondered if I might have heard of her." Not that he'd needed verification of Strickland's story, but it was gratifying to get it, nonetheless.

"As I say, I never knew her or that side of the family. Father said she was a cold-hearted bitch who was only interested in his money."

"I'm sorry to hear that. Must have been difficult for you to grow up without a mother around."

Forsythe laughed. "Spare me the sympathy, Detective. You and I both know you don't care about me or my childhood. But you do seem intent on deflecting attention from our female suspect. Hiding something?"

"No sir. I promise you we'll check all leads and suspects. Chief Quinn runs a tight ship."

"And he should continue to do so if wants to keep Mayor Lehmann happy."

Adam smiled again. "I understand you're friends, sir?"

"I don't have friends, Detective. Acquaintances, associates, employees. And I keep them all in a tight circle, cracking the whip as needed. You'd be smart to keep that in mind."

"I have too many things on my mind right now to add one more." Adam rose to his feet, noting the flash of irritation in Forsythe's eyes. "I appreciate you giving me some of your valuable time, sir. We'll keep you posted on the investigation."

Adam made his way back through the crime scene tape to his car. Even if Beverly Laborde were a thief and a liar, he couldn't see her as a killer. He felt himself wanting to protect her from this soul-cannibal, but holding back evidence wasn't his style.

Stopping back by the police station, Adam headed to his computer to start checking databases but stopped when he spied a report someone had dropped on his desk. It was a preliminary autopsy report. Nothing that didn't jibe with what he'd seen from the photos the Hartford PD had sent along. Except for one thing—needle marks on the victim's arm?

He switched to his Hartford notes, but they didn't mention anything about drug use or drug paraphernalia found in the house. Now that was interesting. Maybe Reggie and Beverly were both innocent, and the killer was a drug dealer. Lucky for Adam, that was in Detective Given's jurisdiction and all the best to him.

Adam logged into his computer. Armed with the names that now filled in some of Beverly Laborde's past, he had something to sink his teeth into, research-wise. He looked up Guinevere Gras and searched for any references to Zayette. Regarding the latter, he found the newspaper accounts of Beverly's mother and father killed in a wreck after their car was hit head-on by a cement truck.

He rubbed his eyes at that one. When he was younger and a beat cop, how many tragic and gruesome car crashes had he helped investigate? They never got any easier for him. And notifying the shocked family members didn't either, especially the kids. The article said the Zayettes had a daughter aged six. About the same age Adam was when he lost his mother to cancer.

Otherwise, as far as he was able to tell, Gras and the Zayettes were upstanding, hard-working, honest folk. No rap sheets, no hints of scandal. Nothing like a Beverly Laborde skeleton anywhere in their closet.

He leaned back in his chair, thinking. Now came the hard part, writing up a report. He didn't know yet what he was going to put in and what he'd leave out. Or even if he'd leave anything out. But he honestly didn't feel like staying here late into the evening to do it. He needed some space to think this through and would deal with the chief tomorrow.

After grabbing his jacket, he made his way to his car, opened the door, and then slammed it shut after he climbed in. As he fiddled with the buttons on his radio, he said aloud, "Beverly Laborde, why did you have to choose this town and this time—and to complicate my life?"

21

Saturday, September 18

Despite Harlan cheering her up yesterday, Beverly kept waking up every twenty minutes and gave up after only two hours of sleep. How many hours did that make total over the past several nights? Eight, nine tops. It was no wonder she was quickly working her way through a thermos of caffeine from the waitress in the tea room.

Beverly had developed a bond with the waitress, Gloria Gelling. They had far more in common than on first blush. Thanks to Adam sending Gloria's husband to jail, she was now hoping to go back to school to earn a bachelor's degree. When Beverly asked Gloria about her area of study, she'd said business, but with a minor in acting. Beverly was amused by the classic stereotype of the waitress who wanted to be an actress, but they were soon exchanging tips on makeup and disguises.

Any other day, Beverly would have enjoyed stopping by the quaint shops in Woodstock. But today, she barreled southeast along U.S. 4 until she reached the destination she'd programmed into the car's GPS. The entrance was on a slight hill and looked down at the estate below.

And what a spread it was. The sprawling alpine-style house was flanked by a covered pool and hot tub in the back, with a small pond just beyond. Farther back on the property lay a separate stable and fenced-in paddock. When Beverly called a local realtor earlier, pretending to be a buyer, she found this property was valued in the low millions. Reggie Forsythe's ex-wife must have gotten a bundle in the divorce.

Mindful of Mr. X's comments about security and her recent experience at Forsythe's place, she looked around for security cameras or motion detectors. She wasn't an expert in home security, but she didn't think she saw anything unusual. Someday, she'd have to get Mr. X to give her a tutorial.

She checked her makeup in the car's mirror. Just the basics, nothing flashy. The ponytail was a nice touch, pulled back with a barrette in the shape of an old-fashioned typewriter key. Smoothing her pantsuit as she climbed out of the car, she came close to forgetting to rescue the notepad on the passenger's seat.

She rang the doorbell and pasted a professionally bland smile on her face. She'd called ahead, but when no one answered, she began to think she'd misunderstood the directions she was given.

But then the door opened to reveal a short woman in a gray dress with a white apron. "May I help you?" she asked in heavily accented English. Her complexion, dark hair and eyes, and the accent made Beverly guess the woman hailed from somewhere in Central America.

"My name is Beverly Zayette. I have an appointment with Imelda Forsythe."

The maid motioned for Beverly to follow her. The maid led her to the great room, curtsied, and left Beverly alone. Beverly thought she caught a flash of fear in the maid's eyes, eyes that had stayed downcast from the moment she answered the door.

The great room was great, indeed. Ceilings approaching

fifty feet at the apex, filled with wooden beams and floor-to-ceiling glass windows that afforded a breathtaking view of the mountain peaks in the distance. The furniture pieces grouped in front of the massive stone fireplace were trying hard to look casual, but Beverly recognized the designer—Dongyul Ping. His smallest end tables started around one grand. The chandelier was the size of a moose, appropriate since it was made entirely out of antlers.

The most curious thing about the room was the lack of antiques. Not a single Tiffany lamp or even a nineteenth-century painting. Strange, for a woman who'd married into a family of antiques businessmen. Maybe she'd purged that link to her ex-husband along with the divorce.

Beverly reached out to touch what looked for all the world like a Brazilian rosewood mantel above the fireplace. Wasn't that wood illegal to purchase?

A voice from behind startled her. "You're that reporter who called."

Beverly faced the owner of that voice, a tall woman in her mid-fifties dressed like she was ready to mount an entry in the Grand National. Black breeches, red vest, black dressage coat, and tall riding boots. Seeing the glints of steel in the woman's expression, Beverly was glad Imelda Forsythe wasn't carrying a whipping crop.

Beverly replied, "Beverly Zayette, Mrs. Forsythe. I'm so grateful you were willing to see me for an interview."

Imelda cantered into the room and indicated a chair for Beverly to sit down. Imelda herself leaned against the same mantel Beverly had examined, reaching around to pull a golden cigarette holder out of a case and light up a smoke. As Beverly took another quick glance around the room, she also noted that in addition to the lack of antiques, there wasn't anything silver.

"Now, Ms. Zayette. What magazine did you say you were

writing for?"

"It's a national startup publication, with each issue focusing on luxury homes in a different region."

"A print publication?"

Beverly nodded.

"Good. I hate those digital things. It's like someone is spying on you, watching every word you read. God help you if your hobby is collecting guns. Or you have a curiosity about poisons."

Beverly nodded again. Imelda's thoughts weren't all that unrealistic, but she was as paranoid as her ex. Beverly said, "You sound like my ex-boyfriend. He hated everything computer."

"Ex-boyfriend, huh? I've got plenty of those myself."

"Let's face it, it's hard to find a good man."

"Whatever a good man is. Good can mean different things, can't it? Good as in rich, good as in sex, good as in letting you do your thing and not asking any questions."

"Pick any two, right?"

Imelda laughed derisively. "Pick any one. They're all mutually exclusive. Take my ex-husband, for example. He was good at being rich."

"You do have a nice home, Mrs. Forsythe."

"Thanks to a prenup, I got a nice stash, but it wasn't enough to buy this place. One of my ex-boyfriends was good at investing and gave me some helpful advice."

"Prenups are essential. You were smart to go that route."

"You bet your life, I was. Oh, I didn't divorce Reggie for the money, I mean I knew he was a crook. But I didn't care about that when I married him. I wanted his money."

"You haven't remarried?"

"I've had my share of men, but why should I hurry? Besides, men are my favorite sport."

"You say you knew your husband was a crook. Wasn't it taking a chance to marry someone like that?"

Imelda took a puff on her cigarette and made a perfectly round smoke ring. "I hate boring. And that's one thing he wasn't. If we'd had any neighbors within hearing distance, they would have called the cops on us daily, thanks to our fights."

Beverly was beginning to see that Imelda was a match for Reggie Forsythe in more ways than one. Those fights between them must have been fun to see. She murmured a hopefully sympathetic, "Hmm."

Imelda was good at smoke rings, puffing out two in rapid succession before she added, "I have no idea what all Reggie was into. Who knows? As long as I got my baubles and vacays, I couldn't care less."

"Surely, nothing too evil? I mean, you impress me as being savvy. You would have noticed something like that."

"Reggie was capable of anything. I wouldn't put it past him to have killed someone. He did have a cruel streak. Possibly with psychopathic undertones. That's what my therapist said, right before he asked me out on a date." Imelda smirked.

"Must be an interesting family, the Forsythes."

"Oh, his father was all right, I suppose. Had a tender side when he didn't know you were looking. Who knows? If his first wife hadn't divorced him, things might have been different. I don't think he ever got over that."

That comment brought Beverly up short. But Grammie *had* to divorce him, she couldn't have stayed with such a man. Could she? For the first time, Beverly stopped to think that perhaps her grandmother had an indirect hand in pushing Forsythe senior into his downward spiral. Had he truly loved her? Did the act of her leaving devastate him?

Imelda picked up a brass bell on the mantel. It resembled a Buddhist temple bell and had a dark shimmer as she rang it. On cue, the maid who'd greeted Beverly entered the room, her eyes still downcast as she approached Imelda. She stopped three feet in front of her mistress as if an imaginary line were drawn on the floor.

Imelda barked at the maid, "Palma, did you lay out the extra riding hats and gloves for our guests?"

"I was just going to start on that, Madam."

Imelda scowled. "Oh, for god's sake, I reminded you about that yesterday. The guests will be arriving in an hour. Drop whatever else it is you're doing and get on it. Right now."

Palma bowed. "Yes, Madam."

Imelda took another puff on the cigarette and blew smoke in Palma's face. Beverly doubted it was accidental. After Palma curtsied and fled the room, Imelda pulled the last of the cigarette and threw it into the fireplace. "They say good help is hard to find. That woman is insufferable. Botches such a trivial task as that."

Beverly fought the impulse to slap Imelda right then. But she needed to ask some real estate questions if she hoped to protect her cover story. Plus, it would help get her mind off the tears she'd seen in Palma's eyes.

Imelda was an excellent interviewee and witty at times as she talked about the houses in the area. Beverly dutifully wrote everything down. Who knows? She could try to sell the article at a future date.

When she estimated she'd given it enough effort to look realistic, she closed the notepad. "I know you have guests coming, so I don't want to overstay my welcome. My next project should be writing a profile of your ex-husband. Maybe I'll get a Pulitzer for investigative reporting."

Beverly said it with a smile as if joking, but Imelda looked thoughtful. She replied, "If you need to dig up dirt on the man, you should look up one of his former associates. Had a Greek name. Xenakis, I think. And one other, Kannan Hendrick. If you want to find him, he's in Hartford at 101 Blessing Road."

Imelda laughed. "Now, there was a man who had no sense. Guess that's why he ended up where he did."

Beverly thanked her again and headed out into the crisp air that felt a few degrees colder than when she'd arrived. Snow would soon fall on the mountains in and around Woodstock, which the ski resorts were no doubt hoping for.

Beverly had never been a fan of snow. Pretty, yes. But its cold beauty only masked the hardened landscape of muck and withered grass lying underneath. A lot like Imelda Forsythe.

22

Adam stared at the screen on his home computer. It was blank. Again. He'd typed several hundred words, deleted them, then typed several hundred more and deleted them, too. He jumped up from the desk and stalked into the kitchen. He needed more coffee. And some protein.

After grabbing the rest of his spinach-feta omelet breakfast and refilling his mug, he straddled one of the bar stools with the checkerboard backs that Zelda hated so much. Finding he wasn't really hungry, he dumped the omelet into the garbage and set the plate down on the counter so hard, he half-expected he'd cracked it.

Okay, so he hadn't slept great and might be a little cranky. Dreams of wide cornflower-blue eyes brimming with tears kept waking him up, and he gave up around four a.m. and got up to watch the news. Then he wished he hadn't, because the top story was the murder of Reginald Forsythe, III.

RF the younger had embellished his story about the female intruder even more to the point where she'd now become a murderous professional thief who was obviously after Forsythe heirlooms and treasures. And the poor, innocent murdered victim was in the wrong place at the wrong time and killed for trying to protect his son's property. Right.

If Adam was honest with himself, he had to look the hard truth in the face—what did he really know about Beverly's past? Except that she was genetically tied to the underhanded, shadowy Forsythe family. What if she were a murderous professional thief, after all? Maybe it was in the genes?

He'd entertained the idea she and Reggie Forsythe were in this together, but it wouldn't make sense for Forsythe to try to pin the blame on this "female intruder," if that were the case. Still, could she hate him so much she was willing to put herself at significant risk just to embarrass him? That was some obsession.

Adam grabbed his computer again. He also picked up the notes he'd jotted down from the case, including those following yesterday's trek to Beverly's former town and Forsythe's home. What the hell was he going to put in his report to the chief? If he mentioned Beverly's family connections to Forsythe, it would be enough to haul in her for extensive grilling and several days warming a seat in a holding cell. Once the mayor, Forsythe, and their combined and formidable legal teams descended on Beverly, she'd be like a prize calf handed over to make ground veal.

But if he didn't put his discovery in his report, and it later came out, it would be bye-bye Detective Dutton, hello unemployed Dutton. Everything he'd worked for would be dust under the departmental rug that they couldn't sweep away fast enough. Right now, the only person who knew what Adam knew about Beverly was Strickland at the hardware store. And Adam hadn't yet told anyone he'd gone there in the first place.

Adam caught his ghostly image reflected back on the computer screen. With his dark circles, unshaved scruff, and faded Boston Bruins t-shirt, he looked like a homeless wino. At the moment, he was feeling like one, too. And as for the smell . . . Adam pinched a piece of his shirt and lifted it to his nose. How many nights had he worn this? It reeked of last night's pre-bedtime Buffalo wings.

Adam ripped off the shirt, and soon his sweatpants and

boxers followed it into the clothes hamper. He took extra time showering and shaving in hopes it would spark some inspiration regarding his report. But two coats of Zest couldn't wash away his dilemma, and he was soon back to square one.

Striding into the kitchen for his third dose of caffeine, Adam stopped to pick up a small framed photo off the bookshelf he'd made out of an old guitar case hung on the wall. The wood-frame house in the photo was nestled on the edge of a creek, with windows looking out over the water. A couple of weathered Adirondack chairs perched on a gravel patio, just waiting for someone to sit down. Or to cast a telescopic fishing rod out over the creek.

He'd fallen in love with that house when he and Zelda were engaged, and he'd shown it to her with hopes she'd love it as much as he did. But she'd hated it. Too rustic, too many insects, too far away from town.

If he'd listened to that little cautionary voice in his head right then, he could have saved himself a great deal of grief later on. But he was besotted with Zelda at the time and caved on just about everything. Usually, his instincts were spot-on, but that was one instance they totally failed him.

Adam put the photo down and continued to the coffee pot, where he drained the last of it. He blew on the mug to cool the liquid, but the rising steam wafted back into his face. A ray of sun from the window bore through the curtain of steam from the mug, parting it like a caffeinated Red Sea.

Instinct. Such a simple word, that. But in his line of work, it could mean the line between life and death. Backup or no backup? Draw your gun or wait? Shoot or not shoot? Where Beverly Laborde was concerned, Adam's instincts were somewhere between stay the course and abandon ship. What he needed was an investigative navigational chart to help him avoid the whirlpools that could suck him down.

He sat back down in front of the computer and did a search on Reggie Forsythe. He'd conducted some preliminary trolling, but he wanted more. He needed to know if Reggie was as much of a shady character as some believed. And as Beverly firmly believed.

As Adam perused the various news articles, everything seemed aboveboard, officially. The man's connections cast a wide net into the political and business communities, with only a few known rotters among them. But a man couldn't be judged on his acquaintances alone. Look at Adam—he associated with all kinds of people who were one circumstance away from being on the other side of prison bars, like Stork.

One small paragraph buried in a news item toward the back of a newspaper a couple of years ago caught Adam's eye. It wasn't so much the content, which tiptoed around the question of a possible unethical business practice of Forsythe's, as the name Adam saw in the next-to-last line of the article. He opened his address book and scanned through the alphabet until he got to the Q's, and dialed the lone number there, Creighton Querry.

After eight rings and no answer, Adam was ready to hang up, when a booming bass voice answered. Adam said, "Cray, long time, no Seagrams."

There was a pause followed by a barking reply so loud Adam had to pull the phone away from his ear. "That you, Dutton? You must have stepped in a big pile of shit to be calling me after what happened a year ago."

"You do bill yourself as a cleaner-upper private eye."

"I came damned near close to going to jail on account of you. That was one big steaming dog pile, Dutton."

"All a misunderstanding. I made it square, didn't I?"

Just when Adam thought Querry's rumble couldn't go any deeper, it did. "I should hang up on you."

"And yet, you don't."

Another pause, and then a grunt. "This better be good, Dutton."

"Two words. Reginald Forsythe."

"The one that was murdered?"

"Yes, and no. I'm more interested in the son at the moment."

"What, did he kill his own father?"

"I don't know. It's not my case directly."

"Ah, one of those."

"Exactly."

"What do you want to know?"

"What did you find out about that Gortran case you investigated? Your name made the papers."

"I wish it hadn't."

"Should bring in more business."

"The opposite. Business dried up after. I only recently started getting nibbles. I've been working as a bouncer at the Copper Club in Stowe."

"Think Reggie Forsythe was behind the sudden drop-off?"

"I don't think it, I know it, but I can't prove it."

"I'd like to hear what you found out on Forsythe. Might help the case I'm working."

"Not over the phone. Same meeting place. I've got to be at the club tonight, but I could see you earlier."

Adam glanced at his watch. "Can you make it in an hour?"

"Yeah, okay. If it'll help nail his useless ass, I'm in."

Adam hung up with Querry and considered what he'd said. Another case of Forsythe getting revenge on someone who'd crossed him? If so, he missed his calling as a mob boss. Adam focused on the computer screen and decided what he wanted to do about his report. He began typing, and this time he wasn't going to delete any of it.

23

Beverly turned her car onto Blessing Lane and counted down the house numbers. It started with 900, but when she'd reached the 600 block, the row of houses suddenly ended, replaced by a rolling field hemmed in by a low stone wall. A few feet further down, rows of headstones popped into view. She pulled her SUV in front of the wrought-iron arch marking the pathway into the cemetery and looked at the sign on top. It read Deer Park Cemetery, 101 Blessing Lane.

Had Imelda Forsythe given her the wrong address? Beverly got out of the car and walked under the arch, looking at the various inscriptions on the stones. Several Buels, Howes, and Lathrops. All family burial plots, if she wasn't mistaken.

It was an eerily beautiful setting for a cemetery. Ash-gray stones dotted the field of brown grass like monolithic soldiers, and vivid red trees bled against the cloud-shrouded hills in the distance.

Beverly wandered down the rows and stopped in front of one grave that was newer than the others. The name on the headstone read "Kannan Hendrick." What had Imelda said? "If you ever want to dig up dirt on Reggie Forsythe, you should look up Kannan Hendrick. Now there was a man who had no sense. Guess that's why he ended up where he did."

The death date on the tombstone was fifteen months ago. What had Imelda meant by the man had "no sense?" Whatever it was, Reggie's ex-wife believed it had landed him here.

One thing that stood out was a lack of flowers or a flag on Hendrick's plot unlike other grave sites. Beverly reached down to brush off a piece of withered grass clinging to the edge of the stone. As she straightened up, a voice from behind her almost made her jump out of her skin.

"You didn't bring no flowers."

Beverly spun around to face the man. His long white hair spun a tangled web like spider silk down the middle of his back, and the skin stretched over his emaciated frame hung as if pasted there by sheer will. He looked like he'd crawled out of one of the graves.

She wasn't superstitious, but this man who'd popped out of nowhere was giving her the creeps. Even with the gun hidden in her purse, she was acutely aware of how isolated it was out here. Just her, a few squirrels, and this cadaverous stranger. She gaped at him, then said, "Excuse me?"

"Flowers, I said flowers. You're the first person I seen here visiting old Hendrick since he was planted. The man should have some flowers."

"Oh. I uh, I didn't have time to stop at a florist. But I'll do that later. Are you the caretaker here?"

"Yep. You kin?"

Beverly thought fast. "Distant. A third cousin. I don't know much about him other than family gossip."

He scratched his chest. "Gossip followed old Hendrick around like a cloud of smoke. After his passing, too."

Beverly bit her lip. "Yes, I believe I remember something. It's sort of hazy."

"They said it was a robbery gone bad at his house. But robbers don't usually bash in somebody's skull like that, do they? They got guns or knives. Or they turn tail and run if they's cowards."

"The police don't know who did it?"

"Damned if they know. Damned if I know. And if I did, I'd keep my mouth shut. Wouldn't want to end up like poor Hendrick."

"If not burglary, then surely there was some reason for him to be murdered."

The caretaker lowered his voice, even though they were the only two people there. "I heered Hendrick was in thick with some powerful people. People with lots of secrets they want kept. And old Hendrick, he was into drugs. Not only weed but some of that harder poison. And those powerful people thought he couldn't keep those secrets to hisself if he was all drugged up half the time."

"Maybe it was a drug buy gone bad?"

"They didn't find none in his house. So I haveta think something else was going on. Seems to me someone wanting to cover up his tracks to keep those secrets I told you about would just plant something to frame Hendrick. Even if only a little bit of weed."

Beverly couldn't argue with his logic. "I'm sorry I didn't get to know my cousin better." She took a wild guess. "I mean, he didn't have many close friends, did he?"

"Guess I shouldn't speak ill of your kin, Miss . . ."

"Ginny. And it's okay to speak freely."

"I had a great-aunt name of Ginny. Not near as pretty as you."

Beverly hadn't missed the caretaker giving her the eye. She hoped it was the look of a man admiring a filly he wasn't planning on riding. But she moved her right foot in front of her, in case she needed to heave a quick knee to his groin. "You were going to tell me about cousin Kannan?"

The caretaker reached under his shirt and pulled out a chain with a pendant on the end. No, not a pendant, as she got a closer look. More like a Spanish silver coin. The caretaker said, "Got this from him. He was into collecting old things."

"He had an antiques store?"

"Not a store, no. Just collecting. He did some buying and selling, too. That's where those powerful people come in."

"If he gave you that, you must be his friend."

The caretaker poked the chain back under his shirt. "Didn't exactly give it to me, you see."

"Oh?"

"After the police was done with him, he ended up in Smithson's Funeral Parlor. No one claimed the body. Sat there in the freezer like a side of beef."

Beverly looked over at his grave. "Then how—"

"An anonymous cashier's check came in. Said it was for his burial. But there weren't no talk of what to do with his personal effects."

"You helped yourself, I take it?"

"No, no, what type of ill-bred lout you think I am? Smithson gave it to me."

"I'm afraid I still don't see what you mean. Why would the funeral home director give it to you?"

"Not so much gave it, as lost it. As in poker."

Beverly didn't know whether to laugh or to play the shocked relative. She compromised with a noncommittal, "Oh, I see."

The caretaker rubbed the corner of his mouth. "I guess if you're family, I should—"

"You keep it. You won it fair and square." She wasn't an expert on antique coins, but she'd seen enough of them to have a ballpark estimate of what this one was worth, no more than three or four hundred.

The muscles on the man's face relaxed. "That's mighty kind of you. What can I do you for, in return?"

She wasn't sure she liked where the conversation was

heading, so she turned it back to her "cousin." "You can pay me back by telling me more about cousin Kannan. He sounds fascinating. How did he get into buying and selling antiques?"

"I'm not so sure he bought 'em if you get my drift."

"Stole them?"

"Not so much stole 'em. Repossessed 'em."

Like the younger Reginald Forsythe did several times over, closing down competitors' shops, then carrying off the loot. Was that what Imelda meant when she said Hendrick had dirt on Reggie? That would mean Kannan Hendrick, currently lying under his own pile of dirt, was a literal dead end as a source of proof detailing Forsythe's shady activities.

She said, "One of those people whose antiques he'd 'repossessed' decided to get back at him?"

"Could be. Or worse."

"Worse?"

"One rumor had ole Hendrick involved in a setup that snaked a path all the way to the Statehouse up in Montpelier."

"Surely you don't mean a member of the government killed him?"

"Naw, they're too sissified. They get others to do their filthy business. To take care of their messes." The caretaker pointed over at Hendrick's grave. "And to make sure they're good and buried."

"I had no idea my cousin was so colorful. He must get it from his mother's side of the family. I mean, the rest of the Hendricks are so deadly dull. Like me, for instance."

The man cackled. "Everyone's always shocked when their relative-whoever ends up in Sing Sing."

"If you're right about that rumor and the Statehouse, I guess I shouldn't be shocked. I don't suppose you got any names? I might get a book deal out of all of this." Beverly smiled and batted her eyelashes. First a magazine article, now a book deal. Beverly-the-writer, her second career.

"No names. If I did, I wouldn't say so. Don't want to end up like ole Hendrick."

Beverly was disappointed he didn't have any additional info, and since his leer was getting leerier by the minute, she decided she'd better cut and run. But first, she eyed a freshly dug gravesite nearby that was covered in dozens of bouquets and walked over. She picked one of the baskets with pink and purple flowers and carried it over to Hendrick's grave and planted it on top. "They won't miss it."

The man grinned. "A little flower theft, ay? Well, now, maybe you ain't so far from Hendrick's line of work as you thought."

Oh, you have no idea. Beverly smiled again and made her excuse of having "to get back to work," and left the grave, the place, and the man, as soon as she could.

The deeper she dug into the whole Forsythe affair, the uglier things seemed to get. First theft and profiteering, then murder, and now shady dealings that could involve a person or persons in the Vermont Legislature. What the hell had she gotten herself into?

24

Not having seen Creighton Querry in a year, Adam had forgotten how much the man resembled a bear. The fist he was shaking at Adam was covered in thick, curly black hair from his knuckles all the way up to his forearms, matching his shaggy mane and beard. His arms were like strips of shag carpeting rolled up in tubes attached to the three hundred pounds of meat packed on his six-five torso. Adam doubted anyone gave this particular bouncer any guff.

After Adam let Cray's tirade-of-a-greeting wind down to a dull roar, Cray growled. "What do you have to say to that, Adam?"

"I say we let bygones be bygones and that you lower your voice before you scare the children."

A few wide-eyed tot faces stared in their direction, and he smiled at them and waved. Cray liked to meet Adam in odd places, but this was one of his favorites, the Geddy Ice Palace. Being a weekday morning, few skaters dotted the ice except for a group of preschoolers teetering around the rink, some holding onto the rails.

Adam tapped on Cray's arm to point toward a stand of empty bleachers where they could sit. Adam was born on ice skates, so he loved the cold, but Cray was already grumbling about his frozen ass. The big baby.

"So, Cray," Adam said.

"So, Dutton. Any money in this for yours truly?"

"I make a cop's salary, and the department has started rationing pencils. What do you think?"

"Figures."

"Besides, you said it would be worth it if we nailed Reggie Forsythe, right?"

"Can you promise that?"

"I never promise anybody anything."

Cray squinted up at the rink's overhead lights as if willing them to get brighter. And warmer. "S'good policy."

"To be honest, I'm not sure what I'm working with here. Either Forsythe is the bad guy—a thief and his father's murderer—or he's an innocent victim. But there are too many turd pellets being dropped around by this rat, and it stinks to high heaven."

"You looking for background, corroboration, or leads?"

"All of the above."

"Uh-huh." Cray scratched his hairy chin. "Okay, let's start with the Gortran case you brought up. The one I wish now I'd never worked on."

"What happened?"

"Started out innocent enough. Had this geezer, Kirk Gortran, who kicked the bucket, and his heirs were tidying up his estate. What they didn't know was that said geezer had handed over two items to Forsythe's shop to sell on consignment."

"You mean, remit payment when they're sold."

"Usually, if you're an honest dealer."

"Forsythe sold them and didn't tell anyone?"

Cray nodded. "Anyway, Gortran was estranged from his heirs but hadn't changed his will and testament. The heirs were so thrilled to be rid of the guy and get the loot to boot, they didn't notice the missing items at first, which weren't listed in the will. Plus, they were from out of town, so they were in a rush to gobble up the goodies and scram."

"How much money are we talking about?"

"Hard as it is for me to believe that people would shell out that much for a couple of pieces of furniture, around three hundred grand. Something about George the Third, marquetry, rosewood, tulipwood, the stuff that makes my eyes glaze over."

"How in the world did the heirs figure it out?"

"His youngest grandkid, now in her 40s, had a childhood memory of hiding in this cabinet thingie, one of a pair—they call them commodes in the biz—and wondered where they'd gone to. When they found a note in Gortran's papers about him making an appointment with somebody to sell the things for him, they got suspicious. That's when they hired me to track them down."

"Straight to Reggie Forsythe?"

"More of a crooked line, but yeah, it led to Forsythe."

Adam rubbed his chin. "The newspaper article I read about the fiasco was sketchy. Lots of talk of lawyers and misunderstandings."

"Forsythe and his lawyers were crafty. First, Forsythe claimed he'd never had any furniture of the kind and didn't know any Gortran. Then, when I dug deeper and tracked down a company, Pierson's, that moved the pieces from Gortran's house to Forsythe's shop, the shyster claimed it was a paperwork error. Then he blamed it on a green assistant and some new accounting software they'd recently installed."

"Naturally. All nice and plausible."

"Quite. The heirs were going to make a stink out of it, and they're the ones that called the newspaper. But I got the impression somebody high up the chain of the conglomerate that owned the paper is palsy-walsy with Forsythe. Naturally, Forsythe comes smelling like a rose. Everybody feels sorry for him having his rep smeared over such an 'innocent' goof, and the heirs get their money."

"And you were the guy caught in the middle. Did you at least get paid?" Adam was beginning to feel sorry for ole Cray. He was actually a top-notch private eye.

"With my usual retainer, hourly rate, and per diem, it came out to two grand, not two percent of their take."

"Not bad, though."

"Not bad? I figure the lost wages from the past fifteen months of nonexistent clients makes my fee for the Gortran fiasco more like minus a hundred dollars an hour."

"About that—what makes you think Forsythe had a hand in your client load drying up? You sounded adamant over the phone it was his doing."

"I had two other cases going on at the same time as the Gortrans' case. When that article came out in the papers, both of them called me up and essentially fired me."

"Maybe it was just the publicity."

"One of them was a repeat client who knew me and my work well. He was apologetic, but he was vague about why he was cutting me out. The other one said something more interesting. Said he'd been warned about me. And that working with me might be bad for his health."

"But no one mentioned the name of Reggie Forsythe?"

Cray blew on his hands to warm them up. "One of them let slip a name, sounded like Hendrick or Hatrick. I did some checking and couldn't find a link between Forsythe and this lowlife, who turned out to be named Kannan Hendrick. But the more I dug, the more I realized Forsythe had his slimy tentacles under quite a few rocks with many other slimy lowlifes. What was I to do? Especially when I found out this Hendrick guy died under mysterious circumstances not long after. I do value my health."

"That's when you became a bouncer."

"Earning half my former salary. But the perks are great. Yelling at drunks, washing vomit off my shoes."

Adam watched a couple of the innocent tots on the ice, oblivious to the scuzzy drama unfolding in Cray's story. Some of the kids were skating precision figure-eights like he did at about their age. Not bad. Might be a future Olympian or two out there. "You called Hendrick a lowlife. What was he into?"

"Drugs, primarily. Consuming, not dealing. Although possibly he ended up doing a little of both."

"And the mysterious circumstances of his death?"

"You can look it up. Hope you'll find more than I did. But I think he surprised a 'burglar.'"

"I'll do that. You said, drugs, right? Did you ever hear any rumors about either of the Forsythes doing drugs, say, heroin?"

"Smack? Do people still do smack? I heard it was all opioids nowadays."

"Needle marks were found on Forsythe senior's body."

Cray frowned. "The newspaper accounts of Forsythe's murder didn't mention that. Thought it was another mysterious 'burglary' gone bad."

"They wouldn't, and you know why."

"You police types didn't tell 'em, natch. Maybe your mystery burglar was really a drug dealer."

"The Hartford PD are working that angle, but no ties found so far. He seems clean, except for the marks."

Cray shook his head. "You get all that money, and what do you waste it on? Drugs, hookers, dead-guy art, and pricey booze you piss out in an hour."

Adam noticed Cray was shivering. Apparently, all that extra beefy insulation of his wasn't helping. "Look, Cray, I can't give you any money for your efforts, but if something good comes out of all of this, I'll work your name into the papers. Only this time, it'll be good PR."

Cray snorted, and Adam nudged him out of his seat and toward the door. Fortunately for Cray, it was a tad above freezing outside the rink. Might be even close to fifty. Vermonters would be out in short pants washing their cars any minute.

As Cray drove off, Adam considered his next move. He'd found little on Beverly Laborde so far and hadn't yet heard from his queries to Interpol about any overseas rap sheets.

He craved a little more insight into the story behind Guinevere Glas and her antiques store. Revenge for fraud that led to the death of Beverly's beloved grandmother felt more like a genuine motive for murder than Reggie Forsythe's bowl-theft revenge. And Adam believed he might know where he could mine for some nuggets of information about that very thing.

§ § §

Bradd Simrell may have retired from the antiques business years ago, but both he and his house were antiques in their own right. The early 1800s stone structure matched the stony expression on the man's skeletal face. At first, he wasn't going to let Adam inside until Adam flashed his badge.

Adam still didn't know enough about antiques to tell whether the furnishings in Simrell's house were real or reproductions, but he did notice the two very real dog cages in separate corners of the front room. Each held a hungry-looking Doberman.

Adam decided to stay standing near the door for now. "Thanks for speaking with me, Mr. Simrell. I won't take too much of your valuable time. As a former antiques store owner in the area, I wondered if you'd heard of Guinevere Glas?"

Simrell replied, "Don't know why you'd be asking now, but

yes, I met her once. Had a cute little girl with her, a granddaughter, I believe. Shame what happened to Mrs. Glas's store."

"And what might that be?"

"Had to close it down. Heard she went into a nursing home and died shortly afterward."

Had both Beverly and the hardware store proprietor who now owned Glas's former building been wrong, and Forsythe wasn't involved? Could be there was another side to this story. "You're saying she closed it down due to health reasons?"

Simrell belched, which was followed by a cough. "Things happen, don't they?"

"Just to be clear on this point. You're saying unequivocally that Gras was sick before the store closed?"

"As I said, things happen." Simrell had never once looked Adam directly, and his fingers kept curling and uncurling.

Adam's lie detector had flipped to full-fib setting. He asked, "I don't suppose these 'things' might be connected to the name Forsythe? Particularly one Reggie Forsythe?"

Simrell scratched his chin. "I think he may have been one of the people who bought out her shop, or part of it. Nothing wrong with that, now, is there? Good business practice."

"Not especially good for Glas. More so if Forsythe shut her down under false pretenses."

The finger curling and uncurling picked up speed. "That's some incendiary talk right there, Detective Dutton. Better be careful what you say. Words have power. They can be weapons when used the wrong way."

"And liberating when used for truth and justice."

Simrell laughed. "A regular Captain America, you are. Well, Captain, I think I've said all I'm going to. And I wouldn't hang around if I were you. The doors on the crates with my dogs over there are controlled by this."

He grabbed a remote control from a nearby table. "It would be a shame if they accidentally got out while you were still here."

"They look like nice puppies." Adam thrust his hand into his pants pocket and pulled out a couple of dog treats, tossing one into each cage.

Simrell gaped at him, and Adam flashed him a phony smile. He didn't tell the guy Adam had begun carrying the treats on field assignments after being attacked by dogs on another occasion.

"Thanks for your 'help,' Mr. Simrell. Oh, and if you should change your mind and want to discuss Reggie Forsythe ..." Adam dropped one of his business cards on the table next to the doggy-remote and let himself out.

Back in his car, he stared at his briefcase on the passenger seat. He'd printed out his handiwork from earlier this morning when he was typing up the report to give to the chief about Beverly and Forsythe. Make that reports. One had her connection laid out in black and white, the other omitted it.

He just wasn't sure yet which version he was going to hand over. Following strict protocol meant going one way and following his gut, another. Damn that Laborde woman. She had him so tied up in knots, he felt like a Macramé Man.

On the one hand, Beverly had likely lied to him about that theater ticket and not told him about her Forsythe family connections. On the other hand, from all accounts, Forsythe was a weasel wrapped in a barracuda suit. No arrests, sure, but enough rumors of fraud, theft, and other scandalous dealings to fill a dozen tell-all books. People connected to him died under somewhat mysterious circumstances, like Kannan Hendrick, or were afraid to even talk about him, like Simrell.

If Beverly Laborde's background was outed in his report, she might be in danger from both sides of the law. Most likely, she'd go into hiding and disappear. It was better for her if she kept her profile low, which also gave Adam more of a chance to keep his eye on her and to slog through all of this.

He still believed—lived by—the words of the oath he'd repeated to Lehmann, "I will always have the courage to hold myself and others accountable for our actions." But he'd never met trouble with a capital "T" like Beverly Laborde before. Whichever version of the report he gave to the chief, he had the strong feeling his career would never be the same again.

25

Before she left Harlan's store, Beverly had him write down the names of other members of the Northeastern Antiquities League who'd closed their businesses. She'd made her own list, but wanted to see if Harlan had additional names, and he did. After a few phone calls, she'd learned one was now deceased, but she managed to find three people still alive and willing to talk to her.

Happily, all three lived within a half-hour of Beverly's old stomping grounds in Hanover. So, not only did she know her way around, she managed to see all of them in two hours. They shared their stories with her, stories that were as bad or worse than her grandmother's. They all suspected Reggie Forsythe, but none had proof. Everything had the picture of being aboveboard and legal, but they knew he was behind the efforts to have them shut down.

Hearing about more victims of Forsythe's reign of terror strengthened Beverly's resolve, but the elusive proof was as tenuous as ever. Adam Dutton's lovely mocha eyes aside, he wasn't looking into Forsythe's dealings. The police were fixated on the "mystery woman" and that damned bowl. And though she'd seen Forsythe leaving his home at the time of his father's murder, that wasn't concrete proof he killed him. All she had was maybes, rumors, hearsay, and Mr. X's testimony. Nothing that would stand up in court.

What she needed was evidence. Cold, hard evidence. And something one of the bankrupt former antique store owners told her led her to believe she might know where to find it.

Beverly scrunched her eyes closed as she recalled her interview with that owner, a woman just a few years younger than her grandmother. The woman broke down into sobs as she recounted the day the moving van from the bank handling the bankruptcy pulled up to her store.

Beverly opened her eyes to yank a piece of paper from her pile of notes, glaring at it. One line of legal mumbo-jumbo in the state licensing requirements governing antique stores caused all of this. The state guidelines ten years ago didn't have it. But five years later, it was there.

The woman Beverly spoke with earlier mentioned the name of the state representative who'd championed the change. A freshman rep, who, as far as she could tell, got elected, didn't do much else other than ram through this one licensing code, and then didn't seek re-election two years later.

Beverly looked up ex-Representative Arlen Strudwick and realized he lived only a few miles away from Forsythe's home. That was interesting. The bankrupt store owner had tried contacting Strudwick once, even found a phone number, but he wouldn't return her calls. When Beverly checked the phone listings to see if he had a new number—zilch. Unlisted, most likely. But she had one phone number he used to have, and it was better than nothing.

Using her prepaid burner cellphone, she punched in the number and waited nervously. After five rings, a man's voice answered, and Beverly asked, "May I please speak with Arlen Strudwick?"

"This is he," the man replied, adding, "But if you're a telephone solicitor—"

"I'm not," Beverly hurried to say. "I'd like to discuss an important matter."

"And what might that be, Miss—"

"Kornelson. I want to know if Reggie Forsythe was behind your efforts to amend the state code overseeing antiques stores."

She expected him to hang up, but he didn't, though he did pause a moment before replying. "That's an old story now, Miss Kornelson. Why would you be interested in such an obscure issue?"

"Because I know several people whose businesses and their very lives were destroyed by that 'issue.' All I want is closure and justice for them. You were a representative, sir. Doesn't that mean you pledged to represent the best interests of those who elected you?"

She heard he was still on the line from his rasped breathing, but it was a good minute later before he spoke again. "I'd rather not discuss this matter over the phone."

"I'll meet you." Beverly imagined Mr. X's frowning expression, urging her not to do anything foolish.

"Are you familiar with the Acworth Archives? It's just over the Vermont border, south of Hanover."

"I'm familiar with it."

"Can you be there in an hour?"

"Yes."

"There is a room in the basement for meetings. I'll see you there in one hour. And I don't tolerate tardiness, Miss Kornelson." The phone call ended with a click as he hung up.

Beverly's game plan in her anti-Forsythe crusade kept changing fast, and she hoped she wasn't making foolish mistakes in the process. As she pulled up to the Acworth Archives an hour later, she knew this could be one of them. A look in the visor mirror told her that her brown, curly wig and headband were in place. No time for prosthetics, so she slipped on the dark glasses.

She was five minutes early but headed through the lobby to the basement. The room Strudwick had mentioned was empty. She wandered around the stacks but didn't see anyone. No Forsythe, something she feared was a possibility.

Strudwick could have called him immediately after talking to her, and this was all a setup. But years of being on the run—from her past, from her fears, from her attempts at a little vigilante justice—had taught her all the "tells." A hitch in Strudwick's voice made her believe her he wasn't a threat.

She went ahead and sat at the table, clutching her notes. On the dot of three, a man in his late 50s plodded into sight. He wore a gray plaid golfer-style beret, cream-colored Burberry overcoat and a maroon scarf with white polka dots, and carried a satchel. And he was alone.

He entered the room and sat in a chair but didn't remove his jacket, hat, or scarf. She asked, "Representative Strudwick?"

"Miss Kornelson, I presume." He peered at her. "I'm in rather a hurry. I hope this won't take too long."

"Then I'll get right to the point. I have eyewitness testimony," she gave a silent apology to Mr. X for twisting his words to fit the situation, "that Reggie Forsythe, and perhaps his father, hand-picked you, funded you, and managed your election campaign. All for the purpose of getting you into the position where you could do their bidding. Namely, the code change I mentioned." She was flying blind and taking a wild leap in the process.

"That sort of thing happens every day, Miss Kornelson. It's hardly a crime."

"Not a legal one. But a moral and ethical one. By changing that teensy piece of regulation, you made it possible for the Forsythes to work behind the scenes, via the Northeastern

Antiquities League, to shut down competitor businesses. And by so doing, plunder their antiques at rock-bottom prices. I firmly believe it led to the premature deaths of at least one store owner. If not two."

Strudwick gazed through the glass window toward the stacks. "Both Forsythes are formidable. I met the elder Forsythe while golfing. He found out I was an attorney with a struggling practice, thanks to some unfortunate gambling debts. I was a man with a wife and six kids, one with special needs and three in college. Before long, I got a call from Forsythe's son. He laid out the whole plan, including enough money to get me out of debt with plenty to spare."

"So, you said yes."

"You don't say no to Reginald Forsythe. Either of them."

Strudwick reached to the floor and lifted the satchel to the table, pulling out a manila envelope marked NAL. He stood up in his chair, leaving the envelope on the table, and grabbed the satchel. "For the record, Miss Kornelson, I never intended to hurt anyone."

As he turned to leave, she asked, "Why didn't you seek re-election? Surely they were eager to pressure you to help with more of their unethical agenda?"

"I pleaded personal reasons. Helping take care of my daughter, who has Down's Syndrome. Maybe my conscience did get the better of me a little. Fortunately for the Forsythes, there were plenty of other patsies for them to run in my place."

He waved at her and plodded back through the basement toward the stairs. Beverly opened the envelope and pulled out transcripts of phone conversations and a tape. A quick read revealed that Strudwick recorded conversations between himself and Reggie Forsythe. If the tape had their original communications, then this was damning stuff. Things were starting to look up.

26

Jinks dropped a file onto Adam's desk. He looked at it with a raised eyebrow. "Part of your case?"

"Part of yours. After you told me what Creighton Querry said about that poor Kannan Hendrick schmuck who died under mysterious circumstances, I remembered something from another case I was working back then. Drug dealing."

Adam opened the folder and flipped through the papers, as Jinks added, "The digital files are in the database. But these are the original newspaper clippings."

They were dated fifteen months ago. The first one referenced what Cray had said and what Adam had verified, that Hendrick was both a drug user and dealer. And that he was allegedly killed by a burglar, but no prints and no witnesses.

The second was the autopsy report. Hendrick was strangled by a rope of some kind that wasn't found with the body. And there were visible needle marks and some traces of drugs in his system—heroin, opioids—but no drug paraphernalia was found among his possessions. It was if someone had removed them, but why? Tainted drugs that might be traceable? Shades of Reginald Forsythe's body from his autopsy.

Adam scanned another document in the file and then pointed to a passage highlighted in yellow. "What's this?

Douglas Marcell, Esquire?"

"We had a possible suspect in the Hendrick case, but this lawyer jumped in and got him bailed out. The suspect promptly went AWOL. The attorney, Marcell, was in private practice at the time but was once part of a firm—Lassetter & Lorens."

"I'm not following."

"I had to double-check, but guess who Lassetter & Lorens has represented? Take a wild guess."

"Forsythe?"

"Both of them, *pater terribilis* and *filius horribilus*."

Adam raised one eyebrow, and she grinned, "I flunked Latin. So, pretty interesting about Hendrick, huh?"

"Doesn't directly tie Reggie Forsythe to Hendrick or the murder of Forsythe, senior, but, yeah, it's interesting."

Jinks studied his face. "Okay, what's up? You've got that constipated look."

"Constipated look?"

"When you're thinking, but not liking what you're thinking."

Adam stuck out his tongue. "Constipation would be easier to fix."

"It's that Laborde woman, isn't it?"

His eyes widened. "We've been colleagues too long. I shouldn't be that easy to read."

"I don't know her, haven't even met her, but she's trouble of some kind. Put on your mental sneakers and tread lightly with that one. You know the chief and the mayor are hovering, looking for a sacrificial lamb."

"You calling me a lamb now, Jinks?"

"Bull, then."

"I don't think male sheep are called bulls."

"It's all bullshit to me. I just don't want you stepping in it."

That made Adam smile if just a little. "And you'll be my

pooper-scooper backup. Thanks, Jinks."

"Remember my warning. Beverly Laborde sounds like one smooth operator. The most dangerous kind of woman."

After Jinks left, Adam sat staring at both versions of his report he'd typed up about Laborde and the Forsythes. Jinks was right about one thing—Adam didn't like what he was thinking. And what he was thinking was that he had damning details no one else in the department knew. He'd never withheld anything from Jinks before and not even the chief, not of this magnitude.

He needed to confront the source of the problem head-on before it got the better of him. He grabbed his car keys and headed toward the Apple Valley Resort, but once he arrived, he didn't see Beverly Laborde's rental car anywhere. Just his luck he'd missed her.

Fortunately for Adam, he didn't have to wait long for that luck to change when he spied Beverly's SUV pulling into the resort parking lot. When he got out of his car and walked over to hers, she rolled down the window. "Why, Adam, I was just thinking about you."

"Why don't we have this discussion in my car," he motioned behind him.

Beverly hesitated a moment. "Is this one of those 'I should have my attorney present' moments?"

"Not yet."

He waited as she climbed out the SUV, holding a paper cup, and followed him to the passenger seat of his Subaru. When the doors were closed, he said, "Why didn't you tell me Reggie Forsythe was your uncle? Making his father, the late Forsythe the Third, your grandfather?"

She chewed on her lip. "I didn't know you yet. I didn't trust you."

"You didn't seem too surprised when I referenced your

'late' grandfather. Yet it only happened this morning."

"It? What do you mean?"

"He was murdered, his body found at his son's home."

"I was estranged from both my uncle and grandfather. They had no contact with us after my grandmother's divorce."

"Where were you this morning, around ten?"

"I went sightseeing. The leaves around here are gorgeous. I bought some apple butter and Creamsicle fudge."

"And you weren't on Forsythe's property when his father was murdered? His security camera got a glimpse of a woman intruder."

"If I were that woman, Detective, you'd have me in handcuffs right now."

She was cool, he had to hand it to her. "Was that whole sob story about your grandmother true, or was it a ploy to gain my sympathy?"

"Every word of it is true. My uncle was the main force behind shutting my grandmother's business down. It was a way to get back at her after my grandfather brainwashed him against her. But my uncle didn't stop with Grammie's antiques shop. I've found five other businesses that were turned in to the state licensing board by the Northeastern Antiquities League through his vendetta. He used the same legality he'd bought and paid for to close them, too."

"What do you mean 'bought and paid for'?"

"I have evidence that proves he influenced an elected official to spearhead the legislation."

Adam leaned back on his headrest. "If what you say is true, then it's beyond the scope of my powers. That's higher up the ladder. The Bureau of Criminal Investigation is stepping into the murder mess, and any ethics probes involving the legislature would have to come from the Attorney General or FBI."

"Does that mean you're not interested?"

"I've been tasked with finding out who tried to sell Reggie Forsythe a Revere bowl, then pulled a switch with a fake at the last minute. And if that person should happen to be tied to the murder, then that becomes my business, too."

"And how is your task going, Detective Dutton?"

He noted she'd stopped using his first name. "I personally believe you're our bowl thief, but I can't prove it. When I get the evidence—eventually," he drew out the word, "I'll have to turn you in."

"Just doing your job, naturally."

He used a softer tone. "Beverly, why did you do it? Why take such a big risk to get back at your uncle? For such little gain?"

She looked down at her hands. "Speaking purely hypothetically, I imagine your thief thought this was a way to embarrass that pompous ass. Hit him where it hurts. He's a man used to scamming others, why not turn the tables?"

"He's also a powerful man with a wide reach and possible criminal connections."

"If by criminal, you mean murder, I'd say yes, he does."

Dutton narrowed his eyes. "Whose murder?"

"Rumors from someone he's worked with."

"Who?"

"I'd rather not say. Especially since you're not taking me seriously about any of this. You practically accused me of playing you in some twisted game."

"The Fox and Geese game, perhaps?"

She pushed a strand of hair behind her ears. "If you believed that, you wouldn't be here, and I'd be in jail right now. Which begs the question—why are you here?"

"I'm worried about you."

"Oh, really? Sure doesn't look like it from here."

"You've put me in a bind, you know."

"The ole rock-and-hard-place?"

"Try Rock of Gibraltar and concrete wall. If what you say is true about Forsythe—"

"If?"

"And if I find out he murdered his father, then I'll be at the front of the pack chasing him down."

She scanned his face. "You don't believe I murdered my grandfather?"

"I didn't say that. But it seems unlikely. To me. There are others I'll have to convince otherwise."

Some moments he hated his job. This was one of them. If it were up to him, he'd wrap Beverly Laborde in his arms, comfort her, and tell her everything was going to be okay. Instead, he had to keep his distance. *Don't get involved*, they were told over and over. Don't *lose your objectivity*. The cold professional must stand on the back of the sympathetic lover to keep him down and inert.

He said, "That evidence you mentioned. Which magically proves Forsythe bought off a state legislator. What is it?"

She flung open the car door and set one foot outside. "I'm going to keep that to myself, for now. But if you get serious about bringing down that worthless piece of garbage, that I refuse to claim has any shared genetic material with mine, then you know where to find me."

As she hurried into the resort, she didn't look back. God help him, neither should he.

27

Beverly waited until Adam drove off as she watched from the resort lobby. Then she returned to her car to fetch the envelope from Strudwick, which she locked into her room safe. Nausea kept her from wanting supper, so she grabbed a bottle of wine and poured herself a glass. After kicking off her heels so hard they flew across the room, she sat in one of the seating area chairs with her feet propped up on the table.

The nausea was soon followed by a headache, and she rubbed her temples. She didn't want to scarf down more ibuprofen. As if that would help with nausea. Not that anything would.

"Oh, Adam," she said aloud.

She'd tried so hard not to fall for him, fall for anybody. Certainly not a cop. Part of her couldn't blame him for not trusting her. She'd lied to him, hadn't she? But why could he not see that Reggie Forsythe was at the center of all of this, that Forsythe should be his main concern? Surely the powerful reach of that man couldn't have trickled down to Adam, too?

With that disturbing notion, she gulped down some of the wine too fast and coughed as the burning hit her throat. She relished the sensation, matching her mood. But no, she couldn't, wouldn't believe Adam was bought off. Not a man who'd suffered what he had at the hands of some crazed psychopath and come back to his job as dedicated as ever. And Harlan wouldn't think so highly of him if Adam was that easily bribed, would he?

Harlan. Maybe she should take him into her confidence. Tempting, but she didn't want to get him involved. He might feel obligated to tell Adam, too, and he was too honorable a man to put on the spot like that. Better to go it alone.

She let the wine trickle down her throat as she toyed with ideas of what to do next. As she fingered the glass, she knew there was no way she'd just sit around and wait for that knock on the door and the offer of a shiny new set of handcuff bracelets.

The big question was to flee or stay and fight? She could disappear right now if she wanted to. But images of Grammie and all the other antiques store owner-victims paraded across her brain like ghostly visions in a cloud. Making up her mind, she drained the rest of the glass, rescued her shoes, and grabbed the keys to the SUV.

Hoping she didn't miss a turn in the creeping twilight, she followed the instructions as she had last time and pulled in front of the castle. Yin and Yang were nowhere to be seen today. Perhaps there was a barn?

Mr. X opened the door right away. "What a pleasant surprise, Miss Beverly Laborde. You must be missing the yak hot chocolate. Shall I make another?"

She took the same chair as on her last visit, and he made the drink in short order. It was even more comforting than wine. "I guess I should get right to the point. How did you know about the Lady of Chartres statue? And how did Reggie Forsythe learn about it?"

"As I said, it's my business to know. But I originally ran across that Rogers Rangers tale years ago when doing some research for a Sotheby's auction. As to Reggie . . . " He rubbed his hand on the armrest. "I'm afraid he learned that from me."

Beverly held her cup frozen in mid-lift. Was Mr. X's story

of being on the outs with Forsythe all a lie? Had she just made another tremendous blunder? She felt dizzy and hugged the cup to her chest.

"Beverly," he said gently. "It's also my business to recognize fear. I spent years trying to create it in other people. You have nothing to fear from me. Frankly, had I known Forsythe would believe in that legend, I'd never have mentioned it."

"You don't believe in it, yourself?"

He smiled. "It's more likely than many other legends I've encountered."

They sat in a more comfortable silence for a few moments until Mr. X said, "I heard that Reginald Forsythe-the-elder was murdered two days ago. It seems a woman was caught on camera entering the home around that exact time. Funny, that."

"You do keep tabs on the Forsythes, don't you?"

"It was on the news, but I heard it via other channels. According to those channels, the description of this woman didn't match you. But disguises aren't all that difficult. Perhaps you learned such techniques when were you acting in those plays at Dartmouth?"

He'd investigated her background. Out of habit, or was it something far more worrying? She put one foot sliding forward as if to head toward the door but stopped. "You did a background check on me?"

"I find you fascinating." When her eyes grew wide, he added, "Not in that way, my dear. Perhaps if you were taller and had a Y chromosome instead of two XX's." He smiled at her and leaned back in his chair. "Tell me, Beverly, how long have you been scamming?"

"Scamming? What makes you think I'm a scammer?"

"Beverly, please. It takes a con artist to know one. When you arrived with your questions, it was easy to guess you were the woman in the red wig who switched Reggie's Revere bowl."

Whether it was despair she'd felt after Adam's refusal to go after Forsythe, the resort wine, or a drug in the hot chocolate, she didn't know—but she found herself being honest with Mr. X. "When my grandmother died, and I learned Forsythe and the Northeastern Antiquities League were behind it, I had to do something. So I pretended to be a seller, showed the buyers whatever object I had they wanted. Even let them have it appraised."

Her mouth was dry, and she took another sip of the drink. "Then I'd take it back, saying I was rethinking selling. This made them more desperate to have it, so they invariably upped the price. Then, I gave them a replica instead. I don't regret it for one minute. They are all scoundrels and deserve far worse. I've never scammed innocent people."

"They never noticed?"

She gave a half-smile. "The only one who did was Reggie Forsythe."

"Even for an actress, that's a dangerous modus operandi."

"I didn't care. I still don't." She furrowed her brow. "Why haven't you asked me if I murdered Forsythe?"

"Because you didn't. Reggie did."

"He told you?"

"Never. But his father taught him well. Taught him how to bulldoze anyone and anything in his path. And that being sentimental was a sign of weakness."

Beverly nodded, and he continued. "The relationship between the Forsythes was strained for a while. F3, as I called him, was far more cautious, felt they should take things slower."

"Was buying off Representative Strudwick F4's idea?"

Mr. X curled his lips in amusement. "If you were the criminal type, Miss Laborde, you'd make a good addition to the Northeastern Antiquities League. You are a dogged researcher.

But yes, it was his idea—" he smiled again. "That is, F4's idea. F3 was content to bring down competitors the old-fashioned way, buying them out with an offer they couldn't refuse, undercutting their business, or spreading rumors. It appears the father-and-son 'disagreements' took a fatal turn today. Not that I didn't see it coming."

He rose from his chair. "More hot chocolate? Or something stronger?"

She'd be driving later but decided to risk it. "A gin and tonic, if you have it."

"Ah, a gin girl, are you?" He disappeared once more in the back, returning with two glasses. "Here you are. You know, I liked F3 at times. Unlike his son, there was a real human being in there. He enjoyed playing marbles, like a little boy. And sometimes, he'd break into song. He was a Harry Belafonte fan."

"Sounds like the music he listened to when he was married to my grandmother."

Mr. X studied her face, tilting his head to one side. "You're Regina's child. I saw a clipping on F3's desk once about your parents being killed in that accident. But neither of the Forsythes ever talked of his family. I only found out Reggie had a sister on my own quite by accident."

He shook his head. "Dear Miss Laborde. How horrible that you had to see your own grandfather like that, even if you were estranged. And to have your uncle be a rotter, too. By the way, you're lucky Reggie's security cameras aren't state-of-the-art. He's had the same ones for years. A true technophobe. Hates to use the phone. Always afraid someone will be listening in."

"I'm not sure I'm lucky. The Ironwood Junction police have me as their number one suspect. I made the mistake of keeping my Amtrak ticket stub where Reggie Forsythe could see it. So the police were on the lookout for women arriving from Amherst, the closest station to his Massachusetts store."

"A car would be more discreet."

"I don't own a car. Or a house. It's rentals, taxis, and hotels all the way."

"Paying cash, of course?"

"Of course."

The warmth from the hot chocolate and the gin were beginning to spread through Beverly's veins, and she settled into the cushions. "I paid a visit to F4's ex-wife, Imelda."

Mr. X peered at her over his glass. "In disguise?"

"I pretended to be a reporter for a real estate magazine. She had some nice things to say about F3, too. But I got the impression she and F4 were like oil and water."

"Think snake oil and radioactive water, and you've nailed it."

"She mentioned Kannan Hendrick. Gave me his current address, which turned out to be a headstone. Did F4 kill him?"

Mr. X swirled the gin around in his glass. "That happened after my retirement. I honestly don't know."

"But do you think he could be responsible?"

"I do. Hendrick was one of F4's hires. Reggie didn't have the same discerning judgment his father did. F3 was a better judge of character as far as his 'colleagues' were concerned. F4 mistakes desperation for competence. Hendrick was a sad case. Lost his wife, kids, house, and most of his money in a bitter divorce when his drug demons got the best of him."

"And loose lips sink ships, as the World War II posters used to say?"

"Indeed." Mr. X studied his glass. "This Ironwood police department. Have they called you in for questioning?"

"No, but Adam . . . Detective Adam Dutton told me if he found evidence I was the Revere con woman, he'd have to bring me in."

"Adam? 'Have to' bring you in? Sounds to me like your feelings toward this detective—and his toward you—are complicated."

"You know what they say, keep your friends close and your enemies closer."

He took a sip of his drink. "Have you told Detective Dutton about your ties to the Forsythe family?"

"He discovered that himself. He was not pleased. I tried to tell him I had evidence tying Reggie to essentially bribing a congressman—"

"That might not have been wise, Miss Laborde. For you or for your Detective Dutton."

"What do you mean?"

"If word gets back to Reggie, he might target you or Dutton. In his tiny mind, he is an untouchable god and not afraid of anyone." Mr. X sighed. "I wish I could help you with your legal dilemma, but I'm afraid I don't have a close relationship with law enforcement. I tend to stay as far from them as possible."

"I understand. I really don't know why I came here, other than to find out more about the silver Lady."

"Miss Laborde, when con men suffer setbacks and trials, sometimes the only other people who understand are other con men."

She ran her finger around the rim of her glass. She didn't know what to do about Adam, Forsythe, or her future, but she did feel more hopeful.

She asked, "Where are Yin and Yang? I didn't see them when I arrived."

"They're in the barn. The yaks' shaggy coats make them tolerate temps down to minus forty, but they don't like warm weather like our recent Indian summer. Anything above fifty-five, and they're miserable. The barn is air-conditioned."

"An air-conditioned barn. Pampered beasties, those are."

"Not as much as the Apple Valley Resort customers. I doubt my yaks will be getting a seaweed wrap and pedicure anytime soon."

The mental image of that made Beverly laugh. "Maybe I'll just stay here as your assistant and become a yak farmer."

"You would always be welcome. But wouldn't you miss your 'line of work' and your mission? It might be a little dull for you."

"Dull sounds pretty good right now. You're right, however. I've come too far to drop my quest. My grandmother deserves revenge for what they did to her."

He leaned forward. "I have found the revenge-dish everyone says is best served cold is based on a false premise. I subscribe more to the saying that 'if you desire revenge, you should dig two graves.' I hope you'll keep that in mind, Beverly Laborde."

28

Sunday, September 19

Despite having to work on a Sunday at the police station, it was just another day, another donut. Adam scowled at the box of pastries in the break room, or what remained of them since it was near noon. He hated the things and came close to chucking the entire box into the trash.

Adam bumped into Jinks as she headed into the room to grab a couple of raspberry-stuffed Danishes. "If my doctor asks, I had something from the grain group, the fruit group . . ." She poured some milk into her travel coffee mug. "And some dairy and protein. Coffee has antioxidants, too, right?"

Adam motioned to the mug. "Going somewhere?"

"Nashua. A possible break in my case. I hope it's worth driving ninety minutes each way."

"That's great, Jinks." His kudos sounded flat, but he hoped Jinks wouldn't notice.

She looked more closely at him. "Dark circles. Either it's ragweed pollen, or you pulled an all-nighter."

"Couldn't sleep. I should take some melatonin."

"Cognac works better. Get you a one-ounce snifter."

"I'll keep that in mind." He ran a hand through his hair but dropped his hand to his side when the chief's assistant, Cherry, came in. Her words weren't helping his growing headache. "Mayor Lehmann is in the chief's office. They want you. Now."

Jinks shot him a sympathetic look and said, "On second thought, driving to Nashua will be fun. Driving anywhere would be fun. As long as it's away from here."

The tension in Chief Quinn's office wasn't just thick enough to cut with a knife; it was like walking into a room with bricks for air. And it wasn't because the chief also had to work on a Sunday—though one of the reasons the chief was pulling a weekend shift stood as close to him as a sleazy shadow. Lehmann. A man who never grasped the idea of "personal space."

The mayor started off right away, "I just got off the phone with Reggie Forsythe. He spent an hour being harassed by the media camped outside his house. As he was escaping their clutches for a meeting with the Hartford PD, one of the TV crew shouted a question regarding whether there were any suspects."

"What did he say?" Adam beat the chief to the question.

"What could he say? The same old story about some mystery woman who broke past his security and managed to conk his father on the head. But he embellishes it more with each telling. I want to know where you stand on your investigation into the con woman who stole Forsythe's bowl. It must be the same person."

The chief looked at Adam, who sat up straight in his chair. "I haven't seen the photos from the security cameras yet."

Chief Quinn opened a folder and passed some papers over to him. "Those were faxed from the Hartford PD this morning."

Adam studied them. Brown curly hair, bulky coat, and the face was odd, misshapen like she'd fractured her jaw. It was hard to see the color of her eyes, but if this were a disguise, then she was likely wearing contacts. There was something familiar about that woman. He was reminded of the same feeling he'd had at the NAL meeting.

Adam handed the photos back. "Doesn't fit the description Forsythe gave of the con woman."

Lehmann growled. "Someone who is that devious could resort to disguises. Forsythe thinks so."

Chief Quinn asked Adam, "And that Laborde woman? Does she have an alibi for the murder?"

"She says she was out sightseeing the whole day."

"Alone?"

Adam nodded.

Quinn said, "No solid alibi. Then she could have murdered Forsythe's father."

Adam chose his words carefully. "I don't have any hard evidence that she did. Or that she stole Reggie Forsythe's property."

Adam met the chief's direct gaze with one of his own. He didn't like hedging the truth, but neither did he like the way the chief appeared to be cozying up to the mayor. The same mayor was in a political bed with Forsythe. How far down did that Forsythe clout reach? Could Adam trust his boss to stay objective? He didn't want to throw Beverly onto some altar as a sacrificial lamb to save Forsythe's worthless hide. Or Lehmann's.

The mayor sneered at Adam. "Forsythe told me you paid a visit to see him yesterday. Not too long after the murder. He hinted that you were disrespectful. And that he felt you were hiding information from him."

The chief clenched his jaw. "You didn't mention you'd talked to Reggie Forsythe."

Adam cleared his throat. "I must have misfiled that report. I realized it this morning and was going to hand it to you, but I stopped for coffee first. And I assure you I was not disrespectful." Okay, so he hadn't misfiled the report. And he'd done more than stop for coffee. But he certainly hadn't been disrespectful. Cheeky, maybe.

Lehmann huffed, but the chief waved his hand toward the door. "I appreciate you coming by, Titus. But if we want to help catch the person who killed Forsythe's father, as well as this female thief, we've got a lot of work to do. We need to get right on it."

Adam was surprised when the mayor accepted Quinn's implied dismissal, turning on his heel and marching out of the office. Adam waited until the man was out of earshot. "If you want my honest impression, Chief, whatever that woman was doing at Forsythe's house, it wasn't to murder his father."

"Really? How do you see that?"

"I talked to the CSIs at the crime scene. The murder weapon was too heavy to hoist easily by a petite woman like in that photo. Plus, it doesn't make any sense she would go to all that trouble to do it when his son might be there. There are far easier ways to kill the man when he's out in public."

"People do strange things in the heat of anger."

"Like Reggie Forsythe, you mean?"

Quinn sat down in his chair and leaned his arms on the desk. "Are you suggesting patricide, Dutton?"

"And if I were?"

Quinn placed his hands on his desk and spread his fingers wide. "The thought occurred to me. Probably my counterpart at the Hartford department, too. But even if—and I stress the word if—that is the case, we have to tread lightly. Forsythe is too well connected."

"With too many high-priced attorneys."

The chief grimaced. "I don't care about my future as much. I could retire now and have enough of a pension for my wife and me to live on. But as long as Lehmann is the mayor, and he and Forsythe have us in their sights, it'll be hard for you to advance. Ever considered moving? You know I'd be good for a reference. Not that I'm trying to get rid of you. You're a damned good cop. You don't second guess yourself even if I don't agree with you."

Adam's stomach stopped doing flip-flops, and he nodded his thanks. For a moment, he was sure Quinn was ready to give him a pink slip. Adam said, "Off the record, say I ran across someone who said they might have evidence linking Forsythe to influence-peddling in the state legislature."

Quinn jumped in, "Who is this source?"

"A confidential informant. If it turns out to be nothing, I prefer not to cause any additional waves, considering you're already in the middle of a tsunami."

"Who or what did he allegedly try to buy off?"

"A state rep, but I don't want to mention names yet. As you say, these are all well-connected people. But if I find that evidence has legs, you'll be the first to know."

Quinn frowned. "Lehmann and Forsythe, the terror twins, are bad on their own, but now I've got jurisdictional headaches popping up. You should have asked me before you went to see Forsythe."

"I was in the area doing some research on Laborde as you asked. Felt it might be good to see Forsythe in his personal lair."

Quinn's lips twitched. "Lair, huh?"

"I'm starting to get the impression lair might not be the right term. Try snake pit."

"Let's hope we don't end up snake bit before this is all over with."

Adam couldn't agree more. He headed back to his office but had too much nervous energy to sit at a desk. He hadn't paid his favorite newspaper reporter, Sam Cowie of the *Herald-Post*, a visit in a while. Perhaps Sam would have some gossip about the Forsythes. And hopefully, Sam liked stale donuts.

Before he left, he glanced at the paper coffee cup sitting on his desk with a lipstick stain. Beverly had left it behind in his car after their meeting in the parking lot of the resort. Maybe he wasn't playing by the book by withholding some of the details about Beverly in his reports. But that didn't mean he couldn't follow proper procedure in other ways.

On his way out the door, he dropped the cup off in the lab, asking his favorite lab tech, Joe Brimm, "You think you can get the prints and DNA off this and run it through the databases for me?"

Joe looked at the cup as Adam placed it on the table. "Sure. When do you want it?"

"Yesterday, Joe."

"Tell me something new, Adam." Joe grinned at him. "You go play cops-and-robbers with your shiny police toys while I toil away in my dungeon of science."

"You do that. And I'll bring you back a Crackerjack prize for your trouble."

"Just make sure it's a good one. I always wanted one of those decoder rings, but all I got ever got was those little plastic monkeys."

Adam didn't have the heart to tell him they didn't even include prizes inside anymore. It was all digital now. Not that he was dissing digital. Those digital databases often save the day. But so far, they hadn't included any data on Beverly Laborde or whatever name she might have been using in her past.

The DNA bit was standard police procedure, and he wasn't sorry for doing it. Then why did it make him feel like such a traitor?

Shaking his head, he strolled to the break room to grab some of those stale donuts for Sam and headed out to play a little cops-and-robbers.

29

Beverly checked herself in the mirror, making sure her blond wig tied into a braid was safely in place. She'd opted for a professional brown pantsuit for this outing, two sizes too large to accommodate her bulky "tubby pack" underneath. The new fake mole on her cheek was just the right touch. And of course, she wore her wrist-length leather gloves. Elegant in a Grace Kelly way, and no fingerprints.

She grabbed the box from the passenger seat and headed into the office marked "Garvin Kirschner, Esq." She'd been surprised to find out the law offices were open on a weekend, but the secretary said something on the phone about a critical case with a high-powered client that was making them put in extra hours.

A few minutes early for her appointment, she took the opportunity to study the office as she waited. Typical law joint. Lots of dark wood paneling, shiny fingerprint-free glass, and beige carpeting. The only interesting thing in the lobby was the triptych painting on the wall of three stylized Egyptian women silhouettes with touches of cherry red.

A frowning secretary, obviously not happy to be working those extra hours, greeted her and motioned for her to follow, and they headed toward the back. Garvin Kirschner was younger than she'd imagined, decked in a three-piece suit, gold tie, and sporting a buzz cut worthy of a Marine.

After the secretary had left them alone, he asked, "Miss

Hood, you said something on the phone about an item of interest you wanted to show me?"

Beverly placed the box on his desk. He eyed it but didn't reach over to open it. So she did it for him and pulled out the contents. "I believe your client, Coral Dockett, reported this bowl as stolen?"

Kirschner stared at it, then picked it up and looked at the bottom, and the word "REVERE" etched in a rectangle. "Where did you get this?"

"It came into my possession. Legally, I assure you." That was mostly true. She'd come across the bowl in a pawn shop, recognizing its worth even when the store owner hadn't, and she'd paid a couple hundred dollars for it. But a stolen bowl hadn't been hers to buy, had it? And if Forsythe had recognized it as being stolen when she showed it to him months ago, that proved he knew it was stolen and just didn't care.

Beverly added, "I believe there is a reward of ten percent, no questions asked?"

Kirschner walked over to a file drawer, pulled out a file, and extracted two pictures from it of a silver bowl. He compared the first to the bottom and then the second to the interior of the bowl, fingering a small, jagged scratch. "This is the same bowl, all right."

He puckered his lips into a question mark expression. "You could have simply sold it on the black market."

She'd bet the full value of the bowl that Kirschner, Esquire, himself would have done it. And she would have considered it if the rightful owner were another Forsythe. But from what she'd read in the newspaper article on the burglary at Miss Coral Dockett's home, the woman was a sweet old lady who was devastated at the loss of her favorite piece. It was in her family for generations.

Beverly replied, "The reward will be plenty. Cash is

preferred."

"Ten percent of the eighty-thousand reward is eight thousand, Miss Hood. We don't keep that amount of money on-site, but I can write you a check."

She pulled out a card and handed it over. "Have it wired to that address."

He read it, then said, "You don't look like you're from the Seychelles."

She smiled. "Appearances can be deceiving. Then we have an agreement?"

He placed the bowl back in the box. "I'll get my secretary to write you up a receipt."

Feeling lighter—both literally and figuratively—than when she'd come, she drove the hour back to the Junction listening to an interesting program on Vermont Public Radio about monarch butterflies. She was on the road to the resort when she spied a familiar figure seated in a car in the parking lot of an abandoned clothing store two miles outside of the Junction.

Reggie Forsythe was arguing with a man she didn't recognize standing next to the car. Beverly turned the wheel sharply to point the car onto a side road, ending up on the street behind the two men. Closing the door quietly, she crept forward, getting as close as she could to the lot while hiding her presence around the corner of the building. She strained to hear what the men were arguing about.

She heard Forsythe say, "You know I don't like meeting this way," and the stranger's reply, "I like it neutral. Just out for a stroll, ya know? All nice and normal."

Then the two voices lowered, still angry, and Beverly decided she should hightail it out of there in case they headed her way. But then, she caught the stranger's words, "Adam Dutton?"

Feeling uneasy, Beverly inched back to her car, climbed in,

and drove it slowly down the street toward the front of the parking lot. At the sound of a car peeling away, she nosed her SUV forward just in time to see Forsythe's car disappearing. Then the stranger got into his maroon car, which had a rifle rack mounted in the window, and cranked up the engine. Should she follow Forsythe or the stranger? Or neither?

Since the stranger had mentioned Adam's name, she made up her mind to follow him instead of Forsythe. The man drove aimlessly around, as near as she could tell. She wrote down the license number on a piece of paper in case she lost him—or in case she decided to abandon this bizarre chase altogether.

Her quarry slowed down, and she saw he was on a cellphone. Then he pulled over to a curb, and she did the same while keeping her distance. Moments later, Adam strolled out of the building that she now saw was the local newspaper office and climbed into his car. He drove off down Elmwood Lane, taking him through one of the prettier tree-lined parts of town.

The stranger followed behind Adam for a mile or so. They passed cars carrying leaf-peeping tourists but when they reached a lonelier stretch in the road, the man gunned his motor, pulled in front of Adam's car, and swerved over into a shallow ditch. Adam slowed down and pulled in behind him.

Beverly nosed her SUV into a curved cutout along a steep bank with some tall trees, hoping it hid her well enough. Adam got out to check on the welfare of the other driver—who promptly charged out of his car, a gun in hand.

As Beverly watched helplessly, the man pushed Adam to the back of the man's car, popped open the trunk, and motioned for Adam to climb in after he'd forced Adam to hand over his police weapon. Beverly's heart sank when she noted the car was an older model that likely didn't have an escape trunk release. But his kidnapper would have done that by design.

When the driver took off again, Beverly followed, keeping as far in the distance as possible without losing the other car in a line of more tourists with their out-of-state plates. She wanted to call someone, but she needed to concentrate on the car with Adam. She was terrified that if she got distracted, she'd miss the car when it made a turnoff.

With her eyes glued to the car in front, she felt around in her purse for her cellphone to have it handy. When she found it, she also felt the cold metal of her gun and slid it out of the purse onto the passenger seat.

This was pure madness, she knew it, but she didn't care. She was not going to leave Adam to the mercies of another maniac who might torture him again. They drove along a road for about a mile, with Beverly keeping her distance so the other driver wouldn't hear her or spot the tail. She wasn't really how far they'd gone because she didn't want to look at the gauges even for a moment.

Finally, as she rounded a bend in the road, she spied the tail of the car pulling off onto another road. She followed on the narrow road, offering a prayer of thanks it was paved—barely—but didn't see the other car and panicked she'd lost it.

She drove for what felt like another half mile and then saw a flash of maroon through the trees ahead. After pulling off onto a turnaround slot at the side of the road, she slid out of her SUV, slowly and quietly, holding her breath.

Realizing she was making a habit out of skulking through the woods around these parts, she threaded her way through the pines and oaks until she got close enough to see the kidnapper opening the trunk of his car. He immediately sprayed a liquid into Adam's eyes as Adam attempted to jump out.

Adam fell to the ground, holding his hands over his eyes, and the now-masked kidnapper promptly grabbed Adam's wrists and slapped handcuffs on them. He half pulled, half-dragged Adam into a small cabin behind them.

Beverly was terrified for Adam and unsure what to do. She looked up the number she'd added to her cellphone's address book for Eliot Jinks. But when she called it, she got a canned voice responder that Jinks was out of town for the day and to leave a message. Beverly hung up. She could call Mr. X, but he was too far away. It would take him over an hour to get here, and that might be too late.

Should she call the Junction PD anonymously, give them the GPS coordinates of the cabin, and flee before they arrived to keep from being questioned? What to do? One thing she did know beyond a shadow of a doubt—Adam didn't have much time for her decision.

30

Adam grunted as he was thrown onto a hard, wooden floor, not so much from the warped board poking him in the back but from the lingering burning of the pepper spray. He'd experienced it before—he'd had to, in order to get licensed to use the stuff back when he was a beat cop. But he'd hoped he wouldn't have to feel that searing pain and watering eyes ever again.

Despite the mild temperatures, beads of sweat trickled down his back. He focused on the pain, the sweat, the sensations. He needed to stay alert, to wait for any opportunity.

That was what failed him during his last kidnapping. He'd made a rookie mistake, allowing his panic to affect his concentration. Just remembering the "last time" called up images he'd worked hard to forget. Flashes of water cascading on his face, struggling for each breath. The smell of burnt flesh as his captor pressed the hot iron into his side, the sound of shoveled earth being dropped on his sealed coffin.

Adam squinted at his captor, willing his eyes to work. They worked enough for him to see the man was training a gun on him. Adam's gun. Adam dubbed the man Goldie, from the one gold tooth shining in the other man's mouth. It was like a distant star blazing through Adam's bleary vision and the black ski mask on the man's face.

Goldie saw Adam staring at the gun. "Looks like I got the

best of you in more ways than one."

Adam managed to raise himself to a kneeling position and focused on his breathing to calm his body down and help fight off the reaction to the spray. The last thing he needed right now was to hyperventilate. He managed to croak out, "Who are you and what the hell kind of game are you playing?"

"Twenty questions. Only I'm the one who gets to ask the questions, and you have to give me the answers. Or I'll start firing slugs into you if I suspect you're lying. I think I'll start with the knees." Goldie grinned and waved the gun in the direction of Adam's knees.

"What questions?"

"Ah, ah, ah. I ask, you answer. First question. You are indeed Adam Dutton, Detective with the Ironwood Junction PD?"

"Yes."

"Good. Now you're getting the hang of the game. Question number two. A certain silver bowl was stolen recently. You know the one. The thief was a lady, red-haired, kinda pretty, kinda youngish. And you're now going to tell me the identity of that woman."

Adam hoped his training in interrogation and spotting lies would stand him in good stead and help him make up his own story. "If I knew who it was, she'd be in jail right now. My boss is breathing down my neck. The mayor is breathing down my neck. And both want to find that woman. Believe me, I'd gladly have turned her in. Might get me a commendation."

Goldie stared at him as Adam did his best to stare back through the pepper-induced haze. Goldie nodded. "Okay. Do you have any suspects?"

This one would be a lot harder. Adam was beginning to get a very good idea of how cruel and heartless a man Forsythe was, and he didn't want that man anywhere near Beverly. Adam was glad it was him kneeling there and not her.

He replied to Goldie's question, "We have a few suspects. If you're working for the person I think you are, I'm surprised you aren't more interested in the woman he says killed his father."

"That was going to be question number three. But my employer says the two may be the same girl."

"We're working that angle, too. My boss and the mayor are having me make up a list of possible suspects."

"Who you got at the top of that list, Dee-teck-tive Dutton?"

"No one yet. As you say, the first thief was tall with long red hair. The second woman was shorter, heavier, and had curly, brown hair. Maybe it's some type of burglary ring." Stall, stall, stall. Adam wasn't sure how much longer he could play this game.

"Okay, so no numero uno suspects. I got that. Why don't you tell me who all's on your list and let me decide who's the winner?"

"You got something to write it down?"

Goldie grinned. "Nice try, Dutton. Like I'm going to drop this gun here and start writing down names. I'll remember fine. You just start naming." Goldie waved the gun toward Adam's knees again. "Now."

Adam was starting to see more clearly but kept up the pretense of being half-blinded. He said, "You wouldn't have any water, would you? I can't see a thing."

Goldie laughed. "Got my friend Jimmy Beam in the car. Want some of that thrown in your eyes, Dee-teck-tive?"

It was pretty clear Goldie wasn't going to stop with the kneecaps, and it didn't matter whether Adam told Goldie what he wanted or not. It was a fishing expedition that didn't need any witnesses.

Adam said, "If I turn up dead here in handcuffs, my colleagues won't stop until they find my killer."

"They won't find you in handcuffs, Dee-teck-tive Dutton. I got some high-quality smack in my car. You're going to be found dead after an overdose here in your little secret hideaway where you come to get high."

Suddenly, the track marks found on the bodies of Forsythe and Hendrick made more sense. If it wasn't Goldie who did it, then he must yet be part of that equation somehow.

Adam squinted, gauging the distance between himself and Goldie. The man had put Adam's handcuffs on in front of him instead of behind his back, thank god. He'd only get one good chance to make this work, so he sagged a bit and bowed his head. He pleaded, "No, please, no, I can't take any more."

That made Goldie laugh harder, which is what Adam was hoping for. With a quick upward thrust, he got both knees up off the ground and hurled himself at the other man's stomach, headbutting him in his groin. He was rewarded with a loud "Oomph" from Goldie, who dropped the gun and staggered backward, moaning in pain.

Adam grabbed the gun with his handcuffed fingers and stood with it pointed at Goldie, whose eyes grew wide with the realization it was Adam who now had the upper hand. Goldie straightened up and started a ragged limping toward the door.

Adam fired a warning shot, but that only made Goldie limp harder and faster, so Adam aimed for his body. He was sure the second shot got Goldie. But with Adam's eyes still watering and not at a hundred percent and his hand shaky, he wasn't sure where he'd hit the other man.

Goldie apparently had enough stamina left to open the door and push himself through, making Adam curse. Ordinarily, it would be a cinch to chase the man down, but in Adam's current state, that task was much more daunting. But damn it all, he'd give it his level best effort or die trying.

Adam made it to the doorway in time to see Goldie's car roaring off, which made Adam curse some more. And then he saw a woman standing in the yard. Despite the blond hair, extra padding, and beauty mark, he knew it was Beverly Laborde. Goddamn that woman. What the hell was she doing here?

31

Beverly had just decided to dial 9-1-1 to call in the cavalry when the loud echoing sound of a gunshot rang out in the air. A few moments later, a second shot rang out. No time to call the cavalry. *She* was the cavalry. She pulled the gun from her pocket and held it in front of her, trying to remember everything her instructor told her.

But then the door of the cabin swung open, and the masked stranger limped outside with a red stain forming on his upper left arm and shoulder. Confused, Beverly pointed the gun toward the stranger, ready to shoot, when a movement inside the cabin doorway made her glance over. It was Adam. They stared at each other for a moment, then looked over toward the stranger's car at the sound of the motor being gunned. The car was soon out of sight.

Adam looked back at Beverly. "What the hell are you doing here?"

She smiled weakly. "Rescuing you. Guess you didn't need me. You did it all by yourself."

He walked toward her, his head cocked to one side. "How did you get here? Where's your car?"

She pointed behind her. "Back there. I followed you after that man threw you in his trunk."

"I've heard of being in the right place at the right time, but this is taking it to the extreme, don't you think?"

Beverly couldn't tell if he was joking or if he believed she was an accomplice to the kidnapping. Perhaps he didn't trust her, after all. Then she noticed the white residue on his face and his bloodshot eyes. She took the sleeve of her sweater and gently dabbed at his skin. "What was that liquid he sprayed you with?"

"A form of pepper spray. From the strength of it, I'd guess First Defense MK-4. Burns like the devil. I take that back. Even the devil would react to this heat."

She studied her handiwork. The residue was gone, but his eyes remained red. "I have some bottled water in my car. Would that help?"

He said, "Very much," and she darted through the trees in the direction of the car, staying close by his side to make sure he followed her and didn't trip over any roots. When they reached the SUV, he doused his entire face with the water, not an easy task with his handcuffs on his wrists.

"Better?" She asked.

"Better. Thanks."

Her words came out in a rush. "Adam, I'm not part of your kidnapping, I swear. I drove by a parking lot where Forsythe and this goon were arguing, and I got curious. I overhead the goon say your name, which made me worry. I followed him and saw that fake crash maneuver he did to get you to stop. Might not be the smartest notion to follow him, but I'm not sorry I did."

He grinned at her. "Oh, I'd say it was a good idea, myself. What were you going to with that gun, by the way?"

"Call me Annie Oakley. Shooting from the hip."

"Do you even know how to use that thing?"

"My instructor told me I was a natural. But then, I think he was gunning for a tip." She studied him as he leaned against the car. He seemed to be okay, and his breathing was normal. "Why did this guy kidnap you? What did he want?"

"He's one of Forsythe's gorillas. As psycho as his boss, if not as bright."

She winced. "Mr. X warned me about this."

"Who's Mr. X?"

"He's a former associate of the Forsythes. Left because he couldn't stand Reggie."

"Sounds like I should meet this Mr. X of yours."

"Then you believe me about Reggie being an evil SOB?"

"If I didn't before, I do now. And I did, by the way. I've done research on his associates, many of whom wound up murdered." He opened the passenger door. "I think part of me has always believed you even when I probably shouldn't."

Once they'd slid inside the car, Beverly handed him a piece of paper. "That's your kidnapper's license number. And make and model."

He thanked her and tucked the paper into his shirt pocket. "You don't make a bad blonde."

She touched her hand to her head and grimaced. "I'd forgotten I had this on."

"What was it this time? Another Revere bowl?"

She gave him a slight smile. "A simple transaction where I needed to remain anonymous."

"So that's what they call cons these days. Transactions."

Her improving mood dimmed a couple of notches. "I'm not a crook."

"The chief called you a female Robin Hood. Or that's what he dubbed the woman who stole the Revere bowl."

"I like that. Robbing from the rich and giving to the poor. Or returning items to people that were rightfully theirs to begin with."

"How did you get into this line of work, anyway?"

"Can you think of something better to do with an art history degree?"

He laughed.

They came to the intersection where the narrow road joined up with the main highway. She asked, "Should I take you back to your car?"

"Yeah. I've got a tool that'll help me unlock these." He held up his cuffed hands. "Deciding what to do after that is a little harder."

"What do you mean?"

"I'll have to report this to the chief, but he's in a rough place. And we've already talked about how thrilled he is at the idea of the planet-sized can of grubs that Forsythe's investigation will open up. Plus, my only witness to the kidnapping is you. I'd like to keep you out of this, if possible."

She glanced at him. "If it means nailing Forsythe, then you should tell your chief about me."

"I'll hold out as long as I can. I might bring Jinks in when she gets back. But first things first. Chief Quinn."

Beverly drove Adam to his abandoned car, which was in the same place as when the goon kidnapped him. She told him she was going to follow him into town, and when he started to protest, she shushed him. "I'm going that way, anyhow. Plus, your eyes might not be back to normal."

After a muttered comment from him that *he* was supposed to be the knight in shining armor, he relented. He grabbed the tool from his trunk and unlocked the cuffs. But before he got into the driver's seat, he added, "Forsythe is going to spend the rest of his days in prison, Beverly. I promise you." And with that, they headed back toward town.

32

Monday, September 20

Talking with the chief was difficult, but not as painful as it could have been. The chief agreed they'd need more concrete evidence to go after Forsythe than a kidnapping from a man who asked suspicious questions but hadn't once mentioned Forsythe's name. Adam didn't bring up Beverly's role but told Quinn he had several leads that could help.

After heading home and only once—briefly—thinking about asking Beverly to join him for supper, he'd called it a night and slept soundly, no nightmares for a change. Maybe he should thank Goldie for helping to purge a few demons haunting Adam since his captivity two years ago. This time, he'd won.

He pulled up to the Apple Valley Resort on the dot of ten, and Beverly bounded out to the car with a big smile on her face. She climbed in, and he looked over at her. "Back to dark hair. I think I prefer it that way."

She laughed. "I should try purple. Go punk or Goth."

Adam pointed the car east, and they drove for several minutes in companionable silence. Adam spoke up first. "Are you sure you saw blood on Goldie's arm and shoulder?"

She sounded confused. "Goldie?"

"Sorry. That's the nickname I gave him. One gold tooth right in front."

"Goldie, it is. Yes, you most definitely got him at least once."

"No gunshot victims turned up at any area hospitals. It's a good bet he drove far afield or had someone tend to him off the grid."

Beverly asked, "You didn't recognize him? Or find his photo in the mug shot database?"

"'Fraid not."

"You look awfully bright-eyed. I hope neither your eyes nor your boss gave you much trouble this morning."

"Correct on both counts. But we need a much stronger case against Forsythe. And we don't know how much his failed interrogation of me is going to affect his plans. We have to work fast."

Beverly held up the envelope she'd brought with her. "This is the evidence I mentioned. A tape of a phone conversation between him and the representative."

"Is that the only copy?"

"The only one I've got. I'm not aware of any others."

Adam pointed to a group of geese overhead flying south. "Great bird watching this time of year."

"I guess I can add birdwatching to fishing on your list of interests."

"And I don't know any of yours, other than following detectives around."

"That's my new job."

"Doesn't pay much."

"That remains to be seen."

He glanced at her, noting her smirk. "You're good at this detectivy thing. You should put out your shingle. And you'd still get to wear disguises on occasion."

"Now there's an idea. What does it take to be a private eye in Vermont?"

"It's tougher than other states. You'd need a license, fingerprinting, a background check, two years of related experience, and a written exam."

"Lot easier just to do what I've been doing."

"In the short term. Don't you think about your future?"

She fell quiet. Then she said, "I don't think about it much. One day, one week to the next. Unfettered, no responsibilities, no landing site."

"No permanent address?" He knew what he'd uncovered in his research but wanted to hear her reply.

"A room I rent for legal purposes. But my primary residence is a post office box."

"Kinda small to squeeze into."

She punched him lightly on the arm. "Speaking of futures, I saw you talking to a woman with short red hair the other day. Cute, stylish. Seemed like you knew each other well."

"Zelda. My ex-wife."

"I hope it was an amicable split."

"She believed it was. She married the mayor."

"I'm sorry, Adam. I didn't mean to bring up a sore subject."

"S'okay. For the best, I guess." He slowed down when they came to an unmarked four-way intersection. "Which way?"

"To the right. I remember it from the dead sycamore tree over there."

With Beverly guiding him along the increasingly lonely and increasingly more narrow roads, they eventually pulled around down a long driveway to a house looming in front of them. No, make that a castle.

He asked, "This is the place?"

"Um-hmm. See Yin and Yang over there?"

He spied the two animals in the fenced-in yard. "Are those yaks?"

"You really are an outdoorsman. A-plus for your animal identification skills."

Adam looked around the castle-like dwelling and spied several high-tech security systems that would be hard to see if you weren't in the business. A motion detector greeted them from the bushes at the head of the driveway, and floodlights under the eaves of the house doubled as cameras with thermal imaging.

The door opened and revealed a man about Adam's height clad in black slacks, black shirt, and a black scarf. With a Scandinavian blond mane and cool, gray eyes, he looked more like a Nordic god than Greek, as his name would suggest.

The man said. "So this is your Adam Dutton, Beverly. Do come in."

He led them to a den that could be a movie set in Hollywood. "Beverly enjoys my yak-milk hot chocolate. Would you care for some? It's non-alcoholic. And unpoisoned."

Adam looked to Beverly, who said, "It's quite good. And it is a pretty chilly morning out there."

Mr. X brought back a tray with three mugs. Adam took one and sipped the drink. Tangy, gamey, salty. With the sweetness of the chocolate, it worked.

Mr. X propped his feet up on a footstool. "What can I tell you about Reggie Forsythe? That is why you came, I presume?"

"I had an encounter yesterday—"

Beverly jumped in, "He was kidnapped."

Adam continued, "By a man asking me questions. About what I knew regarding the suspects in the theft of Forsythe's bowl and his father's murder."

Mr. X tutted. "Reggie is getting sloppy. That is why he and his father argued so much. Reggie is always in a hurry, wants what he wants now. He's been lucky so far not to make too big of a slip-up. But that may be coming to an end. Tell me, what did this man look like?"

"Five-eleven or so, two-thirty, lots of muscle, and a laugh like a hyena. And one upper gold tooth in the front."

"Gabriel Karlstad. Forsythe used him once several years ago. I found the man to be a caveman. Strike that—that's being unkind to cavemen."

Adam pulled a small notebook out of his pocket and wrote down the name. "He lives around here?"

"If you call that living. He spends most of his days and nights in an encampment near Sutton's Grove. A quasi-gypsy group. But no one asks any questions. Live and let live."

"I know the place." Adam nodded. "I nicked him with one bullet. Would this camp have someone who could dig that out?"

"Undoubtedly."

"I wonder what he reported back to Forsythe?"

"I doubt he did. And if he did, his failure might have sealed his fate."

"That means Forsythe may not know for sure that we know he's involved in the kidnapping and likely his father's murder."

Mr. X set down his cup and tented his fingers together. "I don't envy you the task ahead of you, Detective. The murder will be hard to prove and fraught with peril."

Beverly picked up the envelope she'd laid on the table next to her. "This has proof of Reggie Forsythe bribing Representative Strudwick."

Mr. X looked at the envelope. "A transcript or tape?"

Beverly replied, "Both."

"I assume you haven't made copies yet?"

When she answered no, Mr. X said, "I have duplication

machines in my office. I could make a copy for you, and you could listen simultaneously." He looked over at Adam, his eyebrows raised into a question mark.

Adam hesitated at first, but then he relented, and the trio traipsed back to a room with enough high-tech gear to put the NYPD to shame. Mr. X placed the tape in a small duplicating machine and reached into a drawer to grab a blank one. Then, as he began the duplication process, he cranked up the volume on a set of speakers.

A man's voice started off, and Adam recognized it immediately as Forsythe's nasal tenor. The other man's voice sounded older, less assured. Adam could get his hands on a video of Strudwick speaking and compare the two later to make sure it was him. But the gist of the conversation was clear. Forsythe and Strudwick discussed a bill coming up that would change one of the regulations overseeing antique stores. Forsythe laid out everything Strudwick was to do, when he was to do it, and how he should do it.

And then he reminded Strudwick of the man's dire financial situation and how much money would be wired to his bank account if he did everything exactly as Forsythe said. As a parting shot, Forsythe added that he hoped Strudwick's wife and children were doing well. And how Forsythe was sure that Strudwick would like them to continue doing well. The veiled threat wasn't lost on Strudwick, whose voice quavered as he agreed to Forsythe's plan.

When the tape finished playing, Mr. X popped the original out and handed it back to Beverly. He took the new copy and said, "I have a nice secure place for this. I guarantee it will be safer there than in any police evidence closet."

Adam didn't know how much he should trust Mr. X at this point. He came across as being eager to help them nail Forsythe, but could this all be part of an elaborate trap? His face must have registered his distrust because Mr. X added, "I will be most happy to see Reginald Forsythe pay for his sins."

Adam said, "Why haven't you turned him in, yourself?"

"That should be obvious, my dear Detective. It would mean turning myself in, too. I'm not proud of everything in my past, but it's my past. My future is what I'm worried about. And that means being a regular, legal antiques dealer and yak farmer."

They returned to the den, and Adam drained the last bits of the chocolate. Even lukewarm, it was pretty good. "All right, then. We need a plan. First, we'll have to find out what Mayor Lehmann's connection is to Forsythe. Is it just his ambitions needing Forsythe's backing or something worse? Second, I need to find Gabriel Karlstad and get him to sing to save his own skin. Third, we need a motive for Forsythe to kill his father, and if we're lucky, proof."

Beverly said, "You can leave that last one to Harlan and me."

Adam asked, "Harlan?"

"As you said, the murder isn't technically in your jurisdiction, so your poking around asking questions about Reggie Forsythe would look too suspicious to him, his attorneys, and the Hartford PD. I think we need to talk to Reginald Forsythe's widow, and she'd clam up in front of a cop."

Mr. X said, "You could use the evidence you have in hand to get him convicted for influence peddling. That would avenge Beverly's grandmother."

Adam had considered that, too, but discounted it. "As a last resort. Even though his father wasn't a saint, I want Forsythe to go down for his murder."

After Beverly and Adam had left Mr. X's castle, Adam asked her, "Interesting man. I think he was quite taken with you."

Beverly giggled. "He is an interesting man, I'll give you that. But you're more his type."

"What do you mean?"

"He's gay. You didn't see the way he was eyeing you?"

Adam shook his head. "Glad I didn't."

"Oh, come on. A handsome guy like you has never been hit on by another man before?"

"Once. In a bar. Not a gay bar, just a bar bar."

"What did you do? Punch his lights out?"

"No, I arrested him."

Beverly's jaw dropped open, and when her eyes narrowed, he laughed. "Not for that. He was wanted for credit card fraud."

33

Adam looked over at Beverly, who was crammed into the floor of the passenger seat. He said, "I must be insane to let you talk me into this."

She grinned. "I kinda like you being on the crazy side. It'll be fine. You'll see."

"We may have only fifteen minutes, twenty tops."

"People can get up to all kinds of mischief in twenty minutes."

"That's what I'm afraid of." But Adam parked the car toward the back of the long, circular driveway next to a path leading around the back. He opened the driver's side door and held it open long enough for Beverly to maneuver across the seats and slide out the door. Then he headed toward the front while she ducked around the back.

Hoping that the mayor's golf game would take another hour or more, followed by the usual nineteenth-hole cocktails, Adam rang the front doorbell. The look of shock on Zelda's face would be amusing on any other occasion.

She held open the door but didn't invite him in which made him sweat for a few moments. He asked, "May I come in? It won't take too long."

Her curiosity apparently overriding her suspicions, she motioned for him to enter and led him toward a living room. It was immaculate and decorated in contemporary-chic Vermont, with metal and wood furniture and showroom-pristine fabrics.

He'd looked up her house in the local real estate assessment database. The place had six bedrooms, four baths, over five thousand square feet. Much bigger than his two-bedroom, one-and-a-half baths. It also had an office, which is where he and Beverly had agreed was the best place to do a bit of slightly unauthorized sleuthing.

Adam started coughing and apologized to Zelda, saying, "Ragweed pollen. Maybe a glass of water?"

Zelda headed toward what must be the kitchen, and Adam took the chance to scurry down the hall to unlock a side door nearest the office to let Beverly in. She'd offered to use her bump key on the way over, which had made Adam reply, "You have a bump key? How in the world did you . . . no, better I not know how you got it."

When Zelda returned with the water, he was back seated on a sofa, trying not to look out of breath. She sat opposite him, perched on the edge of her seat. "Does my husband know you were coming today? He didn't mention it."

"I didn't tell him. It's about your husband that I'm here. Something he said the other day when we ran into each other."

"Oh?" She leaned so far forward, he was worried she might fall off.

"He suspected I might be having an affair with you. At least, that was the implication."

"Good heavens, where would he get that idea?"

"He saw us in the street. After you came out of the wine shop three days ago."

"But that was a random encounter."

Adam looked directly into her eyes and said softly, "Was it really random?"

"Of course," she said, reaching her hand up to touch her hair, the bracelets on her wrist jangling. "Do you think I planned to see you that day?"

"As I recall, you're not a big wine drinker. More of a whiskey connoisseur. Yet not only were you buying wine, it was my favorite type."

"Coincidence. Nothing more."

He rubbed his eyes. "Zelda, I know I wasn't the warmest guy to be around when you initiated the divorce. Who would be? But I wanted you to know that if you're happy, then I'm happy for you."

She twirled a short strand of hair. The bracelets jangled some more. "Happy? As happy as anyone is."

"I'd forgotten how adept you are at non-answers."

"I'm happy, deliriously happy, over-the-roof happy. There. Is that what you wanted to hear?"

He leaned back and noticed how her eyes followed his body as he moved to make himself more comfortable on the sofa.

This wasn't the mayor's first marriage. He'd divorced his previous wife after only two years. Rather, she divorced him. One day when he'd bumped into the woman at a bar, she'd regaled Adam, in her drunken state, about the mayor's shortcomings in bed. Not what Adam needed to hear, and he'd extracted himself as soon as humanly possible. Although a corner of his brain did do a tiny victory dance.

Zelda dropped her hand and rubbed her leg. She still had nice legs, he had to admit, as he eyed her short skirt hiked above the knee. She said, "Have you been spending time with that suspect—Beverly something?"

"Doing my job, as I always do."

"Is that all? Just doing your job?"

"We have a mutual friend in Harlan Wilford, one of the main reasons she came. But Beverly is merely passing through town."

"Beverly. Sounds schoolmarmish. Is she older, near

Harlan's age?"

"She's around my age or a little younger. Why all this interest in a suspect?"

"Is she pretty?"

"I'm not sure that's relevant to this conversation. I want to talk about us."

Zelda got out of her chair and sat close beside him. "Adam, I've been thinking about you a lot lately. Not only at the wine shop. I just ... I guess I'm getting sentimental. Remember that summer we carried a picnic up Franconia Notch and you tripped and fell into a bog, so we went skinny dipping in the Concordia falls?"

"Yeah, I remember." One of many moments he'd shared with his wife that brought a smile to his lips.

Without warning, she reached over to wrap him in a bear hug. He managed to extract his arms to pat her gently on the back. And then he looked over her head and saw Beverly waving from a hallway. She made a cutting motion with her hand, then disappeared.

Zelda released him and rubbed her hand across his cheek. "We could do it, you know."

"Do what?"

"Have an affair. If Titus believes we're already having one, why not?"

His jaw dropped open. "Zelda, you do know that's crazy, don't you? And that's not why I came here today."

"Not crazy at all. You are an amazing lover, Adam. Thoughtful, passionate. Titus wouldn't have to find out."

"In a relatively small town like this, you think he wouldn't find out?"

"Not if we're careful."

"Zelda, I ... " He rubbed a hand through his hair. "I care about you. But not that way."

"You said you wanted me to be happy."

"I do, I do." He bit his lip at his choice of words. "I fear that my coming here was a bad idea. I should go." He stood up and then reached down to give her a light kiss on the forehead. "This is what you desired, wasn't it? The house, the fame, the fortune, the glamor? Don't squander it all on a sordid affair."

Adam dabbed at the corner of her eye, where a small tear was threatening to fall. "You gave me ten wonderful years, Zelda. I'll forever be grateful for that." He reluctantly headed out the door, part of him hating to leave her like that, part of him wanting to run as far and fast as he could.

Re-enacting their arrival in reverse, he opened the driver's side and waited for Beverly to hurry over and crawl onto the floor of the passenger seat. She waited until they were out of sight of the house to sit up in the seat and pull off her gloves. She was quiet for the first few minutes.

"How'd it go?" He prompted.

"Prospecting pays off sometimes."

"Good, good." He paused. "About what you heard in there. I wasn't being dismissive of you."

She waved him off. "Guess what I found?"

"Gold, I hope. Not Goldie."

"Your Mayor Lehmann is going to have to surround himself with an army of smart people if he wants to be governor. He's not an Einstein. Keeps his papers in unlocked drawers and documents everything. Possible blackmail fodder for later, who knows?"

"What did you find?"

"Evidence that the mayor knows full well about Forsythe's shady dealings. I didn't see anything that indicated he was involved per se. But he's freely consorting with a known criminal. He'd done a little research himself. All written down. Is he a Luddite or something? No computers in his office. Only a set of expensive, matching executive-type furniture. The place was like a museum."

"Too bad you couldn't make copies of those documents."

"Didn't have to." She reached into her pocket and pulled out her cellphone. "I took pictures."

"You are a wonder, Beverly Laborde."

He caught her looking at him before she looked away and said, "Was it awful? Being there with your ex?"

He laughed, but it was bitter and humorless. "She wants to have an affair."

Beverly sucked in her breath with an audible hiss. "That's what the hug was about. And here I thought it was a goodbye hug."

"It was. As far as I'm concerned."

She put the cellphone away. "Where do we go next?"

"We don't. I do. You may be one tough lady, but I'm not going to risk taking you in the Sutton's Grove camp to hunt for Gabriel Karlstad. Gun or no gun."

"You can't go in there alone, Adam. I won't let you. You should take Jinks with you."

"She's still in Nashua. That break she'd hoped for in her case came through. But don't worry. I have someone else in mind. He's helped me out on more than one occasion. We'll be fine."

34

Beverly tried one more time to convince Adam to take her with him on the hunt for Gabriel Karlstad, but he wouldn't budge. So she tried a different tack. "I recognized one of those names, you know."

"What?" he asked, giving her quick sideways glance before concentrating on the road again.

"From the documents in Mayor Lehmann's study. I came across the same name while doing research on Representative Strudwick."

"Which name?"

"Richard Nagra."

"Never heard of him. What's his connection?"

"He runs a moving company called Pierson's. He was another of Strudwick's financial backers, along with Reggie Forsythe."

"Did you say Pierson was the name of the moving company?"

"Yes, why?"

"That happens to be the same name of an outfit involved in a furniture consignment scandal Forsythe was involved with. Accused of, at least. He was able to explain it all away, naturally."

Beverly pondered that news for a moment. "So, Richard Nagra, via Pierson, creates a line from the mayor to Strudwick to Forsythe. And here I was feeling sorry for Nagra."

"Whatever for?"

"His reputation took a nosedive in the past year or so. Along with his business." She tried to recall all the details of the articles she'd read about Nagra in the Mayor's study. There hadn't been much to go on. "When did this consignment scandal take place, Adam?"

"A little over a year ago, about a year and a half."

"Perhaps it's mere coincidence, but Nagra's fall from grace coincides with that time frame. Could Forsythe have threatened him in some way? To shut down his business?"

"The only reason to do that is if Nagra wasn't in on the scam and found out later. Or, if he was a willing participant, he asked for more money to stay silent. Doubt Forsythe would take too kindly to blackmail."

They drove in silence for a moment, then Beverly said, "Nagra lives near here. Or he did once, so say Mayor Lehmann's documents."

"Oh no, you're not going to talk me into another harebrained scheme like breaking into the mayor's house."

"We didn't break, we just entered. And you were invited in with hugs and kisses." It wasn't fair to tease him like that, but she was still perturbed at the scene she'd walked in on, with Adam's arms around his ex. "We'll stop by, ask the man a few questions, and then you can go chase after Goldie."

Adam grimaced, but then he picked up his phone and called the office to get an address for Nagra. Beverly heard a high-pitched woman's voice on the other end, trilling like a cedar waxwing in flight.

As Adam hung up, she said, "You need earplugs before talking to that woman."

He grinned. "Sergeant Gray is notoriously cheerful. Whether it's five in the morning or eleven at night, she's always the same, even on the worse cases."

"Did you get an address for Nagra?"

"You were right. He lives about ten miles from here."

Adam pointed the car around in the other direction but didn't talk much. Beverly watched the houses speed by, until they thinned out to one every few acres or so, before she couldn't stand the silence any longer. "This is what being a detective is like? Boring car rides, minimalist conversation, consorting with shady women?"

"I'll grant you the last one," Adam's lips curled up into a small smile.

"What does Jinks do when she's riding shotgun?"

"She hums."

"Hums? You mean songs?"

"I wish. It's more of a tuneless hum, random notes she strings together. I haven't the faintest idea why."

"Would you like me to—"

"God, no. She drives me nuts."

Beverly grinned. "Score one for Detective Jinks. I'll have to remember that."

It didn't take them long to reach the address Sergeant Gray had looked up for Adam. Nagra's reputation had fallen off, and so had his homestead. Several shingles on the roof were buckled or curled, the peeling green paint on the shutters revealed gray wood underneath, and the posts on the wraparound porch were cracked.

Beverly followed Adam out of the car. He opened his mouth as if to tell her to stay behind, but instead just shook his head and motioned for her to come with him. The walkway skirted around a small creek, and Beverly clutched the railing across a boardwalk bridge, trying not to look down. When Adam looked at her strangely, she hurried along and maneuvered alongside him as he planted himself next to the front door.

Three series of knocks later, and the door opened. But it wasn't what Beverly was expecting, and she could tell from the slight shifting in Adam's posture that he was surprised, too.

Beverly couldn't help herself from thinking the person in front of them could be described as a mythological troll. She guessed it was a woman from the purple striped stockings and gray skirt, but the electric white hair and cavernous wrinkles were more androgynous. The woman was half Adam's height.

He asked her, "I'm looking for Mr. Richard Nagra. This is his last known address."

"It's his all right." The woman scowled at them.

Adam asked, "May we speak with him?"

"If you can find him, sure."

Adam clenched his jaw as he added, "Where did he go?"

"Damned if I know. I'm the caretaker here. He put me in charge to keep an eye on things, said he was only going to be gone for two weeks. That was two months ago."

"No calls or letters from him since?"

"Not jack shit."

Beverly didn't think she'd heard a troll curse before. She bit her lip and concentrated on Adam's questioning. "Did you call his business, Pierson Moving Company?"

"Every day. Said they don't know where he is, either, even filed a missing person report. I tried to get them to fork over more money, but they hung up on me."

"Money? You mean to pay you for being the caretaker?"

"I've eaten my way through the pantry. The only things left are cans of sauerkraut. Electric company's come by twice to turn me off, but I sweet-talked 'em into keeping it on."

"Did he say where he was going when he hired you?"

"Squat. I called up the mayor. They hung up on me, too."

Adam did a good job of keeping his voice nonchalant as he pressed the troll further, "Why call the mayor?"

"They was a message from the mayor on Nagra's answering machine. Figured they must know each other."

"What did the message say?"

"Didn't make no sense. Said, 'Forsythe says you're in.'"

"Only that, nothing else?"

"That and 'don't screw this one up.'"

The troll gawked up at Adam, her scowl so deep it was like a like the edges of a pit opening up among the caverns of wrinkles. "You're a cop, right? 'Cause I can smell a cop a mile away."

Adam nodded, and she added, "You find him. Find Mr. Richard Nagra. I want my money. And if he don't come back soon, he might not have a house to come back to."

"If you're threatening arson, Miss——."

She cackled at that. "No names. And if this house was to burn to the ground, you wouldn't find me around nowheres. Just like Nagra." With that, she stepped back and slammed the door in their faces.

Beverly looked at Adam, who shrugged, and they headed back to the car. Beverly forced herself to walk quickly over the footbridge and only grabbed the railing once. Adam put a hand on her shoulder and said, "If you're afraid of more trolls under the bridge, I think we're safe." Beverly whirled around, knowing she hadn't mentioned her troll impression out loud. Guess they were thinking alike.

She licked her lips. "What did the mayor mean by that 'Forsythe says you're in' bit?"

"I'm more interested in the second part, the 'don't screw this one up' comment. And whether it's tied to Nagra's disappearance. Not proof but intriguing all the same."

Beverly said, "Did you have one of those troll dolls when you were a kid?"

"A girl at my school had a two-headed one. Butt-ugliest

thing I ever saw."

"That would fetch a ton of money today. The two-headed ones are rare. The original dolls were made by the Danish company Thomas Dam and called Dam Things. They're said to bring you luck."

Adam motioned with his thumb back at the house. "Tell that to our friend back there."

"You don't believe in luck, Adam Dutton?"

"You make your own luck. No prayers or rabbit's feet or four-leaf clovers can take the place of sweat. As in hard work and perseverance."

"But look how lucky it is I bumped into you at the Apple Valley Resort."

"Is it? I arranged that you know."

"Could have been Detective Jinks, but it was you."

"And you think that's lucky?" He eyed her with a look that was half-joking, half something more.

"Depends upon whether you buy me dinner or not." She winked at him, and his jaw dropped open.

"Are you flirting with me, Miss Laborde?"

"I don't flirt, I manipulate."

He unlocked the car door but paused before slipping into the driver's seat. "I'm not sure we should be seen together in public too much."

She frowned at him. "Why not? Embarrassed to be seen with me?"

"Hell, no. Worried Forsythe's goons will see us and put two and two together."

Beverly followed his reasoning for a moment and nodded. "You may be right. But I want a rain check."

"Checks I have plenty of, rain not so much lately. But you're on."

She was a little disappointed but knew he was right. This

was no time to get careless and make them both more of a target than they already were, both physically and politically. But the minute this whole nasty business was over, she was going to call in that rain check and maybe . . . No, that was all. Never think too far ahead, never plan, never trust anyone. It was the only way for her.

35

As Adam drove Beverly back toward town, it was such a lovely day—several degrees warmer than average—that Adam entertained the idea of opening up his car's sunroof. As long as Beverly was in the passenger seat, he might as well show off the best feature of his car.

Adam moved his hand to push the button for the roof but stopped with his hand in mid-air when he looked in the rearview and spied a black car bearing down on them. The vehicle moved uncomfortably close to Adam's bumper, so he put his foot down on the accelerator to put more space between them. "Tailgaters," he grumbled.

They rounded a curve in the road, and Adam thought the other car had turned off. But then he caught sight of it as it closed the gap between them. Adam said to Beverly, "Can you get a good look at the driver of the car behind us?"

She craned her neck around to take a good look. "He's sitting up tall in his seat with the visor all the way down. I can only make out his chin. The car is too close to get a plate."

"Keep an eye on him, okay? As soon as you get the tag, let me know, and I'll run it through the database."

He heard the frown in Beverly's voice. "If he were any closer, he'd be in the back seat. Can you shake him?"

Adam accelerated. Looking up the road, he decided to

catch the right-hand turnoff ahead on the north side of the pond that ran parallel to the road. That way, he could turn around and get behind the guy. But he didn't have a chance to enact his plan when the black car whipped around Adam's driver-side bumper.

A sickening crunch followed by a heavy thud told Adam all he needed to know—someone was playing death-by-car. Adam felt the car veering to the right and tried to correct it to bring the tires back toward the road, but the black car bumped them again and hard.

They always say crashes happen in slow motion, but it was more like a macabre roller coaster blur, as their car tumbled over on its side, sliding down the embankment. By now, Adam's frantic turning on the wheel had no effect, and with one last, awful shudder, the car rolled over and tumbled into the pond upside down.

Thanking his lucky stars he hadn't opened the sunroof, Adam was grateful to see they had plenty of air in the car. For now. Within a few seconds, the car stopped moving with a shaking thud.

They were no longer in motion, which was the good news. The bad news was they only had one to two minutes before the car was totally filled with water.

Over in the passenger seat, Beverly was taking panicky gasping breaths. He said sharply, "It's okay. It's survivable. We'll be fine. The pond is shallow, and we're wedged in the mud. We're stable for now."

As the water came up to the bottoms—or rather tops—of the windows, Beverly shrieked, and her words came out in gasps. "I'm terrified of drowning. Ever since I was a child. We were at the beach. A giant wave created an undertow I couldn't escape from. It almost killed me."

Adam reached over and fumbled around to touch her on

the arm as he talked soothingly. "Beverly, listen to me. You're tough. You can do this. I believe in you."

Her breathing slowed, and he said, "We're going to unbuckle our seatbelts, okay? The water's not pouring in yet, but it will." Adam spied trickles of water beginning to leak through car joints.

"What do we do?"

"We unbuckle, we fall to the roof." Adam carefully opened a console next to his seat and eased out a safety hammer before it slid toward the upside-down roof. "Then I use this on my window. When you see the window shatter, hold your breath. The water will start pouring in when I knock out the rest of the glass. Then we'll swim out."

"I don't know if I can do this."

"Sure you can. When I get ready to swim out the window, I'll grab you and pull you with me, okay? I won't leave you behind. I promise."

"Adam, I . . . " Her breathing got shallower again.

"Beverly, do you trust me?" He looked over at her.

She nodded.

"Okay, then. First, buckles off. Ready?"

He unbuckled his seatbelt and tumbled down to the roof, which was now the floor, then wiggled his body to right himself in the correct orientation toward the surface. She followed his lead and then took the strap off her purse and used the purse's clasp to attach it to the belt on her slacks. They were now both upright—but rapidly getting wet with water up to their waists.

"Okay, then," Adam said. "I'll count to three and hit the glass. Ready?"

She nodded again and took a long, deep breath. Then he counted, "One, two, three."

With a sharp tap of the tool on the driver-side window, it shattered into a mosaic of broken glass, and he used his sleeved arm to clear away the last pieces of glass. With the water now pouring in, he held his breath and was pleased to see Beverly was still doing the same.

Adam grabbed her hand and yanked her with him as he did a fishtail kick with his legs and used his free arm to push them toward the surface. Thank god the pond wasn't that deep, but the ten feet to the surface felt like an eternity. When Adam's head broke the surface, he gulped in the air and released Beverly's hand to tuck under her arm and bring her up alongside him.

The two tread water, glad to be out of the car and breathing good old clean Vermont air. But if they stayed too long in the cold pond, they might get hypothermic. "Can you swim?" Adam asked her. He was glad to see the sparkle return to her eyes as she grinned at him and executed a perfect freestyle over to the shore. How in the world was she doing that while wearing her purse?

Once they were both high, if not yet dry, they sat on the bank of the pond staring at the water where the car was now submerged. Beverly coughed, and he turned to her with concern, but she smiled at him. "It's okay. Swallowed a little water."

He looked at her purse. "Do you have a cellphone in there?"

She pulled out her phone, but it was dead. Adam contemplated diving back down to the Subaru to detach his radio. But when he spied a car down the road heading in their direction, he instead grabbed his badge from his pocket. He stood in the middle of the road waving his arms.

The driver slowed, then stopped, and Adam went to talk to him. With a big thank you to the inventor of the cellphone, Adam used the man's phone to contact the PD and relay their position and SOS. After sending the man on his way, he rejoined Beverly on the bank.

"Look at it this way—trying to kill us so soon after the kidnapping is a desperation move. And a dumb one. They're making it much easier for us to catch them."

Beverly smiled but was shivering. He wished he had a dry coat to give to her but didn't think putting his drenched jacket around her shoulders would do much good. He moved closer to help block the light winds.

"Thank you," she said.

He wrung some water out of his shirt. "For what? Coming close to getting you drowned?"

"That wasn't your fault. I meant for knowing what to do. Keeping me calm."

"You really did nearly drown once?"

"I was six. Grammie and I were at the Bay of Fundy, and I went swimming. You know about the tides, there?"

"Highest tides in the world."

"More so to a short six-year-old. I got out a little too far, a tide came at me, and when I tried to run back toward the shore, I felt the forces pulling at my feet. It was like walking in quicksand. I didn't make it. The waves gobbled me whole, and I spun around and around like I was in a washing machine."

"But you're a good swimmer."

"Now, I am. I wasn't then. I signed up to learn how to swim the day we got back home."

"You really are something, you know that?"

"What do you mean?"

"Most people would be so traumatized, they'd never go near the water again. But you confronted your fears head-on."

She grinned. "Blame Eleanor Roosevelt. She said 'you must do the thing you think you cannot do.'"

"Good advice." Adam looked back over the dark blue waters of the pond. "Why Laborde?"

"What?"

"Why did you take the name Laborde instead of your grandmother's name of Gras or your father's name, Zayette?"

"Truthfully?"

"Yeah, truthfully."

"I saw it in a phone book."

Adam laughed. "As good a way to choose a name as any." He looked toward the pond as if willing his submerged car to pop up to the surface and onto the road. "I'm guessing Forsythe was behind this. Getting someone else to do his underhanded work for him again."

"Goldie?"

"Maybe. But I do know one thing. Whoever it was—well, just like my car, that bastard is going down."

36

Beverly allowed herself fifteen minutes in the Jacuzzi before getting dressed. She wasn't sure she'd ever get warm. The police officers from Adam's department had given her and Adam blankets when they arrived at the pond, yet she was still shivering when they dropped her off at the resort.

But fifteen minutes was all she had, plus saving a few extra minutes for getting dressed, before Adam arrived. He'd called to say he was going to stop by and check on her and make sure she was all right. She'd reassured him she was fine, but her words sounded shaky to her ears. They'd agreed to meet in the tea room when they both admitted that his coming to her room might not be the best idea. In more ways than one, for her.

As Adam looked her over when he greeted her, she was suddenly a lot warmer, especially her cheeks. Good god, that was such a cliché. To mix things up a bit, she ordered a hot espresso with extra shots, and Adam ordered the same.

When the drinks arrived, she pointed to his drink. "Is that enough for you?"

While he stirred in a teaspoon of sugar, he replied, "If I weren't on duty, I'd be adding some Irish whiskey. Or maybe Kahlúa."

"Talking with me is being on duty?"

He stirred the sugar in slowly. "You know, I was proud of you back there. You showed some true grit."

He hadn't answered her question. Was this visit business or

pleasure? "I don't know about that. I remember hyperventilating."

"At first. But you got yourself under control. That's what saves you in life-or-death situations."

"Like the drug dealer who buried you alive?"

The gaze he settled on her, with the intense cocktail of emotions stirring behind those eyes, was mesmerizing and a little frightening. She stammered, "I'm sorry. Maybe I shouldn't have—"

"It's okay." He dropped his gaze to stare at his espresso. "I've talked about it with my therapist so much, it's starting to feel more like a long-ago bad dream."

"Does it help? Talking to this therapist?"

"I'm not much of a talker. But if the mantra is 'first do no harm' with psych people, too, then guess it turned out okay."

When he looked at her again, his eyes were back to their usual warm mocha. He said, "But I didn't come to talk about me, I'm more interested in how you're doing."

She settled back into her chair and gazed out through the picture window toward the mountains. "Hard to believe I've been here a week. I didn't plan on staying this long."

"Grab the goodies and run?"

She smiled. "I know you think it's insane to be obsessed over one little silver statue. One that might be lost to history."

"Is it the money you're after? If you can find the statue and sell it?"

"I never seriously considered searching for it, even after I first found Kornelson's treasure map. It was more of a game. Until I learned my uncle was interested in it."

"Is he? Reggie Forsythe must really be into silver doo-dads. There are tons of them in his house."

"Really? I guess I'd heard that." Beverly wasn't ready to trust Adam completely. She definitely didn't want him to know yet, if ever, that she'd been the woman seen going into her uncle's house.

He said, "You know, that woman on the videotape from the day the senior Forsythe was killed looked awfully familiar."

"I hope you find her someday."

"Perhaps I already have. And perhaps she'd like to tell me why she was there and what really happened?"

Beverly drained the last of her espresso in one gulp. "I can't warm up. I need a refill." She jumped up to place the order, and she waited at the counter until they handed it to her.

When she returned to their table, she set the cup down and wrapped her hands around it. "Harlan told me he was good friends with your father, whom he admired. Wish I could have met him."

Adam didn't reply at first. Was he upset with her for asking? Or was he angry she hadn't answered his question about her being at Reggie Forsythe's house? If it were the latter, he'd be waiting a long time. But then he gave her a small smile, and a little of the tension in her shoulders slipped away.

"Dad and Harlan were fishing buddies. Took me along on several occasions. My father wasn't into antiques like Harlan and your grandmother, but he did like antique cars. Always wanted a working Model-T."

"Grammie drove a 1937 Packard with a red quilted leather interior, even on the roof."

"Guess your grandmother and my father had something in common."

Beverly's smile at his comment faded as she remembered what happened to that car. Adam must be reading her mind because he asked, "Do you still have the Packard?"

"We had to sell it to pay for nursing home care. I'm not sure Grammie noticed it was missing. Like her mind—all gone."

"I'm sorry about what happened, Beverly. But this vengeance kick you're on won't bring her back. And vengeance can be a soul trap. Sucks you in and never lets go."

Shades of Mr. X's words. Beverly reached over to get more sugar and accidentally brushed against his hand. He had such strong hands, tanned, a little weathered, but the kind that invited holding. She drew her hand away. "For someone who doesn't like to talk, you're doing well."

He leaned his forearms on the table. "I mean it, Beverly. It's much safer for you to be obsessed with that statue than with Forsythe."

"I can't give up the cause yet. Besides, Harlan and I have a date to interview my grandfather's second wife."

"I'm glad you'll be with Harlan so he can jump in if things get hairy. He's ex-Army and tougher than he looks."

"Adam, I'm not that fragile."

"I don't doubt that. But between you and me, Reggie Forsythe is a nut case. It's the psycho types you have to look out for. Can't predict what they're going to do next."

Wanting to lighten the mood, Beverly smiled at him. "How did you get here? When I last saw your car, it was under water."

"We'll get an electric winch to pull it out. In the meantime, I've got an unmarked department loaner."

"Were you teased by your fellow cops?"

"More like grilled."

"Grilled?"

"The chief wants to know why you were riding in my car."

She picked at a fingernail. "Oh. What did you tell him?"

"The truth. That you'd given me a tip on Richard Nagra and the Pierson Moving Company, and you wanted to show me where he lived."

"And he believed you?"

"Somewhat. It helped when I pointed out that our mad

driver may have targeted you, too. Makes it look like you're a victim in all of this."

Beverly waved the unfamiliar waitress over to refill the creamer. Gloria must have the day off. "That's not what you thought when we first met here."

"I didn't know for certain yet that you were a female Robin Hood."

She caught hints of a smile playing around his lips and replied, "I still think that title is apt. Robin Hood was a freedom fighter going up against oppressive lords."

"That art history of yours again?"

"I was a straight-A student."

"Did your grandmother approve of your . . . um, career?"

Beverly picked up the newly delivered creamer, thought better of it, and put it back down. "I helped her with her antiques business as long as she had it. I didn't switch 'careers' until after her death. It was my way of giving back to other victims."

"Doesn't sound like the type of career one can sustain long term."

"It's as good as any until something more interesting comes along."

He tilted his head. "You could assist Harlan. You've really impressed him."

"It would mean settling down, and I'm not sure I'm ready for that." She bit her lip at the double meaning. Could she settle down? Would she ever get to the point she'd want to? The man sitting across from her was making it hard to contemplate months and years of more lonely nights in a succession of hotel beds.

"Anyway," he said, "Give it some thought."

"All in good time. First things first—much needed sleep tonight, and then I've got to pick up Harlan tomorrow."

"Hope you can get helpful info out of the widow."

"And I hope you'll be careful at Sutton's Grove hunting for Gabriel Karlstad."

He reached over to shake her hand. "Deal."

37

Tuesday, September 21

Adam was beginning to relish his newfound ability to sleep like a newborn baby. Maybe he should be more worried about the case and other things—like his recently repaired car being dunked into a pond. But for some reason, he felt pretty good. A perfect state of mind to go hunting.

Unlike the trip to Mr. X's castle, this route Adam knew like the back of his forty-two-year-old hand. He pulled up in front of a cabin and waited for his friend to hop in. "Haven't heard a word from you in two forevers, Stork. What have you been up to?"

"This and that. Old man Korn pays me well to look after his property. Lots of fresh air, lots of natural vitamin D."

"You still on that health food kick? You were taking some twenty vitamins for a while."

"Chucked 'em all. Got a juicer. Grind up everything and drink my meals."

Adam gripped his shoulder. "I need to take you out for a steak, my friend."

"Get thee behind me, yada yada. I haven't had a steak in years."

"Steak, horseradish crust, medium rare, and a loaded baked potato."

Stork sighed happily. "Don't forget the maple pie."

"With cinnamon ice cream."

Adam's companion pointed toward the "Y" in the road ahead. "That's the one you need to take. About a mile or so." He added, "Funny you should call me up. I was out here the other day, and a pretty lady pulled a gun on me."

"About five-eight, thirty-five-ish, long dark hair?"

"That's the gal. Forgot to take the safety off that gun."

She'd learned her lesson since the safety was most definitely off at the cabin when Goldie kidnapped him. "What did Beverly want?"

"That's her name? Beverly? Nice name. She didn't come right out and say what she was after."

"What did you talk about?"

"I mentioned my ancestor, one of Rogers' Rangers. She was kinda interested in that."

"I didn't know one of your ancestors was a ranger."

"We're not proud of that part of the family."

"We've all got those."

"That's what I told her."

As they drew closer to the camp where Mr. X believed Gabriel Karlstad might be hiding out, tendrils of smoke curled up into the clear blue sky. When the camp came into view, he counted half a dozen rustic homes clustered around a semicircle off to the left side. No power lines going into the houses. But he spied a few generators, and the smoke was coming out of one of the chimneys indicating a fireplace or wood stove.

Adam looked around for the obligatory mangy dog or half-feral cat, but the area was surprisingly devoid of animals. Not a cow anywhere. Or a yak. Stork pointed toward the home closest to them. "That's where Joe Bibb lives. If any of these characters is harboring your bad guy, it'd be him."

Adam let Stork lead the way since he was known to most of these people. The woman who opened the door smiled at

Stork but looked at Adam with a furrowed brow. "Who's he?"

"Friend of mine, Missy. Is your husband home?"

"Him and Gerry are out huntin.'"

"I see. That's too bad. Hoped I might hit him up for some of that gold maple vodka of his. I was telling Adam here all about it, and he didn't believe me when I said how good it was."

"Joe's the best. Better than that fancy crap they sell in Brattleboro."

Stork nodded vigorously. "I second that."

Missy looked behind her. "We don't got much extry right now but wouldn't want Adam here calling you a liar. Come on in, and I can give him a taste."

Adam hoped Stork knew what he was doing. As Missy led them inside, it didn't take long to tell this was a far cry from Forsythe's mansion. Or the mayor's fancy spread. Hell, it was a far cry from his own small home. Three rooms total, as near as he could see, the front living-dining-kitchen combo and two tiny bedrooms, with a small bathroom between. The walls were covered with mounted guns, knives, and animal heads.

Missy poured him a half glass of the vodka, and he sipped it slowly. The first drops down his throat made him think he'd swallowed hot acid, but after that initial kick, it was quite smooth. He lifted his glass at Missy. "Okay, so I guess Stork here won that bet. And you're right. That stuff in Brattleboro is a poor imitation."

She smiled at him and then added apologetically to Stork, "When you come next, Joe'll have a new batch ready."

"No problem, Missy. I'm a patient man. Though Adam here might disagree."

Missy asked Adam, "Are you a caretaker, too?"

Adam took another sip from the glass. "I look after things."

Stork piped in, "Adam and I go way back to when we was kids. He knows the area around here. And the people, too." Stork lowered his voice. "There was this one feller I saw the other day. Wasn't too sure about that one. Hadn't seen him before, I don't recall. Odd gent. Had this one gold tooth. You might want to keep your eye out for him."

Missy snickered. "Don't worry over him, Stork. I'll tell him to leave you alone. That's just Gabe. And as long as you don't bother him, he won't bother you."

"Does he live here now?"

"From time to time, when he needs a place to hide—" She hastened to add, "To dry out."

Adam kept taking subtle glances around the small room, looking for signs Gabe was there recently. Clue number one was the top of a bloody cloth poking out of the sink. Add one of those knives on the wall and some vodka, and you'd have the means to cut out a bullet and disinfect it afterward.

Stork said, "I'd like to meet this Gabe of yours. So if he sees me around, he'll know I'm okay."

"You just missed him. I'd say to look for him at the Dragon's Teeth Bar where he likes to hang out. But he went into the Junction on some business, he said. He's friends with the mayor, you know that?"

"Is that a fact?" Stork smiled. "More reason to get to know him, then, if he's that all-fired important."

"Oh, he's important, all right. Got a shitload of powerful friends. There's this one in particular."

Stork asked, "More powerful than the mayor?"

"Much. Richer, too. Gabe was doing a job for him yesterday when he was ... " Missy's voice trailed off. "Anyways, I'll tell Joe you came by, Stork."

"You do that. Hope to get some more of this elixir soon." Stork took Adam's glass from him and handed it over. "You should sell it. Might make some good money."

"I told him that myself. Maybe he'll listen to you."

Stork laughed. "Thanks again, Missy. Take care now."

When they were back in Adam's car and down the road, Stork said to Adam, "Missy can be a decent sort if you don't cross her. She and Joe had a black market business for a while. They've dabbled in things you could arrest her for several times over."

"And may have to someday."

"Be a shame. She hasn't known any other way, you see. Abused by her stepfather, abandoned by her mother, a drug user."

"Perhaps she's done dabbling for good, Stork."

"More than I can say for our friend Gabe. Sorry we missed him."

"We'll get him, Stork. That's a promise. But if you do see him before I do—"

"I'll have him hogtied with a pretty red bow and delivered to your office."

§ § §

After Adam parted ways with Stork, he pulled into the parking lot of Miralee's Market for some coffee. It turned out to be good timing when he got a call on his cell from Creighton Querry.

"Cray, please tell me you've got something I can use."

"I got something, but it's not much."

"I'll take whatever crumbs you have."

"I've been pursuing Nagra of Pierson's Moving Company and found the man had a favorite haunt, this little diner in Walbridge."

"The Birdseye, right across the state line?"

"Yeah, that's the one. I chatted up the owner, and she admitted Nagra was a regular, but she hadn't seen him for two months, which was unusual. She guessed maybe it was a family thing or vacation or such."

"And it wasn't?"

"She doesn't know, and I don't know for sure. But she also swears that on his last visit, he was extremely tense and nervous and looking over his shoulder. And that she saw him leave in his usual red Mercedes. Then, a half-hour later, she witnessed that same red Mercedes driving past, but the driver wasn't Nagra."

"Did she get a description of said driver?"

"Not a good one. He had the windows rolled up. But it looked like he was playing car karaoke, singing to himself. She said she thought he had this one gold tooth."

Goldie. Of course. "Your crumbs are more like bread loaves, my friend. Can't pay you—yet—but you get a gold star to go with that gold tooth."

"Yay for me. I'll put in on my calendar. Seriously, though, ya think this helps in building the case against Forsythe?"

"Definitely doesn't hurt, and I'll keep my promise. If this pans out, you'll get credit in the paper."

"When pigs fly, right?"

"Cray, you know my word is good."

"Yeah, yeah. You goody-two-shoes types. Keep me in the loop, 'kay?"

Adam hung up and tried to connect the investigative dots. According to Cray, Nagra, a crooked associate of Reggie Forsythe's and a backer of Representative Strudwick, acted nervously right before he went missing. Enter Goldie, another crooked associate and kidnapper, and you have an intriguing thread from one to the other. Adam wouldn't have been surprised to see Kannan Hendrick pop up in all of this if he weren't already six feet under.

38

After laying out everything to Harlan Wilford, Beverly was pleased when he said he'd be happy to do anything in his power to help. "I always suspected Reggie Forsythe was a demon in disguise. Lord, help me, I never knew how utterly and deviously evil the man was. You really think he killed his own padre?"

When she said yes, Harlan made a face. "And had someone attack Adam, too." Harlan's face turned several shades of red when she told him about Adam. It only took him a minute to grab his hat, call his assistant, Prospero, to come in and mind the store, and they were off.

Beverly wasn't sure what reception they'd receive from her grandfather's widow. But Harlan turned on the charm, introducing himself as a colleague of Forsythe and that Beverly was his associate. He handed over the flower arrangement he'd picked up from a florist along the way, and she motioned for them to come in. But she sat them near the door and didn't offer any refreshments.

Beverly grudgingly admitted to herself that Mairi Forsythe was a fit and attractive seventy-something. Her shoulder-length silver hair sported a stylish bob cut set off by the all-white sweater dress she wore. No mourning-widow black for her. Even so, Beverly couldn't imagine this woman being a finer catch than Beverly's grandmother.

As Mairi started to speak, the Botox couldn't hide traces of frown lines around her mouth. "I don't remember my husband mentioning you, Mr. Wilford."

"Please. It's Harlan. No one calls me mister. I hadn't seen your husband for a while, but we were both in the Northeastern Antiquities League."

Beverly didn't think she imagined the sudden tension in Mairi's shoulders as she replied. "Reginald was quite the businessman."

"He was very successful at what he did, yes. But I'm sure you must know how admired and respected he was." Beverly noticed the corners of Harlan's lips twitching.

Mairi smoothed a small strand of wayward hair. "Some people admired his drive, perhaps. He was hated for his success more than respected."

Beverly grew more impressed by the minute at Harlan's acting job, as he pasted on a fake scowl and said, "I didn't know that. I'll bet people were being jealous."

"Oh, they were jealous, all right. Jealous, cruel, spiteful. I attended many a social affair, the type where the women shower you with air kisses while gossiping behind your back. But I overhead more than they knew."

Beverly spoke up. "Mrs. Forsythe, we were shocked to hear of your husband's murder. Do you think it was one of those jealous colleagues, then?"

"I honestly don't know. The police asked me that, too. They and Reggie said something about a woman who might be involved." Mairi straightened up. "I know for a fact my husband wasn't having an affair, despite what people may say."

Beverly said, "Why else would a woman be involved, do you think?"

"It's definitely not that. My husband was impotent."

Beverly bit her lip to keep from laughing when Harlan squirmed at that revelation. She asked, "You mentioned a Reggie. Would that be your stepson?"

"Yes. Reggie's been handling everything. The police, the attorneys, the media. He's sheltered me from all of it. I can barely go out of the house without asking his permission."

Beverly took note of Mairi's hands as they curled up into fists. Her relationship with her stepson was rocky. That could be helpful. "Were Reggie and your husband that close?"

"Reggie was like a clone of his father. With the personality cut out." She jutted out her chin. "That makes me sound the wicked stepmother. Why should I care? As soon as Reggie gets his three-fourths of the estate, I'll never see him again. And good riddance."

"Three-fourths?" Harlan tutted. "That doesn't sound fair."

"Life's not fair, Mr. Wilford. I'm surprised Reggie didn't put pressure on Reginald to leave everything to him. I'm sure he's thrilled his sister is long dead, so he doesn't have to split anything with her."

Beverly fought back the tears that came to her eyes, and Harlan reached over to touch her hand. He said, "That's just not right. If I had a wife, I'd make sure she was well taken care of in the event of my demise."

"I'll do all right. Enough to live on. Barely."

Beverly leaned forward, pouring on her own faux sympathy. "Dear me. I do hope the police don't believe Reggie was somehow behind his father's death. What's the world coming to?"

Mairi tugged on her earring. "The police didn't say anything about that. I don't think they're seriously considering it. Reggie was rich in his own right. To him, his father's bequest is play-money."

Beverly kept a straight face as she lied, "I saw both Forsythes arguing at an NAL meeting once. One of my friends said they did that incessantly. But due to the generous bequest, it sounds like they patched everything up before your husband's death."

"They did argue, and incessantly is the perfect word. Over everything. Like two horned-steers circling for control of the herd."

Harlan piped up, "Yet, they both loved antiques. Especially silver. Such a nice collection Reggie has."

"Reggie was the silver freak. I don't know why. Silver is so cold, so colorless, so blank. He's become obsessed with some Indian legend. A silver statue, I think. Now, if it were gold, that I could understand."

Beverly rushed to say, "Must make a nice addition to his collection, then?"

"If and when he finds it."

Beverly stifled a sigh of relief at the definitive news Reggie hadn't found it yet, and Harlan added, "Antiquing is a funny business. Obsessing over history, markings, imperfections. Guess it could turn anybody into an obsessive type. Make you a touch crazy."

Mairi laughed bitterly. "Crazy. My family said I was crazy to marry Reginald. He had a reputation for being a little shady."

Harlan replied, "Come to think of it. I've heard those rumors, too. I discounted them. As you say, professional jealousy."

"Maybe not so much." She looked at Harlan, then Beverly. "I haven't cried a single tear. My sister tells me it's because I realize I'm better off. My shrink tells me grief will come in time. But you know I what think?"

Beverly shook her head.

"I loved Reginald too much, at first. But year by year, life ate away pieces of my heart until there aren't any left. Everyone talks about rose-colored glasses. Mine were star-colored. Twinkling indigo and green and red. But stars burn out eventually, don't they?"

Beverly and Harlan left Mairi Forsythe's and stopped at a cafe that they had all to themselves. Harlan ordered an applewood-smoked bacon biscuit and Beverly some chocolate Frangelico crème brûlée. She hoped the Frangelico content wasn't enough to run up her blood alcohol. She didn't need a DWI.

She said, "Forsythe had a double motive for killing his father. Wanting to run the business his way and inheriting a pile of money. Plus, he won't have to deal with his albatross stepmother anymore."

Harlan nodded while munching. Biscuit crumbs cascaded to the table as he replied, "Plenty of motive, zero proof."

Beverly licked some brûlée off her spoon. "You know I actually feel sorry for Mairi?"

"So do I, Beverly. Awful lot of collateral damage those two men left in their wake."

Beverly's hope that they'd turn up some proof to pin on Reggie Forsythe appeared to be dashed. And Adam told her Reggie had used gloves or some cloth to wrap around the candelabra, probably disposed of somewhere they'd never be found.

In the minds of most law enforcement types, the "mystery woman" was still the main, if not the only suspect. For the hundredth time, she told herself she should just run. Run far away and leave Ironwood Junction and the case behind. She dug the spoon into the crème brûlée. At least, that was one excavation that was going well.

39

Adam handed Jinks a coffee. "Sorry it's not Cognac. Looks like you could use it. I heard you solved your missing person case—so why the long face?"

She took the cup with a grateful smile. "Located the missing husband, all right. Got hit by a car outside Nashua the night he vanished. Mr. Hit-and-Run robbed our guy of his wallet with the two grand and all his ID. Our husband gets taken to the hospital as John Doe, where they discover he has head injuries and amnesia."

"Why hadn't he come to your attention sooner?"

Her smile dimmed. "Here's where it gets ugly."

"Uglier than a hit-and-run?"

"Oh yeah. Some other family believed he was their missing husband and father. Matched his description. All banged up like that, bandages and bruises everywhere, hard to tell."

"Okaaaay. That doesn't sound too ugly."

"Wait for it. He *was* their missing husband and father. My family, the Baylors, wondered why he spent so much time up in Nashua. Now they know, unfortunately."

"Let me guess—he had a double life."

"Two houses, two marriages, two sets of kids."

"Has he been reunited with your family?"

Jinks took a long, slow sip of the coffee. "Reunited, yes. But he doesn't remember them. He doesn't remember either family. The docs aren't sure how long the amnesia will last. Or whether he'll ever get his memory back."

"Think he's faking it to avoid the impending fireworks?"

"Could be. Either way, the Baylors are devastated."

"I was going to congratulate you. But I guess it's like winning the battle but losing the war."

"Sucks, doesn't it? Just goes to show there are few people you can trust in this world." She peered at him over her cup. "I hear you had some fun while I was gone. You're making a habit out of getting kidnapped without me."

Adam grinned. "Now that you're back, you can make it up to me. I took Stork out to the backcountry, and we have a name to attach to our bad guy." Adam didn't want to mention that he'd originally learned the guy's identity from Mr. X. "Name's Gabriel Karlstad. One of Forsythe's cronies." He handed her a photo he'd printed out from a newspaper database of the man after he'd won a hunting trophy.

"Where do we find this Karlstad? I'd like to give him a taste of his own medicine. Handcuff him, then tell him to talk, or I'll shoot him in the balls."

"That's what I like about you, Jinks. You're one classy dame."

She saluted, and Adam continued, "He likes to hang out over at the Dragon's Teeth Bar. Might be a bit early in the day, even on a weekend, but somebody there could have seen him."

"What are we waiting for? At the very least, I can pick up hard cider. Ever tried an Irish Vermonter? Some cider, a little Jamesons, and you're ready to make love to a post."

Jinks grabbed her jacket and joined him in his car. Adam estimated it would take them ten minutes to get there, thanks to the Junction's blissfully light traffic. What he hadn't expected to see was Gabriel Karlstad walking easy-as-you-please out of the Tavern. And he was followed closely by none other than Mayor Lehmann, who pumped Karlstad's hand.

Adam and Jinks were out of the car in a flash, Jinks with her gun drawn, and Adam with handcuffs at the ready. Karlstad's face twisted into a scowl, but the mayor looked shocked. It was Lehmann who spoke first. "What the hell do you think you are doing, Dutton?"

"Gabriel Karlstad here is wanted for the kidnapping and assault of a police officer."

Lehmann's purplish-red face made him look like a moldy strawberry. He sputtered out, "There must be some mistake. I've had only the most honest dealings with this man."

Adam doubted that seriously, but he bit his tongue. "This is the guy all right. I wouldn't forget an ugly mug like that." What he could see with the mask, that is. But the gold tooth was enough.

"This is harassment, pure and simple, Dutton. If you're mistaken, I'll have both your badges for this."

"You do that, sir. And have a nice day," Adam called out to him as they pushed Karlstad into the back of Adam's car.

They carted their prisoner to a holding cell after he'd been booked and searched, and he stood behind the bars, glaring at them. "I won't talk without my attorney present. And I want my rights read to me right now. On video," he motioned toward the camera in the corner of the ceiling. Jinks rolled her eyes and obliged.

They left their prisoner alone while they went to fill in Chief Quinn, and then Jinks pulled Adam aside. "What's up with that asshole of a mayor?"

Adam shrugged. "He doesn't like me. Guess I don't part my hair on the right side."

"No, seriously. Apart from the whole Zelda thing which I know about. How deep is he in with this nutjob and Forsythe? They got some political ménage à trois going on?"

"Lehmann knows all about Forsythe and his 'associates.'

But he needs Forsythe's clout to get him elected as governor. When he saw us arrest Karlstad, he probably had voices chanting 'bye-bye election' in the back of his mind."

"And the chief? Has he gone dark-side on us too? I'll resign my commission and work as a greeter at Walmart if I find he's dirty."

"You'd make a great greeter. I can see it now. 'Take this cart, or I'll punch you in the jaw.'" Then Adam shook his head. "Quinn's in a bind. I know it goes with the job, but he's not used to being squeezed in a vise that's this well-oiled."

Adam waved adieu to Jinks and stopped by the lab on the way to his office. Spying Joe Brimm at his desk, he asked, "Got those prints yet?"

"The coffee cup prints? Got a pretty good set. Tried the state records and AFIS. No matches. DNA will take longer. Is that good news or bad?"

Adam pulled a decoder ring he'd bought from Harlan's store out of his pocket and handed it over. "Good, I think."

Joe's eyes lighted up at the decoder ring. He said, "I owe you some maple fudge for this," which made Adam laugh.

Adam called Beverly as soon as he got back to his office. "Great news, Beverly Laborde. We got Goldie heating up a bench in our cell as we speak. I'm betting it's only a matter of time before he squeals on Forsythe. Then we can haul him in."

Beverly didn't answer right away. Then she said, "Sounds great. Good work."

"I can tell you're enthused about this. Please contain your excitement."

She sighed. "It's just that I won't believe it until it's over, you know? I've had so many disappointments before. Things don't often work out like I think they should."

"We've got Goldie, and he's not going anywhere. That was part of the plan, remember?"

"Harlan would agree with you, I'm sure. He was a big help today. If only he could help me find that statue, I'd nominate him for a Medal of Honor."

"Still worrying about that statue after all of this?"

"With my luck, it's likely long gone. Or the whole puzzle thing was an elaborate hoax—as if there are any monuments in this area. Harlan thinks we're aiming too high. He says monuments aren't always big. Sometimes, they're rather small."

"Harlan, the sage. Glad he was with you today. Did you have any luck with the murdered Forsythe's widow?"

"No proof. Lots of motive. Father and son hated each other, argued over everything. Yet the elder's will leaves three-quarters of his estate to his son. Reggie keeps his stepmother on a tight leash and will be glad to be done with her. I suspect Mairi Forsythe knows about her husband and stepson's dealings, too, but didn't open up to us that far."

"Good to know. And to keep in mind for a court trial when she can be put under oath."

"You think it will get to that point? To a trial?"

"I'm betting my job on it."

"I wouldn't want you to lose your job, Adam. I know you love it."

Thinking back to Jinks' comment about being a greeter, Adam added, "I could always work security at the resort. Speaking of which, want to grab some dinner?"

"Maybe tomorrow. I've got a monster headache."

"That's the first time I've ever gotten the 'not tonight, dear, I have a headache' routine about dinner." He said it jokingly, but he was a little hurt. And concerned. "Get a good night's rest then. And hopefully, I'll be giving you a call soon with news we've arrested Reggie Forsythe."

After he hung up with her, Adam leaned back in his chair, his hands clasped behind his head. Was the stress getting to

Beverly? Or was she only tired? She was strong, but everyone had a breaking point. He shouldn't have involved her so much. Or involved her at all. But then again, she'd started the whole thing—and trying to stop Beverly Laborde from whatever she was after was like trying to tame an earthquake.

Tomorrow she'd be back to normal. Adam rubbed his knee, where it had rested on a nail on the boards in the cabin when Goldie had the gun on him. He ignored the pain in his lower back from being bumped around in Goldie's trunk. Tomorrow, after the worst of this case was over, maybe Adam would feel better too. Then why did he get the oddest feeling that the other shoe was about to drop?

40

Beverly popped a couple of pain pills with some apple seltzer water. She hadn't lied to Adam about her headache, but that wasn't the main reason she'd declined his dinner invitation. Again. Fair was fair since he'd declined hers once, too, right? Even if it was to protect her.

Adam thought the whole Forsythe saga was winding down, and it wouldn't be much longer at all until they had that evil bastard behind bars. The case was coming to a close and so was one of the two main reasons she'd stayed in Ironwood Junction this long.

What was it like to stay in one place for longer than a week? Or two? It had been years for her. Five long years. Moving around from one hotel, one hostel, one flophouse to the next. Always trying to stay ahead of her targets and law enforcement. But now, she'd really gotten herself trapped in a web of her own making, surrounded by both targets *and* law enforcement.

Was she getting that careless? Or was this the fork-in-the-road that would finally break her free from her perpetual cycle of criminal hide-and-seek? On the other hand, it was possible she wasn't tired of that lifestyle. Maybe she thrived on it, lived for it. An adrenaline junkie.

Beverly hadn't felt this unsure of herself in a very, very long while. And she didn't like that feeling, not one bit. She was always the one in charge of her own destiny, the lone ship needing no port and no anchor. But once the Forsythe case was finally and truly over, what was next? Get a real job? She had no résumé and no references.

The stress of even thinking about that question and its complicated list of possible answers made her grab Kornelson's treasure map and her notes. Even though she'd studied the damned map hundreds of times, she must have missed something important. Reggie Forsythe allegedly hadn't found the silver statue, so it must be out there somewhere. But she was running out of leads and time.

What was this "monument" Kornelson had referred to, the site of the statue burial? Was it just a play on words as Harland had suggested to her and not an actual place? She ran through her notes, again and again, page after page after page. But all she got from her labors was for the headache to get worse.

Time for the Jacuzzi? No, too hot. Wine, then? Despite the fact it might help her headache, she didn't want her thought processes dulled any further.

She stood up and paced around the room, ignoring how the sudden blood flow was making the throbbing of her head worse. Why had Adam's phone call not cheered her up? Why did she still have a bad feeling about all of this? It wasn't just the headache, she was sure of that. Then what?

Images from the past several days kept coming back to her no matter how hard she tried to keep them at bay. The red-stained rug under her grandfather as he lay on the floor with his head bashed in. Adam being kidnapped and pepper-sprayed. The panic as she and Adam almost drowned in that pond— she'd never forget the smell of the mud, the fish, and the algae, and the rotten-egg odor from decomposing debris in those murky waters.

Adam had said she was tough. Well, she *was* tough. She hadn't let a little murder, kidnapping or near-drowning get her down, right? *Well, then, if you're such a Superwoman, explain why you're so jumpy.*

She was so deep in thought, it took her a while to realize her cellphone was ringing. It was Mr. X. "Beverly, I need you here. And I need you here now." His voice sounded unusually agitated.

"Whatever has happened? Are you all right?"

"I can't explain over the phone, but you must come right away. Don't dawdle. And don't talk to anyone. I'll be waiting anxiously and won't rest until your arrival."

After he hung up, Beverly sat there, wondering what was going on, wondering what she should do. Once again following her sixth sense formed from those years of being on the run, she grabbed her suitcase, notes, map, and purse. Then she practically flew out the door, through the lobby, and outside to her car.

"Hold on, Mr. X, I'm on my way," she said aloud as she peeled out of the parking lot so fast, the SUV's tires screeched their disapproval. What she needed was to stop second-guessing herself, even as she wondered once again if she was doing the right thing.

41

Wednesday, September 22

Adam woke up in a great mood. Jinks had solved her case, despite it having a mixed ending. He was close to wrapping up his case. And as dug into his biggest breakfast in days, the sun shining through the window cast a hopeful prism on the wall next to him. Even when he arrived at work, his favorite parking spot at the PD was open, and he even harbored a secret hope Beverly might agree to meet him for dinner.

That all changed the moment he opened the door to the police station lobby. The senior receptionist, Arline Newton, greeted him with, "Chief wants to see you. Emergency." And when the ever-chirpy Sergeant Gray saw him walk by, she wouldn't look him in the eye.

Adam hurried into the chief's office, a feeling of dread working its way up his spine. Quinn didn't wait for him to sit down. "Gabriel Karlstad's high-powered attorney arrived. Guy named Douglas Marcell. Karlstad clammed up except to say he was hired by the same woman who killed Reginald Forsythe. And he gave that woman a name. Beverly Laborde."

Adam blinked several times. He'd expected Forsythe would want to keep Goldie's mouth shut. He must have fed Karlstad a line he'd pay for his defense and make sure he didn't get much time. The alternative being an 'unfortunate demise,' in prison or out. Okay, but how had he figured out Beverly's identity?

His gaze fell on the newspaper on the chief's desk. He hadn't subscribed to the paper in a while and hadn't wanted to listen to the news this morning for fear it would darken his good mood. Maybe he should have. Emblazoned across the top was a headline about the death of former Representative Arlen Strudwick.

Adam picked up the paper and scanned the article. Strudwick was found dead by his wife. Cause unknown, but the local cops hadn't ruled out suspicious circumstances. Adam tossed the paper back onto the chief's desk.

Quinn said, "I sent Jinks over to Apple Valley Resort to pick up Laborde and bring her back for questioning."

"Where is she? In a cell?"

"Beats me. She'd checked out of the resort."

Adam took a moment for the shock of that news to wear off. "Why'd you send Jinks instead of me? Or have me go with her? It's my case."

"I sensed you've gotten too close to that Laborde woman, Dutton. Even lost your objectivity where she's concerned. That whole Mata Hari thing."

Adam leaned forward on his knees, wincing at the bruises there. Before he could reply to that, Quinn continued. "To add insult to injury, the mayor is after my badge and yours. He says our department accused him of consorting with criminals. Then I get a call from Reggie Forsythe. He found out about Laborde being the suspect and was furious when he heard she'd disappeared. What the hell happened, Dutton?"

"How did Forsythe hear of Laborde?"

"I don't know. It's possible his attorney and Karlstad's attorney work in the same office."

"Or his attorney is the same as Karlstad's attorney." Adam had recognized the name of Douglas Marcell. The same attorney who'd gotten the Hendrick-killer suspect out of jail.

"That's awfully fishy, Chief. I don't buy it."

"Look, Dutton. I don't care if a pink fairy came down from above and whispered it in Forsythe's ear right now. I want answers, and I want them five minutes ago."

Adam leaned back and ran a hand through his hair. Where had Beverly gone? Had she been tipped off? Had she been kidnapped? He didn't want to consider the idea that she was guilty and ran when the noose started tightening. No, there must be a good reason why she left.

And what about Karlstad? If Forsythe had him wrapped up in a neat, tidy package, then there went one of their main avenues of proof. Except for Beverly's tape. That could pin something on the man. Beverly's tape. The same original-tape she'd held onto after they left Mr. X's castle.

Adam felt the pieces of the puzzle swirling around in his brain like a blender full of live bees. Weighing his vanishing options, he looked directly into the chief's eyes. "I'd love an opportunity to question Karlstad. Is his attorney still here?"

Quinn grimaced. "Yeah. But it won't do any good. Karlstad will clam up."

"Then it won't take much of my time, will it?"

"Knock yourself out. And after the all-of-two-minutes you're in there, I want you back at your desk thinking of ways to track down Laborde. Jinks is already working hard on it. Help her out."

Adam noted his sudden demotion to being the assistant on the case. But he headed toward the cells as the chief called up a sergeant to take Karlstad to the interrogation room.

Goldie looked up as Adam entered and flashed him a big, gold-toothy grin. "Look who's come crawling back. You're wasting your breath. I'm not talking."

The man hovering behind Goldie could have been plucked from an attorney casting call from the looks of the guy. He had a power suit and tie, shiny monogrammed cufflinks, shellacked hair, and a slick, screw-you smile.

Adam picked a chair opposite Goldie, which he turned around and sat with his body propped against the back. He stared at Goldie for two minutes, his gaze not wavering from the other man's face. When Goldie started squirming in his chair, Adam said. "You familiar with the name Arlen Strudwick?"

Goldie stayed silent. Adam continued, "Not a politics devotee, I see. Strudwick was a state representative. Reggie Forsythe bought him off. Threatened him and his family to get him to do what Forsythe wanted. You might be interested to know that Strudwick was found dead late last night. And I think your good pal Forsythe had him killed for handing over evidence pinning Forsythe to influence peddling."

The attorney's face grew beet red, and he looked like he was ready to jump in at any moment, but Goldie stared at them blankly. However, Adam knew Goldie was paying close attention by the way his hands were gripping the table.

"Then, there's the case of a missing man named Richard Nagra. The name ring any bells with you?"

Goldie just gripped the table harder and continued to stay silent.

Adam continued, "You know what I think? I think Forsythe told you he'd protect you. Get you in and out of jail quickly if you keep your mouth shut. But consider this for a minute. This is the same man who bribed a state official and then killed him. And the very same man who killed his own father. Do you really think he's going to let you walk out jail of scot-free? When you can tie him to my kidnapping and several other offenses, including murder?"

The attorney spoke up. "Detective Dutton, this is not an approved line of questioning. My client doesn't have to answer that. In fact, I don't like the tone of your questions at all."

Adam ran his finger lightly along the table top. "You see, Forsythe doesn't care about anyone other than himself. And he'll get rid of people who get in his way. Or anyone who's a loose end."

Goldie licked his lips and wiggled in his chair. The look on his face made Adam think of those cartoons where you could see the gears literally turning in a character's brain.

"Here's the deal, Karlstad. We can get Forsythe with your help. Then he'll be the one in jail, not you. If you agree to help us, we can put in a good word for you with the court and see that your sentence is reduced. Isn't six months in jail better than being planted six feet under?"

Goldie's expression grew pensive, but then his eyes turned hard, and he blurted out before his attorney could stop him, "You're trying to make me fold. And I won't, you hear me? I won't."

Feeling as if he'd given it his best shot but still defeated, Adam left Goldie and told the sergeant to take him back to his cell. He didn't know whether to be cheered or more depressed when he got a call from his counterparts in Walbridge, New Hampshire, home of the Birdseye Diner. Acting on his tip, courtesy of Creighton Querry, they'd canvassed the area with a drone and found a decomposing body along the banks of the Connecticut River.

The fingerprints matched those of Richard Nagra's—from police databases after the man's run-in with the law a decade ago for leaving the scene of an accident and simple assault. Guess that meant the "troll" caretaker he and Beverly had encountered at Nagra's home was going to be waiting a long, long time for the man to return.

Oh, Beverly. What to do about Beverly? There really was only one thing—he needed to go in search of a missing suspect.

42

Beverly propped a pillow under Mr. X's foot, adjusting it so that his shiny new cast was centered in the middle. "Then you weren't kidding about how you did this?"

"I swear it's the truth. Yang bumped me, and I tripped over a large root. Broke my foot in two places." He pointed to the crutches propped against the chair. "The doctor tells me I have to wear this monstrosity for six weeks."

Beverly made sure he was comfortable and then settled on the sofa across from him, curling her legs up under her. She hugged one of the throw pillows. "I don't know how to thank you for calling me last night about my impending arrest. I'd be in a jail cell or dead right now, otherwise."

He nodded. "My first opportunity to help out a damsel in distress."

"And you get an A-plus. Although I apologize for sleeping until noon. I had no idea I was that tired."

"Quite understandable due to the unpleasant situation you find yourself in. I must also apologize, however. Having you make a late lunch for us isn't very hospitable on my part."

"The least I can do." She'd also spent the better part of the afternoon on cleaning duty since he found it hard going.

Staring at the ceiling, she said, "This is all my fault. All of it."

"I don't think you made Yang trip me, dear girl."

"Getting Adam kidnapped and nearly killed, getting Mr. Strudwick killed. Poor Mr. Strudwick. He had a wife and six kids, one with Down's. He was trying to do the right thing in the end."

"Then it's a blessing he won't have to face the humiliation when this comes to light."

"No, but his family will."

"That is unfortunate. Too many people get caught up in the underworld without thinking about how it might hurt their families."

The faraway look on his face prompted her to ask. "What about your family? Where are they living?"

"My family, such as it is, is scattered around the globe. I was married once to an opera singer, a soprano."

She gawked at him, and he laughed. "Don't look so surprised. It only lasted a month."

"Where are you from?"

"Everywhere. My origins are original. And secret. We'll leave it at that."

Clutching the pillow tighter, she said in a half-whisper. "All I wanted was to avenge my grandmother."

"Don't give up hope, Beverly Laborde. When the world seems its darkest, dawn is just around the corner. That's a song, isn't it?"

"I left Adam with a horrible mess. I can't begin to imagine what he thinks of me right now. I take that back. I can most definitely imagine what he thinks of me, and it involves lots of four-letter words."

"I looked up your Adam Dutton. A fast track to detective, plenty of commendations. And there was a nasty bit of business a few years ago. He survived that, even thrived, when others would have crumbled. All is not lost."

Beverly relaxed a fraction or two. "I hope you're right."

"Of course, I am. I'm hardly ever wrong."

That made her laugh good and hard. When she'd caught her breath, her gaze landed on a silver chalice on the mantel. She said, "Forsythe must have a touch of OCD. His fascination with antique silver, for example. Maybe it's genetic. I've become obsessed myself, like him."

"You mean that Lady of Chartres statue?"

"He's probably found it by now."

"Are you so sure?"

She chewed on her lip. "Not really. His father's widow said he didn't have it yet."

Beverly hopped up and retrieved a folder with her notes and flipped through them until she got to the part with the Kornelson verses. She'd made a list of possible 'monuments' in the area but so far come up empty. Only one left, but it was the least likely, so she'd left it for last. It was too small for a monument. Unless Harlan was right about monuments not always being huge.

Slamming the folder shut with such force that she startled Mr. X, she said, "I'm going to get that statue before he gets his greedy hands on it if it's the last thing I do."

"It may well be, dear. Give it a rest. *You* need to rest."

"But I've just had a brainstorm about those verses I mentioned to you. From the Kornelson papers. It's possible I might know where the statue is hidden." She grabbed her coat and purse and headed toward the door to put on her shoes.

Mr. X called to her, "Where do you think you're going? You're a wanted woman, you know."

"I can't sit around here waiting for god knows what to happen without doing something."

"I will agree to it on one condition. I come with you."

She pointed to his cast. "In that?"

"You can drive. I'll go as a passenger and your backup."

They decided to take Mr. X's car since hers would be more of a red flag. Not that his Beamer wouldn't be out of place among all the Vermont Subarus. Beverly felt confident about finding her way to and from Mr. X's castle now and didn't have to ask for directions from him.

The cold front forecast to be heading their way had dropped the temps into the upper 30s. The wind had picked up, tossing some of the remaining leaves across the road into mini-leaf vortices.

He asked, "Where are we headed?"

"To an old abandoned church."

"Not my favorite places, those."

"Churches? Or abandoned churches?"

"Both. Whatever religion my family followed, I'm a lapsed form of it."

Beverly pulled over next to a pasture to consult her notes and re-program the GPS destination in Mr. X's car.

"Lost, are we?"

"I hardly ever get lost. Not on the roads, anyway."

After an hour of twisting, turning roads that seemed to lead nowhere, the GPS's mechanical voice said, "Turn left in fifty feet. Your destination will be on the right."

After the turn, Mr. X said, "What destination? Looks like a bunch of trees."

"The area would have grown up considerably in a hundred years. But the church should be beyond that thicket. I hope."

Beverly spied what looked like the main entrance into the site, overgrown thought it was, with two large, twisted oak trees. Something made her decide to continue around the bend until she found what looked like a separate pathway, and she parked beside it.

She grabbed her collapsible shovel and metal detector she'd brought along from the trunk and gave Mr. X a wink.

"I've never had a lookout before. Certainly not one with a broken foot."

Mr. X waved at the crutches in the back of the passenger seat. "Those will make a handy weapon in a pinch. You've got your gun, right?"

"Naturally." Beverly patted her bag, which she'd slung diagonally across her shoulder. "The only threat I expect to see, in all honesty, is a rat or two."

"Just promise me you'll be careful."

She gave him a wave, picked up the shovel and metal detector, and plunged ahead through the trees.

43

After countless phone calls, interviews with the resort staff, and chats with employees at other places Beverly might have visited in town, Adam and Jinks were running out of leads. He and Jinks split up tasks, hoping to cover more territory. Later in the afternoon, Adam tracked down a phone number for Mr. X, but no answer.

The hardest trip was to see Harlan. The man was adamant that the sky would be more likely to fall than Beverly being behind Reginald Forsythe's murder and Adam's kidnapping. He was a little upset with Adam, too, for considering the notion. "You and Beverly were getting on so well, Adam. Thought you might be a little sweet on that filly. You telling me you're going to toss her in a cold jail cell when you know she's innocent?"

But that was the thing, wasn't it? Adam didn't think she was guilty, but a part of him wasn't exactly, entirely sure. Perhaps this was just like his father, being duped by that Ponzi scheme. With Beverly's experience at living off the grid and with disguises, Adam would have a hard time tracking her, if she didn't want to be tracked. But why run? She'd been so obsessed with avenging her grandmother and finding that infernal statue before Forsythe did.

The statue. Maybe that was the key. One thing he sensed about Beverly was when she wanted something, she went full tilt after it. Adam considered taking another pass at Dewey's

Pond, thinking that she'd head back there again, but discounted it.

He ran his hand across his face. He'd been on the force for fifteen years, worked his way up from patrol, had his share of commendations. Until now, he'd never once let a suspect get under his skin, let alone consider a personal relationship with her, gorgeous con artist or not. He was slipping, and his judgment was questionable. It would have served him right for the chief to take him off the case altogether. He might still.

Adam got up to pace around his office. With any luck, the added blood flow would help him think or work off the nervous energy derailing his concentration. He needed to focus on that statue and try to think like Beverly Laborde was thinking. He knew first-hand she'd tried Quechee Gorge, and he also knew she'd checked the wooded cabin Stork looked after. She hadn't mentioned other places she'd tried, but they could number in the dozens or more that he didn't know about.

Adam slid into his desk chair and opened the file with the faxed verses from the Kornelson estate. Kornelson had some ties to this area, or he wouldn't have mentioned it in reference to the silver statue. The man had obviously known about the Natick Indian lore. But would he really have hidden the item here in the area? Maybe Kornelson was senile. Or this was all a goddamn joke.

And yet, the Natick were among a group of natives who'd become Christians and were known as "Praying Indians," or so his research had told him. And the missing silver statue was a Catholic icon—Our Lady of Chartres, taken from Indians by the Rogers' Rangers. Either the religious angle meant nothing, or it meant everything to Kornelson.

Dutton jumped up and grabbed a book on local history from a shelf behind his desk. He skimmed the index, looking for an entry he remembered from reading it years ago. There, in a chapter on places of worship, was a photo of the Woodstock Church from 1905 that was used by the Natick natives before it half-burned down the next year. The ruins had remained there untouched for a hundred years. Harlan might have been right—monuments aren't always big.

And what had Stork said? That old man Korn paid him well to look after his property out in the forest. What if Korn was as embarrassed of his ancestors as Adam was with his slave-owner kin in the 1800s? What if Korn's original family name was Kornelson? And Stork said he was a descendant of one of Rogers' Rangers. Coincidence? Or were the two family lines somehow related decades later by a twist of fate—or intent?

Adam grabbed an area property chart from a file cabinet and flipped through to the Korn property. It was adjacent to the land that once housed the Woodstock Church. Maybe this wild idea of his seemed far-fetched, but nothing about this case was normal.

Reggie Forsythe was also obsessed with that statue, maybe a detail Adam could use to his advantage. Even if Adam didn't know where the statue was, all he had to do was make Forsythe think that he did.

Adam popped by the chief's office and got a promise from Quinn to let Forsythe know Adam was following a lead that might take him to Laborde. And that it had to do with a silver Lady of Chartres statue, part of a legend surrounding Rogers' Rangers. Adam gathered some things from his office, checked with Jinks, and was off.

It took twenty minutes for Adam to find the road to the old church and the overgrown entrance bookended by two twisted oak trees. And it took another five minutes walking from a muddy roadside parking place through overgrowth and rotting tree carcasses to reach his destination. Off to the right, a tributary from the Ottauquechee River had carved a channel ten feet deep, a mini-gorge. A lot like "the chasm" in the verses. Of the church building itself, only a skeleton doorway and a few charred walls stood mutely by.

It only took ten seconds for him to spy the splintered remains of the pulpit on its side at the front of the ruins. The remaining floorboards were crumbling, and he had to tiptoe around several dubious-looking cracks, but he made it without falling through.

Using the flashlight his father gave him years ago that Adam was hardly ever without, he peered into a gaping hole previously hidden by the splintered pulpit. The grimy silhouette of an empty square the size of a breadbox—the right size for a small silver statue—mocked him from the bottom of the hole.

Whatever had been here was gone. Adam stood there cursing the gaping hole until he heard a noise off to his left through the trees. It was hard to pick out with the wind rattling tree branches and swirling the dust and leaves around. He listened again. Had he just imagined it? But then the distinct sound of boots clomping through the woods reached his ears.

He pulled out his gun, aimed it toward the sound, and waited.

44

Beverly handed the plastic bag with its heavy contents to Mr. X and tossed the shovel, metal detector, and her purse into his Beamer. She said with a grin. "How's the gimp doing?"

"Better, now that you've returned. Would you call your mission a success?"

"I would say that I—" She turned to face the path she'd just traveled. "Did you hear something?"

"The wind. Your lovely voice."

"I'm sure I heard something back there."

"Maybe nothing."

"I'm going to check it out."

"Beverly—"

"I'll be fine, back in a minute."

She retraced her steps over the rotting logs and tree roots, taking pains not to end up like Mr. X and his foot. A branch whipped back and hit her in the face. She listened again— probably nothing, like Mr. X said. But it was only about twenty more feet, so she forged ahead. Pushing aside the last branch before the clearing and site of the church, she stopped dead in her tracks when she saw a gun pointed at her. Adam.

"I guess my long shot paid off," he said.

"You followed me."

"Just got lucky. I've been looking for you all day. Why'd you run?"

"I felt the noose tightening. What else was I to do?"

"Talk to me. Let me help."

"In case you haven't noticed, you and I aren't on the same side of the law right now."

Adam lowered his gun to his side. "I could have taken you in several times, but I didn't. Why did you think I would now?"

"Goldie told you I masterminded your kidnapping. That's reason enough."

"If I believed it, yes."

"You don't?"

"No, I don't." He shook his head. "Don't give up on me. You've got the evidence Strudwick gave you, for one. I'll keep working on Goldie to convince him to rat out Forsythe. We can do this. But I need your help."

She took a couple of steps closer until a new voice stopped her cold. "It would be best if you both stayed right where you are." The voice added, "And throw your weapon over into those bushes, Dutton. Or else I might be forced to shoot this lovely lady."

Beverly had a twinge of fear as Adam tossed his gun under a thicket of holly bushes. She reached over to put her hand on her purse when she remembered she'd chucked it into Mr. X's car to make it easier to put in the shovel and metal detector.

She followed the sound of the man's voice until a figure came into view. "Miss Beverly Laborde. I've so been wanting to see what you look like without the disguise. Detective Dutton here has been putting all kinds of roadblocks in my way."

"How did you find this place?" She narrowed her eyes at Adam. Had he told Forsythe where to find her? Was he going to make her the sacrificial lamb to preserve his job? She shook off the horrible idea. No, not Adam.

Forsythe walked toward the ruins near the altar and motioned for Adam and Beverly to move closer together.

Adam asked, "Don't have anyone else to play the evil fixer for you this time? No more Nagras or Hendricks or Karlstads?"

"Look how well that turned out. Idiots, all of them. Can't do anything right."

"You mean the kidnapping or forcing my car off the road into a pond?"

"Both." Forsythe directed a cold smile at Adam. "Your chief called me to say you were in pursuit of Laborde and a certain silver statue I've been hunting. I see you found Laborde. So where is the statue?"

Beverly shot Adam a hurt look. He'd given her away to Forsythe? Adam looked at her briefly with those intense brown eyes of his, and a glint of something in those eyes made her relax.

Adam taunted, "You've been a busy man. My kidnapping, two murders—your father, and Strudwick. The antiques world too boring for you?"

Forsythe laughed. "I admit my life's been more lively lately. Although that dolt Karlstad was a mistake. You know what they say, if you want something done right, do it yourself."

Adam said, "I can see why you'd kill Strudwick after you found out he had evidence against you and was ready to do something about it. But why your own father?"

"That was unfortunate. Oh, I'd thought about doing it many times before, but the opportunity presented itself. He'd outlived his usefulness."

"How were you originally going to explain his murder?"

"An intruder. A phantom drug dealer, to be exact." Forsythe turned to Beverly. "Fortunately, you were a godsend, my dear. Tell me one thing—I still don't know why you were there."

Beverly gritted her teeth. "To avenge Guinevere Glas."

Forsythe scowled. "I don't understand. What does my

mother have to do with this?"

"If my grandmother were alive, she'd disown you if she knew how you'd turned out."

"Grandmother? So you're Regina's daughter. Oh, how delightful. My niece is a burglar and a schemer. Must take after my father and me."

Adam spoke up, "No, she got the good genes."

Forsythe sneered, "Now, Beverly, if you believe our family connection will play on my sympathy, think again. If I killed my father, I wouldn't have any problem killing my niece."

He pointed the gun toward Adam. "But not yet. I need that evidence Strudwick gave you. Do you have it with you, Miss Laborde?"

"You think I carry it around in my coat pocket? Sorry to disappoint you."

"Then tell me where it is, or I will shoot Dutton."

Beverly hesitated, still not knowing what to do. Mr. X was trapped in the car, unable to move around with his foot in the cast. She was without her gun, and Adam's was too far away to reach.

She'd have to tell Forsythe where the tape was. She'd tell him anything he wanted to know, even if it meant he got away. Whatever it took to keep him from killing Adam. She opened her mouth to answer his question, but Adam interrupted her.

Adam said, "I know you're dying for any excuse, but it's too bad you won't get to shoot me, Forsythe."

Forsythe cackled. "Oh? Who's to stop me?"

Beverly realized Adam was doing something odd with his hands that she could swear was sign language. She feared he might be losing his mind, but then Adam replied to Forsythe, "*They* are," and nodded toward an African-American woman and three police officers in uniform moving toward Forsythe with their guns drawn.

Adam added, "Did you get all that, Jinks?"

The woman, who Beverly knew must be Eliot Jinks, said, "Loud and clear, Adam." Then she barked out to Forsythe. "Put your gun down on the ground, Forsythe, nice and slow. My friends here aren't too happy about the way your goon treated my partner. You know how cops are when one of their own is threatened. Shoot first and ask questions later."

Forsythe looked up to the heavens as if expecting help from above, but the gun in his hand didn't waver.

Jinks said louder this time, "Put it down. Now. I'm not going to say it again."

Beverly had one moment of sheer terror when she realized Forsythe's gun remained trained on Adam. What if he didn't obey? What if he killed Adam as his last act of defiance?

Then, in one quick-as-flash move, Forsythe twisted the gun around and shot himself in the head. He was like a macabre bloodied tree falling to the ground as he came to rest on the ruins of the church altar.

Beverly was shaking as Adam came over and put his arm around her. "You okay?" he asked.

"Fine. Really."

Adam said to the other woman, "Great timing, Jinks. I'm surprised the chief agreed to the plan."

"He wasn't exactly thrilled. But he trusts you, Dutton. You owe me a big case of Norwegian lutefisk for this."

Beverly took a quick look at the man lying on the altar, as one of the uniformed cops bent over him. "Didn't have much faith in his attorneys to get him out of this mess, did he?"

Adam said, "His attorneys likely couldn't get him much less than thirty-five years. Guess he couldn't stand the idea of prison food."

Beverly punched his arm with a small smile. Unlike seeing her grandfather's body, she didn't feel anything at all looking down at her uncle. She didn't know if he was alive or dead, and she really didn't care.

Her smile faded as she imagined Grammie looking down from heaven on her son. What would she feel? Would she forgive Beverly for her part in arranging his demise?

A cold wind whipped through the trees and made her shiver. Her grandfather and Representative Strudwick all gone. Mr. X's words came back to her, "If you desire revenge, you should dig two graves." He'd meant hers, of course, but there were two deaths triggered by her revenge scheme, all the same. Maybe she'd avenged Grammie in part, but at what cost?

45

Beverly looked at herself in the mirror, adjusting the wig, fluffing out the short, dark hair. After dropping off the SUV at the rental agency, she'd taken a taxi to the bus station and changed her clothes and hair in the bathroom there. No train this time.

She smiled as she remembered Adam's tenderness in making sure she was okay as she endured several interviews at the PD before signing her statement. Both of them were there for hours. Enough to see the mayor storming into the office, then leaving with his tail tucked between his legs. Also sufficient time to see Adam's boss, Chief Quinn, go through five cups of coffee.

Adam had popped in and out, apologizing at having to deal with the aftermath, and Detective Jinks sat with her for a while. Beverly liked Jinks enormously. She was glad Adam had such a wonderful colleague as Jinks to watch his back.

Poor Mr. X. Adam had let her drive him to a cafe where she dropped him off, so she and Adam could endure their police department debriefing. Three hours later, she'd picked up Mr. X after his third helping of pumpkin pie and felt guilty for leaving him there so long. Though he may have found a new friend in Dennis, the cute waiter who'd hovered over him the entire time cooing over Mr. X's broken foot.

Then there was Reggie Forsythe. He'd survived his suicide attempt, something about the bullet entering at a 40-degree angle above his eye, then ricocheting and exiting the other side of his head near the back of his ear. The doctors weren't sure if he'd be able to walk or talk again. Beverly wasn't sure she should be glad about that or wish his attempt had succeeded.

Beverly would never forget that one horrifying moment when it looked like Forsythe was going to shoot Adam. Oh, Adam. She knew he'd take her leaving hard. He'd looked so happy the case worked out the way it did and so eager when he asked her out to dinner.

She'd declined again, using the excuse she had to take Mr. X back home, but it was more than that. He knew it, too, she'd seen it in the look in his eyes.

Beverly was running away. She had what she came for— Grammie was avenged, and there was a somewhat heavy object in her luggage needing attention. When the bus station clerk asked her what her destination was, she'd hesitated. Where would she go now? A note on a schedule board about a special price to Chicago caught her eye, so that's what she told him. Any city was as good as any other.

The psychologists would have a field day trying to ferret out why she was running. Running from what? Happiness? Adam? Love? Maybe she'd find what she was looking for in Chicago or not, but it was another brand new start. Like all the other brand new starts she'd had through the years. The psychologists would say she was constantly reinventing herself whenever she put on a new disguise. They'd be wrong.

When she heard the call for boarding, she lugged her suitcases to the bus, waiting until she witnessed them being loaded to make sure they didn't disappear, and then hopped on board. She regarded the faces of her fellow passengers. Perhaps that woman in the print dress was going to see her grandchildren. The man with the deep worry lines etched in his craggy face, off to take a new job. The young girl with the dreamy smile on her lips was probably meeting a lover.

They were all escapees in a way. Exchanging one setting for another, one reality for another, if only temporarily. Souls fading in and out of time and place.

Beverly pulled out a book and started to read, but she kept reading the same paragraphs over and over and stuck the book in the seat pocket. Looking out the window, she watched the gently rolling hills of Ironwood Junction and Vermont disappear out of her life.

46

Three Weeks Later

Adam glared at his computer, rubbing his eyes. He'd scanned this same page several times but didn't remember what he read. Jinks breezed in to hand him a McMuffin and a large coffee. The station's coffee machine was broken, and it was funny to see all the paper and Styrofoam carry-out cups from local joints clutched in everyone's hands as they navigated their day.

"Any word from Beverly?" Jinks asked.

"Nope." It was three weeks since she'd vanished. He'd got some ribbing from a few of the beat cops, but Jinks stayed silent on the matter, other than to say she liked her.

After the initial political and legal firestorm surrounding Forsythe's shooting and the resulting media carnival, things were settling down. Reporters were making hay out of tragedy, as they usually did, speculating on the motive for the murders. Who knew when, or if, Forsythe would be alert enough for his attorneys to consult with him.

Strudwick's murder would have to wait until the trial if there was one. Beverly's evidence would also have to come to public light some day. But after Beverly told him more about Strudwick, Adam got the chief to hold off on releasing those sordid details to protect the man's family for as long as possible.

The circus would die down eventually and be largely

forgotten by most people. Not by Mayor Lehmann. He protested his innocence, and knowing how thick the mayor's Teflon skin was, Adam was betting he'd survive this politically.

Adam had toyed with the idea of calling Zelda to see how she was holding up but decided against it. When he ran into her in town, she'd gripped his hand briefly without saying a word and then hurried off.

Adam tried not to think about Beverly, but her face kept popping back into his mind. He'd done more research after she left, trying to tie up a few loose ends. Like why did old man Kornelson bury the statue in the churchyard instead of selling it? Then Adam found out the man was exhibiting early signs of dementia, and his only living relative, a greedy nephew, tried to force a Power of Attorney order to take over the man's estate.

Adam occupied the rest of his time with a couple of cases that should have been interesting. For some reason, work now felt like a chore. The intercom on his desk phone shook him out of his glum reverie. Arline Newton, the department receptionist, wanted to route a call to his office phone. It was from a representative of the American Indian College Fund.

The woman apologized for bothering him. "It was so out of the ordinary, I had to follow through. It's not every day we get a cashier's check for fifty thousand dollars. The donor wished to remain anonymous. But the enclosed note had your name and number on it and said you'd be getting something, too."

"This donor didn't identify himself or herself at all? No address?"

"No, they definitely wanted to remain anonymous. But the check was good."

Adam thanked her and hung up, bewildered. American Indian College Fund? Then his heart raced as Arline brought in Dutton's mail and dumped it into his in-box. He flipped through the magazines, official bulletins, and junk mail until he uncovered a small, handwritten package with no return address.

He slit it open and drew out a package of maple fudge, which made him smile. How did she know it was his favorite? And then he scanned the letter inside, which the history-loving Beverly had written in the form of a telegram.

"Found a little silver object someone was interested in buying. Stop. Thought of you working your way through community college and also theft from Indians by Rangers. Stop. Payback time. Stop. Can't find anyone here with eyes as nice as yours. Stop. Ironwood Junction might be a nice place to settle down. Stop. Could use a partner to help nail additional NAL crooks."

He smiled. And then he chuckled. And then he pulled out the large file he'd started compiling on more of the Northeastern Antiquities League bad guys. A partner, huh? Yeah, he'd be ready.

www.ingramcontent.com/pod-product-compliance
Lightning Source LLC
Chambersburg PA
CBHW021645110726
47902CB00007B/1836